RETURN

TO ME

WRITTEN BY
EMMA ATKINS

Copyright

Contents

This book is dedicated to those who helped me believe in myself again.

The Nightmare

Matt

The nightmares are the worst. It's been over 2 years now and no amount of alcohol can wipe them completely. It always starts the same way. It tortures me with happy memories and then shatters me with how it ended. It reminds me of how perfect my life was before that night but mostly it makes me think of *her*.

Every night it starts with my first day at Primary School, the day I met her. For most people I'm sure that memory is a fuzzy story with lots of missing pages. But not mine. I remember it as clear as yesterday.

I was so terrified to leave my Mum at the school gates to join the rest of the children in the playground. I'd pictured that all teachers would be like Miss Trunchball from Matilda and that this would be the worst day of my life. Little did I know by going to school that day it would be the day everything changed.

As I walked through the playground I was surrounded by children who were running around playing games. They were genuinely having fun with each other. I on the other hand was the complete opposite. I didn't want to be there. I just wanted to be with my parents where it was just the three of us. The way I liked.

Each class was assigned a colour such as red, green, yellow etc. I was in class 'blue' which I was pretty pleased about as blue is my favourite colour. Teachers were dotted around the playground holding up their class colour on a large piece of card so the new children knew where to go. I headed straight to the lady who was holding up the blue card. She smiled and looked down at me in a friendly, welcoming way. She looked older than my Mum and was very curvy. She had her red hair tied up in a pony-tail and had shiny, pale pink lipstick on… some of which was on her teeth.

"Hello, what's your name?" She asked as I stared at her pink stained teeth.

"Matthew Parker. But, but I like to be called Matt, please," I remember speaking so quietly. I'm surprised she even heard me. She smiled and nodded as she started writing on her clipboard.

"It's nice to meet you Matt. I'm Mrs Harding and I'm your new teacher," she then peeled off a blue sticker from her clipboard and reached down, sticking it to my school jumper. "There you go, now everyone will know to call you Matt."

The sticker she put on my shirt had 'Matt' written on it. I smiled as I placed my hand on the sticker and pressed it down firmly before following Mrs Harding into the school. She led the way down a corridor where every door to a classroom was a different colour, representing the colour of that class. We stopped as we came to the classroom that had a blue door.

"This is your classroom. Every desk has a name on it, have a look around until you find your name and take a seat. Everyone has been placed in alphabetical order from your first name as it makes it easier for me to learn who you all are," she smiled as she directed me to enter the classroom.

There were a few children already in their seats who were sit-ting quietly and looked just as nervous as I was. For some reason I headed straight for the back of the classroom. I figured as the letter 'M' was quite far down in the alphabet that my seat would be at the back. But I also wanted to hide away from everyone else and I couldn't do that at the front of the class. The delight on my face was well and truly visible when I found giant letter stickers spelling 'Matthew Parker' on a desk that was not only at the back of the classroom but also in the corner. Away from everyone. I quickly took a seat at my desk and then looked at the name of who I'd be sitting next to. The stickers spelt 'Mia

Parsons' and I suddenly realised… I would be stuck sitting next to a girl! Yuck!

Once the school bell rung and this mystery Mia Parsons still hadn't arrived, I remember thinking that I'd somehow gotten away with it. Maybe I wouldn't have to put up with an icky girl next to me for a whole school year. The excitement in my stomach began to rise just as there was a faint knock on the blue classroom door. I knew it, I knew it right there and then that the knocks would be from a very late, Mia Parsons. Frustration took over and I slammed my head on the desk pretty hard. I'm sure some kids would have turned around but I didn't lift my head to see. I closed my eyes and wished so hard that it wasn't her. I just wanted to be alone, just me myself and I until school had finished and I was back with my parents. But then I heard her voice for the first time. All of those thoughts flew out of my head almost as quickly as I'd hit my head on the desk moments before.

"I'm sorry I'm late, my Daddy's car broke down and we had to run here but," the panicked voice rushed her explanation and was quickly cut off by a reassuring Mrs Harding.

"That's ok don't worry, please come in," Mrs Harding said in the same friendly tone she used on me earlier.

I lifted my head as Mrs Harding welcomed her into the classroom and then first laid eyes on Mia Parsons. Her hair was long, light brown in colour and was in two pigtails. She was tiny, smaller than me and looked so incredibly delicate but also terrified. From that moment onwards something inside of me wanted to look after her.

"What's your name?" Mrs Harding asked as she approached Mia with her clipboard. Mia was the only child who hadn't arrived so it was obvious who she was, but I also decided this was not the time to shout out and answer Mrs Harding's question.

"Mia, Mia Parsons," she replied shyly whilst fiddling with her skirt.

Mrs Harding nodding and began writing on her clipboard again before peeling off Mia's name sticker and placing it on her school jumper.

"Welcome to class blue, Mia. I think your seat is in the corner over there."

Mrs Harding pointed at me, and that was when both Mia and I locked eyes for the first time. We were so young but it's a feeling I will never forget and a feeling that only increased ever since that day. My stomach twisted with nerves and excitement. I felt my hands go clammy and my foot started tapping quietly under the desk. Mia approached me slowly, ignoring everyone else in the room and then sat down next to me. Not once did our eyes drift apart from each other. I remember hearing Mrs Harding in the background begin talking to the class, but Mia and I were in our own little world.

Mia eventually broke our eye contact as she looked at my jumper to my name sticker. I followed her eyes and looked at my sticker too, before following her eyes to the name on my desk. I have no idea why but I suddenly felt insecure of my name as she analysed them.

"Which are you?" Mia asked quietly.

"S-sorry?"

"Your name, do you prefer Matthew or Matt. They're different," she points with one hand to my sticker and one hand to my desk.

"Oh, right. I um, I prefer Matt. But if you'd like to call me Matthew then you can."

I remember thinking *'please don't call me Matthew'* but my thoughts quickly disappeared. It was like Mia cast a spell on me as I watched her reach across my desk to where my name was. She carefully peeled off the letters 'h', 'e' and 'w' from my name, leaving simply 'Matt Parker' on my desk.

"There, now everyone will call you Matt," Mia smiled proudly as she admired her handy work. Her eyes then met mine and I swear they sparkled at me. I think I knew from that moment on that Mia was special.

Mia turned to face Mrs Harding and for the first time she started to pay attention to what she was saying. I was the opposite. I was fidgety and couldn't concentrate on anything other than the girl next to me. I wanted Mia's attention back on me, but I didn't know what I could do that wouldn't get us in trouble. I couldn't correct her name on her desk as it was already spelt right. I couldn't ask her for a pencil to use as we were all given stationary. I genuinely didn't know what I could do. That's when I placed my hands in my trouser pockets and felt something.

On the way to school Mum bought me a small packet of M&M's. Mum told me that students were not allowed to have sweets in their packed lunches so as it was my first day and I was so nervous she let me sneak in my favourite sweets. I just had to be extra careful not to get caught, that was the deal.

"Mia?" I whispered quietly enough for her to hear me.

She turned her head to face me slowly taking her gaze off Mrs Harding.

"Yeah?"

"Would you like some?" I asked and showed her the packet of M&M's. I was careful to keep them underneath the desk so that no-one other than us could see them.

"M&M's are my favourite!" She smiled and nodded her head in excitement.

"Mine too!"

I remember thinking how perfect she was and for a girl she was pretty cool. I quietly opened the packet and then tipped some out into her small, cupped, waiting hand. We would causally, but carefully, take it in turns to pick one from her hand and eat them.

"What's your favourite coloured M&M?" I asked her quietly as we kept our eyes fixed firmly on Mrs Harding.

"The blue ones, what about you?"

"My favourite are the blue ones too."

She grinned just as much as I was as we turned to face each other.

"Can we be best friends?"

I nodded instantly, "Yes!"

She giggled at my response and nodded back at me, "Do you

think that M&M stands for Matt and Mia?"

"It does now."

That right there was the start of our friendship. We were inseparable throughout the whole of Primary School. Each of us would take turns in bringing M&M's to school and I'm proud to say that neither of us ever got caught. Every night after school one of our parents would pick us up and we would have dinner at each others houses. Weekends were spent at the playground which was in the street that separated our houses. We'd both lived in this town our whole lives yet we never once bumped into each other before. Little did we know that we were only a couple of roads away from each other the whole time. We didn't have many other friends, we were content with just each others company and didn't need anyone else.

The nightmare then shifts to High School. Luckily we both got into the same school and were once again in the same class. We took a few different subjects but the majority of lessons we were together.

Things got interesting between us when we hit puberty. I always knew I liked Mia, and I mean *really* liked her. But the feelings I had for her multiplied when I was a teenager. I had no idea if she felt the same way or not and therefore, being a stereotypical male, I didn't talk to her about how I felt and decided to keep it to myself. In my head I came up with every scenario you could imagine of me telling her how I felt. All of which resulted in her hating me and never seeing her again. But then one day she wasn't the same. Well she was still my Mia, but something was on her mind I could tell.

I decided to take her to Epsom Downs on the weekend to try and get it out of her. We'd always thought that Epsom Downs was our place to chill, unwind and forget everything. We could sit there for hours, during the day or for sunrises and sunsets. It didn't really matter to us. We would just enjoy each other's company and admire the view of London.

It was the 4th of July and we were both 16 years old at the time. We had a picnic together and then had a walk through the woods. It was maybe around 4pm when we decided to go into the lake with our inflatable doughnuts and played around until the temperature dropped. I remember walking back to our towels just laughing and joking with her as always. I had my arm around Mia's shoulder and I pulled her against me because she was shivering slightly. Halfway walking back to our things she placed her arm around my waist too. I tried to hide the fact that her touch gave me goosebumps, but it's so hard to hide anything from her.

"Look at you trying to act all manly when you're just as cold as me!" Mia chuckled at my goosebumps.

"I wasn't cold until I tried to warm up what feels like a damn ice cube, you're freezing Mia," I told her as I shrugged off the fact that every time I touched her it gave me goosebumps.

Mia giggled next to me when we reached our towels. She watched me bend down and pick up her towel first, wrapping it around her tightly. I remember rubbing her shoulders trying to get her warm as I totally lost myself in her beauty. Her eyes were staring back at me looking just as love struck as I was. But surely that was my mind wishing that's how she felt? This is Mia, there's no way she would like me. I'm her best friend; she could have anyone if she wanted, why would she pick me? I managed to snap out of it and quickly removed my hands from her before turning around and picking up my own towel.

"Are you still hungry, we have some left over sandwiches," I began and then she interrupted me in the best possible way I could ever have imagined.

"I think I have feelings for you," she blurted out.

I've never felt it before, but it genuinely felt like my heart stopped. A tingly sensation spread throughout my body and my smile was from ear to ear.

But then I stopped. I've dreamed of this so many times, it has always only ever been a dream. I *must* have fallen asleep and I'm just dreaming again. Right?

"What did you say?" I questioned eventually, keeping my back to her still.

"I-I think I like you and more than just a friend," she repeated sounding terrified.

I stayed silent at first still in disbelief that this was actually happening.

"Mia," I began to turn around when she let out the saddest sob I had ever heard from her.

"I'm so sorry, Matt. I shouldn't have said anything. It's just been eating away at me for what feels like forever and I just can't take it anymore,"

"Mia, stop it's ok," I interrupted her this time.

"I can't lose you over this, I just needed you to know and," confusion set in and her sobbing stopped as she tried to work out if she heard me correctly. "What did you just say?"

"It's ok, Mia. I feel the same way."

"You do?" Mia questioned as a tear rolled down her cheek.

I stepped forward, closing the gap between us and wiped the tear from her cheek with my thumb.

"I think I always have," I whispered before kissing Mia for the first time.

The nightmare then skips from the happy memories of how things started to our last day together.

The day everything stopped.

It's July 4th again only this time we're both 23 years old and we're resting on the bonnet of my car at the top of Epsom Downs. On that day, our last day, we'd enjoyed the sunset over London and it was now dark. All I could hear was the gentle sound of nature and Mia's quiet, calm breathing next to me. It's such a peaceful, soothing sound and is a sense of comfort for me.

"Just think, this time next year we will be celebrating our anniversary in America. The whole country will be setting off fireworks for July 4th so it will be like everyone is celebrating with us," I told her.

"What if we don't like America or we don't want to be out there for as long as we planned, would you be disappointed?" Mia asked.

"I don't care where we are, if I'm with you that's all that matters to me," that's honestly the truth. I only ever need to be with her I don't care where we actually are. "But just incase we *are* in America for July 4th next year, shall we get some practice in?"

I grinned mischievously at her, little did she know I had a surprise for her.

"What do you mean?" Mia frowned.

"Why not celebrate tonight with fireworks?" I questioned cheerfully. Mia's face was full of confusion which was quickly replaced with excitement as she put everything together.

"You have fireworks?" Mia asked as I walked around to the boot of my car. I wasn't able to purchase many as we have been saving for what feels like forever so we can go and explore America together. But I was able to get us a few rockets and some sparklers. Mia watched as I lifted the box of rockets and sparklers up out of the boot.

"*We* have fireworks."

Mia squealed in excitement as she ran around to meet me. She tried to walk and read the packets at the same time and tripped causing us both to laugh at her clumsiness.

"I think it's best I light the fireworks, Miss Clumsy," I poked her nose and began to unravel the rockets from the box.

"Can I do one? Or can we do one together, yeah let's do the blue one together," Mia always talked really fast when she's excited which is one of the million things that I loved about her.

"Ok, ok," I laughed, "We can do the blue one together."

Mia clapped her hands in excitement as I picked the blue coloured rocket from the box. We both placed it far enough away from where my car was and took a match each from the box. We strike our matches and then light the firework together. The sizzling sound of the firework made Mia shriek in excitement as I grabbed her hand. We both ran away from the firework and waited at my car for it to shoot up.

"This is so exciting!" Mia gasped as we waited.

I didn't say anything. I stopped watching the firework and just watched Mia. Her smile was huge as she waited patiently. She looked as beautiful as ever. Her eyes glistened as they focused on the firework which was seconds away from reaching its peak. She gripped hold of my hand as the firework finally shot up into the sky. We watched as the colour blue exploded everywhere with the London skyline in the background.

"Happy anniversary Mia," I whispered as I turned to face her.

Mia instantly turned to face me with the biggest smile.

"Happy anniversary Matt."

Then the physical pain starts as the nightmare shifts to *that* moment.

It was around 11:30pm when we'd finished all of the fireworks and had eaten every last bit of the food I brought for us to eat. That was except for a packet of M&M's. We'd packed everything away and I was currently driving Mia back to her home whilst she'd feed me the odd M&M.

"So are your parents coming to the airport next week?" Mia asked as she munched away.

"Uh-huh. Dad isn't really too bothered but you know what Mum is like. Her precious baby boy is going gallivanting in America for 2 years with his girlfriend. I can already tell she will be a blubbering mess when it's time for us to go through security," I shook my head as I spoke because although both Mia and I laughed we knew that's exactly how my Mum would behave.

"It's cute though, she loves her little Matty-kins," Mia teased as she popped another M&M in my mouth and then pinched my cheeks. "Both my parents will be there too. I suspect that our Mums will cry together and our Dads will head straight to the pub for a pint."

"I think you're right. Don't get me wrong saying goodbye to them will be hard,"

"Um, it's a 'see you later' not 'goodbye' Matt."

"Sorry, your majesty, saying 'see you later' will be hard but we'll be back in no time. I'm so looking forward to doing everything we dreamed about. We'll visit every state in America. We'll see all the famous sights and I'll be making memories daily with this little weirdo who's coming with me," I grinned at her as she gently slapped my thigh.

"Hey, less of the little!" She protested playfully.

"Wait, you're offended because I called you little rather than the weirdo part?" I laughed as I questioned her.

Mia pauses for a moment as she tries to come up with a smart answer and as usual, she does.

"Oh no that offended me, because of that you're not getting an M&M for at least 2 minutes," Mia grinned as she placed a few M&M's into her mouth. She slowly ate them and expressed how much she was enjoying each one just to rub it in my face.

I couldn't help but laugh at her and the way she is. It's impossible to ever get irritated or mad at this women.

"I'm so hungry," I moaned playfully. "I can't keep driving if I don't have any food in my stomach."

"Oh no, that's a shame isn't it," she said sarcastically and placed another M&M in her mouth. "Mmm, my stomach is so full right now, these tastes so good," she exaggerated whilst trying not to laugh.

"Must. Have. M&M. Can't. Go. On," I joked as I pretended I was dying dramatically next to her.

"Fine, fine," Mia laughed in defeat. "Here you go."

Mia placed an M&M into my mouth and I crunched down on it triumphantly.

"Yes! Matt wins again! I knew you would cave. My Mia wouldn't let me go on without an M&M if it was the last thing she did."

I turned my head to face her and took one hand off the steering wheel, placing it on her thigh and giving it a gentle squeeze. She placed her hand on top of mine and squeezed back as she held the packet of M&Ms in her other hand. When we turned the corner the bag tipped out of her hand and the M&M's spilled all over the floor.

"Oh no!" Mia gasped.

"Not the M&Ms!" I joked as though I was devastated.

"Hold on I can fix this, 5 second rule," Mia laughed and unbuckled her seatbelt. She quickly reached for the packet and started collecting them all back up, putting them back into the bag.

I laughed and turned my gaze away from hers back to the road as we approached some traffic lights which were green. We passed them and moved into the junction like we had done every other time we've done this journey together.

Except this time it wasn't just like every other time.

This time as we passed the traffic lights both Mia and I were distracted by the bright lights of a speeding car coming towards us that had jumped their red light.

"Shit!"

I turned the steering wheel as quick as I could to get us away from the car making the tyres screech underneath us. I tried, I tried *so hard* to avoid the car but I couldn't. It happened so fast. In a second I went from laughing to having my whole world flipped upside down.

"Matt!"

"No!"

The car slammed straight into Mia's door, spinning us around instantly. I tried to reach for her to keep her upright but it made no difference. The sound of Mia screaming my name is something that haunts me daily. Mia flew forward and slipped through my grasp. Her head smashed against the dashboard as we continued to spin into oncoming traffic. A second car hit us, straight into Mia's side again but this time it caused my car to flip over.

Glass shattered around us as Mia's lifeless body flew in every direction. The crunching sound of metal and glass breaking was all around us until the car finally stopped upside down.

Silence, complete and utter silence.

"Mia," I managed to say.

She didn't respond.

Her body was at a funny angle, half hanging out of the smashed windscreen whilst I was still loosely strapped to my seat. I tried to get to her but my body wouldn't move as warm blood trickled down my face.

The nightmare skips once more, one final time.

Have you ever had one of those dreams where you wake up and momentarily you don't know where you are or what's even real? That's how I felt when I woke up in the hospital. The first thing I saw was both my parents by my bedside. Their eyes were red as though they hadn't slept for days and their faces were tear stained. But the relief when they realised I was awake was clear for all to see. They both bombarded me with questions, not knowing what the right thing was to do.

"Are you ok?" I remember my Mum asking desperately. "Can I get you some water?"

"Shall I get the nurse? I should get the nurse," Dad told himself but he stayed by my side.

I was so confused. The smell of cleaning products almost made my nose hurt. I rubbed my nose and realised there was a tube in it.

"Don't worry sweetheart, it's just a little bit of oxygen," Mum reassured me. "Do you remember what happened?"

I frowned in response and it hurt. I then realised how much my whole body hurt. Everywhere ached as I moved my body. I raised my head and saw cuts on the skin that wasn't covered by blankets and felt this enormous pain in my head. My parents watched me as my brain caught up and then I felt this sickening feeling in my stomach as everything came flooding back.

"Mia!" I gasped and attempted to sit up only to feel my body scream at me in return to stay still. I had no idea where she was but I knew I had to get to her.

Mum and Dad gently restrained me from moving anymore and I just felt too tired to try. Mum took my hand in hers and looked at Dad as a tear rolled down her cheek. Mum then focused on my hand in hers and Dad looked at me with the most sympathetic, heartbreaking face I have ever seen. It was then that I knew. I knew what they were going to say. There was no reassuring look from them, just unspoken words that told me everything.

"Mum?" My voice broke as I spoke.

"Sweetheart you have to stay calm," Mum's voice wobbled

when she finally spoke.

"Where is she?" I felt a tear roll down my cheek, stinging as it touched various cuts on my face.

"She, s-she was brought to the hospital with you," at that point Mum really started crying and couldn't continue. Mia had become like the daughter my parents never had and I could see that this was hurting them just as much as me.

"Can I see her?"

I'll never forget the way they looked at each other as they tried to find the right words. They had what looked like a mental conversation before Dad turned to face me.

"No, no you can't see her," he put one hand on Mum's shoulder to comfort her and then sighed as he ran his fingers through his hair. "Son, Mia didn't make it. She was pronounced dead upon arrival."

All of the air in my lungs disappeared as my eyes filled with tears, blurring out my parents faces completely.

"I'm so sorry," Mum sobbed as she squeezed my hand tighter.

"She c-can't have," I couldn't finish the sentence. I could not say *that* word. "Why am I here and she's not? Why? How is that even possible? We were in the same accident. She should be here, she should be ok!" I shouted in anger to anyone who would listen.

"The paramedics said Mia wasn't wearing a seatbelt. She wouldn't have felt anything, she wouldn't have been in any pain," Mum did her best to reassure me but it didn't work.

"You don't know that!" I snapped back and then attempted to get out of the bed again.

"Son, you need to stay in bed."

"Matt please, lay down."

"I need to see her, I *need* to," I told them as I sat up and fiddled with the various wires attached to my body.

"That's not possible, Son," Dad's tone is sympathetic but stern enough to make me look at them both.

"Why?"

They look at each other briefly before Dad continues.

"You've been in a coma for 11 days, Mia's funeral was 2 days ago," Dad rests his hand on my shoulder as he guides me back into bed.

I feel numb. Totally and completely numb. Mum started re-arranging my blankets around me just as the Nurse walked in.

"Welcome back, Matt. It's good to see you're awake," she said cheerfully as she picked up a clipboard and started checking the machines. "How are you feeling?"

I didn't respond.

I *couldn't* respond.

"He's just a bit overwhelmed," Mum explained.

"That's understandable," the Nurse nodded sympathetically.

Everyone is treading on eggshells around me with such sad faces. I feel like I can hear *everything*. The sound of the Nurses pen writing on the paper. Every bleep from the machines around me. Shoes echoing from people walking down the corridor and then I hear her scream repeat in my head over and over, getting louder and louder as the anger boils over inside. That's the last time I was going to hear her and that terrifying scream is what I'm left with. I need to get out of here, now. Against my bodies wishes I pushed up from the bed and ripped the tubes from my nose.

"What are you doing?" My parents said at the same time reaching for me.

"Matt stop!" The Nurse said as she rushed over.

"Get off me!" I shouted and swatted her hand away and then pulled out a drip that was in my arm. I yelped in pain but didn't stop disconnecting all of the machines from me.

The Nurse pressed a giant red button on the wall which started making all sorts of noises. I screamed in pain as I covered my ears and closed my eyes, everything's too loud. Mia's scream and this stupid alarm repeating over and over getting louder and louder is too much.

Various hospital staff rush in and I feel several hands on my body forcing me back to bed.

"Make it stop!" I screamed out in pain.

I glanced at my parents momentarily. Dad was holding my Mum as they could do nothing but watch. They looked so helpless, so sad and so worried.

"It's ok Matt, I'm going to give you something to help," A male voice said. I looked to my side and saw a doctor inject something into me. There was a strange sensation in my arm and then I felt everything slowly begin to get heavy as whatever he gave me flowed around my blood stream.

"Just make it stop," I mumbled as everything begins to fade away.

Then I wake up. Sometimes I'm breathing heavily, sometimes I'm sweating and sometimes I even wake up crying. It doesn't take long for me to realise that it's never just a nightmare, it's a memory.

A memory that I relive every single day.

The day that I lost her.

The Confusion

Matt

The plane lands just as I down the last little bottle of whiskey I have. I crave the burning sensation it gives the back of my throat. My body waits patiently for me to stretch after our 10 hour flight but I decide to punish it a little longer and stay still.

"Ladies and Gentleman this is your Captain speaking. We have safety arrived at London Heathrow. The weather is slightly different here compared to where you've just come from in Las Vegas."

I scoff at his comment and look outside. It's raining again, like it always does in this country. I ignore the rest of the announcement and gather my stuff together before checking my phone. There's a text from Mum telling me to have a safe flight. I don't bother responding. They're expecting me to come home tomorrow but I ended up taking an earlier flight.

I left England 2 years ago now to go travelling around America. It was always what we planned, Mia and I, but I didn't see the point of it anymore. It was both our parents who actually made me get on the plane and do what we'd planned. I guess at the time, leaving was probably the best thing for me. I was struggling being around everything that reminded me of her, or us. It was slowly eating me up inside. I think every single day I lost a bit more of myself because everything I was, everything I did, included her. I had to learn how to be a different version on myself and most importantly, learn to live without her. I couldn't do that in a place where I was constantly reminded of her. So I literally packed the absolute bare minimum and walked away from my life without looking back.

Over the past 2 years I definitely started to get used to my own company. Well, I didn't have a choice. My intention at first was to still do what we'd planned and visit every state. But I didn't do that, or more like I *couldn't* do that. I just can't do anything without her no matter where I am in this world.

I ended up visiting New York, Los Angeles and then spent the rest of my time in Las Vegas working in a store on The Strip. Working was never part of the plan but that's a story for another day.

I thought getting away from everything that reminded me of her would make me happy again but it didn't. It somehow made it harder and it just delayed closure.

My god did I need closure.

After I got off the plane and grabbed my duffel bag from the luggage claim area my anxiety levels began to rise. Although I felt ready to go home and face everything again it still hurt every part of me inside. My heartbeat started to quicken and my hands began to get clammy again. This is a feeling I've gotten so use to having but I still can't control it. I can *never* control it.

Everyone around me seems to be in such a rush whereas I'm the complete opposite. People look so happy as they run through the arrivals gate into the arms of a waiting loved one. You can see the joy on their faces once they are reunited, happiness and love was completely surrounding me. It's torture.

"Sir, you need to keep moving," a security guard tells me.

I realise that I'm standing still in the middle of the arrivals entrance just watching everyone around me.

How long was I standing there for?

I give the security guard a nod and before I realise it I'm walking towards a bar within the terminal. It's like my body knows what I need before I do.

"What can I get you?" The barmaid asks with a flirtatious smile. I dump my bag down and take a seat with a bit of a thump.

"Whiskey," I reply bluntly and look away from her.

"Coming right up."

My eyes are drawn back to the arrivals gate again. I feel anger, sadness and loneliness all at once. People of all ages and all races are coming through the gate looking the complete opposite of how I feel. I don't even know who they are but I just feel hatred towards them. All of them.

My eyes land on a woman walking through the arrivals gate who's walking with such determination it makes her stand out from the rest. She then stops abruptly and lets go of her small suitcase as she fiddles with her phone. The lump in my throat begins to rise as she turns slightly in my direction so I can just about see the side of her face.

Mia?

I blink a few times convinced I'm seeing things.

It wouldn't be the first time.

Once my eyes focus again she's still very much standing there looking at her phone. I feel like I'm going crazy, I *know* it's not her. It *can't* be her. Yet here I am, standing up and making my way over to where she is.

"Sir, sir your whiskey!"

The spell is broken. I look back at the barmaid who's holding my drink up looking really confused at me. I turn back to the arrivals gate and scan the crowds for her again but she's gone.

She was just there!

I rub my eyes desperately and look for her again but she's nowhere to be seen.

I'm going mad.

I sigh in frustration and walk back to the bar pulling out a £20 pound note. The barmaid watches as I slam it on the bar and grab the whiskey, downing it in one.

"Keep em coming," I tell her.

"Sure thing," she takes the money and replaces it with another whiskey just as I asked.

It must have been a couple of hours since I landed and probably after at least half a bottle of whiskey later before I felt like I was ready to go home. I grabbed my bag and headed out the terminal where of course it was still raining. There was a short queue for taxis and before I knew it I was climbing in the back of one. It felt strange being in a car and driving on the left side of the road after so long, it felt foreign.

The journey home from the airport was fine until we started to enter the familiar streets of where I grew up. But what made it worst is driving past the place that changed my life forever. The place where we crashed. Just like that night, the traffic lights are green but the taxi drives through the junction with ease.

Why couldn't that have happened that night?

Why did everything have to be the way it is now? Why did it have to be Mia and not the drunk driver of the other car who died? He managed to somehow walk away with no injuries whatsoever. Whereas Mia, she was the complete opposite.

My palms go sweaty again. My mouth is completely dry and I have this horrible twisting feeling bubbling away in the pit of my stomach. I try to focus on my breathing and close my eyes.

Think Matt, think. Think of something that made you happy, something that made you smile.... Even if it is of Mia.

Which is what I've tried so hard to stop doing but it's the only damn thing that seems to calm me down!

We drive over a bump in the road which makes me open my eyes. I then see a familiar coffee shop looking back at me that holds so many memories. I close my eyes again and let my tortured mind think once more of a happy memory we shared.

Mia and I were 13 when we tried it for the first time. We thought it was a good idea. We'd seen everyone else do it and they seemed to enjoy it. It was her idea. I wasn't too keen on it but I decided to do it for her because, well, I'd do anything for her.

"Are you sure you want to do this?" I asked her. "We could do something else?"

"No, I want to try this. Plus there are so many different types we could have. I don't even know how to pronounce some of them, but I want to try," Mia had this thing she could do with her eyes. They would widen but look so sad as she'd stare at you. She did it every time

she wanted something. She just had this control over me and truth be told, I loved it.

"Fine," I smiled as I opened the door. "After you Miss Parsons."

"Thank you, Mr Parker," she grinned as she stepped inside.

Just like she said I had no idea how to pronounce half of these things. We were silent as we tried to read what was on offer, quietly figuring out what might taste nice. Yep, that's right, we were about to try our first cups of coffee together.

"What an earth is a macchiato? Did I even say that right?" I asked her.

Mia giggled next to me and then covered her mouth trying to be mature. "I have no idea. I might have a... oh look you can have flavoured syrups added to it!" She said excitedly.

I smiled as I made my decision. "Ok, I'm going to have a late-e, with vanilla syrup".

"That sounds yummy, I'll have a late-e too but with caramel," she says proudly.

I nodded and we walked up to the barrister together.

"Hello, what can I get for you both?" the cheerful barrister asked us as she smiled.

"Hi, can we have two late-e's please, one with vanilla syrup and one with caramel syrup?" I asked her feeling very grown until she let out a little laugh.

"Late-e's? Do you mean latte's?" She questioned raising her eyebrow slightly.

Mia burst out laughing and I felt myself go incredibly red. I just embarrassed myself in front of Mia, way to go Matt!

"Um, yeah, yeah two latte's please," I mumbled as I got out my wallet.

"No problem. Is this your first ever coffee trip?" The barrister asked as she wrote on to two coffee cups.

"Yeah," I nodded "It was her idea," I pointed to Mia giving her a little shove as she continued giggling.

"I see. Well consider this a treat from me. As it's your first experience in a coffee shop I can only do so much to make it a memorable one. So this ones on me," the barrister smiled.

"Are you sure?" Mia asked and the lady nodded. "Thank you so much. Here, this is our first time tipping someone so this is yours," Mia reached over to the barrister and handed her a £2 coin. The lady took it and smiled back at us both.

"Thank you, that's very kind. Have a good day and hopefully I'll see you again," she had a genuine tone to her voice that made me feel like coming back even if the coffee was awful.

Her colleague prepared our drinks for us as we watched in amazement. We decided to get them to takeaway in case we didn't like the coffee; we didn't want to offend anyone especially after she was so nice to us.

We took our coffees, waved goodbye to the barrister and then left the coffee shop. We walked down the street and took a seat on a bench near a park. We both looked at each other, waiting for the other person to try the coffee first. I wasn't nervous but I also wasn't too thrilled about the fact that it might taste horrible. Especially if Mia liked hers. Then I would have to try and stomach the rest so that I wouldn't look stupid in front of her.

"You first," Mia said looking at my coffee cup.

"Nah-uh, this was your bright idea so you go first."

"Fine," she huffed. Mia looked at the coffee cup for a moment before taking a few little gulps. "It's really nice, try yours."

I was trying to work out if she was bluffing or not. Maybe it is nice? I lifted up the coffee cup taking a large sip and swallowed it. It tasted bitter and was genuinely just awful. But I couldn't let Mia know that because she liked hers and she was so excited about this.

"Wow, that's nicer than I thought," I lied.

"Really?" She questioned sounding shocked.

"Yeah, want to taste mine?" I offered, bluffing my way through this horrible idea of hers.

"Um, no that's ok. I'll stick with mine."

She didn't like it either, I could tell.

"Well, are you going to take another sip?" I asked with a smile pointing to her cup.

"It's um, it's a bit hot right now," she lied again and I nodded.

"Mia, you don't actually like it do you?" I grinned.

She looked at the coffee cup and back at me with a straight face. Slowly the smile began to show and she started laughing, shaking her head.

"No! I hate it. This was a bad idea I'm sorry."

"I hate it too," I laughed "Let's wait until we are much older before trying that again."

"Deal! When we do try it again remember it's called latte not late-e."

We both laughed before putting our coffee cups in a bin and walking back to her house.

That was a good day, every day with Mia was always a good day.

"Which number are you?" The driver asks as we pull into my parents road.

I was genuinely in a world of my own and had no idea we were here already.

Thinking of her always helps distract me.

"It's the white painted house on the left."

The driver stops the car right outside my parents driveway as instructed. I look out the window and see my childhood home staring back at me. It doesn't look the slightest bit different from when I last saw it. The lawn outside is freshly cut. The window boxes still have colourful plants in them. The white paint on the house looks like it's just been repainted and the red door is glistening back at me.

"Everything ok?" The driver asks as I haven't moved yet.

Am I ok? I don't even know. I feel many things at the moment but I don't know if 'ok' is one of them.

"Um, yeah I think so. I just haven't been home for a while that's all," I tell him as I reach for my wallet.

"Ah! Another returned wonderer. Do you know you're the second fare I've dropped off to this area today? Both of you looked just as confused as each other," he chuckles.

"No kidding," I mumble as I pull out a £50 note and hand it to him.

"I think it was only a road or two away from this one, was

it Cherry Lane? The woman had been staying with a relative up north and flew home today for the first time in what she *thinks* was a few years, but she wasn't sure."

"Cherry Lane?" *Mia lived there.*

"Yeah I think so," he nods and gets out of the car.

She's everywhere. No matter what I do there are reminders of her wherever I go!

The driver opens the boot to get my bag out at the same time I open my door. My phone slips out of my pocket and lands by my feet but when I reach down to pick it up something catches my eye.

It's me. There's actually a picture of me poking out from underneath the car mat by my feet. I pause before reaching forward and picking up the picture. My heart stops when I see that it's not just of me, its of Mia too. This picture was taken at her 21st birthday party.

"Anyways I thought to myself, that's strange to not know how long you've been away for, and so I asked her. I felt bad once I did though. It turns out she was involved in an accident a while ago and she only went and lost her memory didn't she? That's rotten luck don't you think?"

My legs feels like they're going to give way underneath me as I stand up from the car. Could he be, is he talking about Mia, *my* Mia?

"Is this her?" I blurt out as I reach forward and show him the picture. He looks at it for no more than a few seconds and then looks back at me with a shocked expression.

"Hey, that's you!" He points out.

"Is *this* her?" I repeat louder and much more desperate whilst pointing to her in the picture.

"Woah man, calm down!" He holds his hands up in defence as I continue holding the picture in front of him.

This man is *really* testing my patience.

"Look, I'm sorry, but I need to know if the girl in the picture was the same girl who was in the back of your taxi earlier today," I tried to sound calmer and less aggressive but I don't think it came off very well.

"Yeah, yeah that was her," he answers quickly.

"Are you sure? Are you *absolutely* sure that was her?"

"Yes, she told me her name. It was um, Amelia? No, Maria? No that wasn't it,"

"Mia?"

"That's it, Mia," he confirmed.

"Oh my god!" I gasp and let my body fall against the car. How, *how* is this happening? Mia died?! My parents told me she died, *her* parents told me she died.

"What did she say again?" I ask desperately.

"Something about an accident a few years ago and she lost her memory."

"And it was definitely this girl in the picture? You're sure on that?" I point to Mia in the picture again.

"Yeah, that was her."

"They told me she died," I mumble in disbelief.

The driver looks at me really uncomfortably and checks his watch.

"Listen man, she looked really sad an all but she's definitely not dead. I don't mean to be rude but I have another fare that I need to get too," the driver says hesitantly as he scratches the back of his head.

"Right, so-sorry."

I pick up my bag and make sure I have the picture in my hand before stepping away from the car. The driver wastes no time in getting in his car and driving away from me.

My legs don't move, my whole body can't move. I just stand there in the pouring rain holding onto the picture of us with the slightest hope that Mia is somehow, *alive*.

The Lie

Matt

My feet feel as though they're stuck to my doorstep. I feel sick, angry, but also incredibly confused. Of course I want to believe that Mia is still alive, that's all I have wanted to believe since the accident. But I don't want to let myself believe it. I don't think I'll fully believe it until I see her and physically get to hold her.

If she is alive, why did everyone lie to me? Our parents practically pushed me onto that plane 2 years ago. Why would they do that if she was alive? How could they do that to me, to Mia and to us?

I'm snapped out of my thoughts as Mum excitedly opens the front door. Behind her is my Dad with a newspaper under his arm. They look delighted to see me, happier than I ever remember them being.

"Matt! You're home!" Mum shrieks as she leaps forward to wrap her arms around me. I don't particularly feel in a hugging mood right now so it's a good thing I'm still holding my bag which restricts me slightly. The picture of Mia and I is tucked safely in my back pocket and out of sight from my parents. For now at least.

"Come in, come in," Mum unwraps her tight grip from my shoulders and guides me inside, closing the door behind me. I'm smothered by the familiar smell of Mum's cooking. It's a Sunday roast, my favourite, but I have absolutely no appetite right now.

"Welcome home, Son," Dad comes forward and gives me a quick cuddle before taking my bag from me. He places it on the floor and gives me a look as if to say, 'you can unpack later'.

"Can I get you a tea or a coffee," Mum asks and then literally sniffs me. "Have you been drinking?"

I don't respond as we all walk through the lobby and into the living room. The room hasn't changed at all, the furniture is still in the same place as when I left. The radio is on quietly in the corner and there are fresh blue and yellow flowers on the dining table in the room. On the walls and mantel piece, like in most homes, there are pictures everywhere. Pictures of me, Mum, Dad and Mia. My eyes are fixed on her as she smiles beautifully at the camera. I total gets lost in her smile, she was so happy.

What happened to you?

"Matt?" Mum nudges me as she waits for a response.

I take my gaze off the picture and look back at my parents, shaking my head and sit down on the armchair. I really don't know how I should approach this, part of me wants to scream and shout at them to get answers. Then there's a part of me that wants to have a calm, frank conversation with them. But right now, I have a problem with just finding my voice.

Mum and Dad both look at each other for a second. The joy of seeing me on their faces is quickly replaced by concern. They both take a seat opposite me on the sofa as they study my expression.

"Are you alright love? Was it a bad flight or are you just not feeling too well?" Mum asks me.

I look back at the picture of Mia. We were so happy and then that accident tore everything apart. But it wasn't just the accident that tore us apart. It appears to have been our parents too. That is if Mia is actually still alive.

"I haven't been alright since the accident," I mumble as my gaze is still on the photograph.

"Oh Matt," Mum says sympathetically as she begins to get up to come near me. "It must be hard coming back after all this time."

"Don't!" I snap and hold my hand up indicating for her not to come any closer. Mum pauses and looks really taken back as well as worried.

"What's gotten into you?" Dad questions sounding annoyed. Ironic really, they lie to me and yet *they're* annoyed?

"What's gotten into *me*?" I ask as I properly stare at them both for the first time. "I guess finding out that everything is a lie has kind of bothered me a bit. So forgive me if you're both not exactly my favourite people right now!" I explain sarcastically.

They know what I'm talking about. I can see it in their eyes. The fear, the sympathy, the sadness, I see it *all*. They look at each other and I can tell just like that day in the hospital they are having a mental conversation about how to approach this. Once again, like that day, Dad gets the short straw and is the first to speak.

"What exactly is it that you know?" He asks calmly.

Dad leans forward, resting his arms on his legs and holds his hands out in front of him. He's testing the waters. He wants to know what I know first before they confirm or deny anything.

"She's alive, isn't she?" I question bluntly and stare directly into his eyes.

I wait, I wait for what feels like an eternity to hear the words I've wanted to hear since the day I woke up in the hospital. The lump in my throat feels as though my airways are slowly closing and then he finally answers.

"Yes, Mia's alive," Dad confirms.

I let out a breath that I didn't realise I was holding followed by the loudest sob I think I've done since that day in the hospital. I run my fingers through my hair and feel so much anger inside of me. I can't take all this pain that's ripped through me for years for nothing. I need to numb this feeling, the pain, the confusion, the deceit... it's all too much. My parents watch me storm over to their drink cabinet and pull out a bottle of whiskey. I take two large gulps and then slam the bottle down onto the table.

"Matt!" Mum gasps as I make her jump.

I ignore her and keep my eyes on Dad.

"Why did you lie to me? You're supposed to lie about things

that don't matter, *Dad*. Like 'no I didn't have the last biscuit' or 'no I didn't use all of the hot water'. You don't lie about *death*. You don't tell your Son that their girlfriend died when she actually didn't!" I shout in pure disgust and take another gulp of whiskey.

"We had good reason to lie. Please, put the drink down and let's talk about this properly," Mum says softly.

"There is NO good reason to lie about something like that you stupid woman!" I scoff.

"Matthew! That's enough!" Dad shouts.

"Whatever," I take another gulp.

"Please stop drinking," Mum sobs.

"You see this, this is what your lies have done," I hold the bottle up at them. "It's how I've coped without her. It numbs the pain of being without her. You caused that, you and her parents caused that with your hurtful, vicious lies!" My voice has such venom in it even I don't recognise myself when I talk.

Mum wipes the tears from her face and looks at Dad.

"We got it wrong, we messed up. We get that now," Dad admits.

"Please let's just talk through this. Put the drink down and we'll tell you everything," Mum begins but there is only one thing on my mind right now. There is only one thing that I want to do, that I *need* to do.

"I have to see her," I interrupt as I put the bottle down and start walking towards the front door.

"I don't think that's a good idea," Dad says quickly as he walks in front of me.

"Your Dad is right, Matt, please sit down we need to explain everything," Mum pleads.

"No! I have waited long enough. You've had over 2 years to tell me everything and you didn't. I'm going to see her and this time you can't stop me!"

"You can't!" Mum snaps. "She doesn't know who you are!"

She doesn't know who I am?

I pause and replay her words over and over as the room falls silent. Of course she remembers me, she's been looking for me. That's why the picture of us both was in the taxi. She has come back to find me, she's probably been looking for me all this time but I've been in America.

"Of course she knows who I am," I scoff as I finally dismiss her comment.

"No Son, she doesn't. She doesn't remember anything," Dad tells me softly.

Even though my parents have lied to me for so long, I can't help but believe them. I called her phone daily for the first month or so just to hear her voice on her answerphone. No one ever returned my calls and then one day the phone was disconnected. If Mia knew about me she would have tried to contact me, wouldn't she? She would have tried to find me. She would, I know she would.

"I don't understand," I mumble, rubbing my head trying to process everything. They both give me a few minutes to compose myself. I may have been away for a long time, but my parents always know when I'm struggling to process something. No matter how much time has passed that hasn't changed. Even when I thought Mia had died, I knew how and I knew why. I hated it, I didn't like it but I *understood* it. This is different. None of this is making sense right now.

Dad clears his throat as he begins to explain.

"The night of the accident Mia suffered life changed injuries. She hit her head so badly that the impact caused swelling to her brain. The doctors said that she was unlikely to make a full recovery and if she did," Dad paused.

"If she did, if she did what?" I ask eagerly.

"If she *did* survive her injuries, she wouldn't remember, anything," Dad finally finishes.

"What do you mean *anything*?"

"Her head injuries were so bad Matt, they didn't expect her to survive. The damage done to her brain wiped her memory, completely. She doesn't remember you. She doesn't remember her parents or growing up around here. She doesn't even know who she is," Mum sobs as she explains.

I shake my head at her words. There is no way in this world that Mia would ever be able to forget me or forget us. All those years we spent together, all the memories we made, she couldn't forget that – she couldn't!

"Th-that's not possible," I mumble shaking my head.

It's then I realise I'm crying as a tear rolls down my face and touches my lips. I wipe it away quickly and look at my parents.

"I'm so sorry Matt. We knew it would completely break you having the girl you love look back at you with no idea who you are. We couldn't see you go through that. She wasn't supposed to survive. That's why we lied to you. We spoke with Mia's parents and decided that it would be the best thing for *you.* The Mia we all knew wouldn't have wanted you to watch her either slowly slip away or look at you like a total stranger. We hoped that in the long run you'd be happy again. That's all we wanted for you," Mum finished.

The room falls silent as I can see the relief from my parents as the biggest lie they've ever told is out in the open after all these years. But her words repeat over and over. *She wasn't supposed to survive. She wasn't supposed to survive.* But she did...

"She does remember me, that's why she's come back," I snap.

"Son, I know you want to believe that but she doesn't," Dad says firmly.

"You're wrong! Look, she's been looking for me!" I stand up and take the picture out of my pocket and show it to them. They both look at the picture of us and then back at me with confused expressions. "She wasn't *meant* to survive, but she did. So why the hell can't her memory have come back too!"

"I don't understand," Dad mumbles still looking at the picture in my hand.

"It turns out my taxi driver took a woman home from the airport today who has been away for a few years after she had a car accident. That woman carried this picture and left it in the taxi. Are you going to tell me that's a coincidence?" I snap.

"That, that's impossible," Mum whispers in disbelief.

"That's what I thought too, Mum, because an hour ago I thought that the girl in this picture was dead. But she isn't. She's here and she's looking for me. Maybe she won't remember me or she won't remember everything. But I will do *everything* I possibly can to help her memory come back and even if I can't, it's not for you or her parents to decide that I can't see her! You've kept us apart for too long already!"

I turn around and walk out the living room, with my parents hot on my trail.

"Matt, Matt where are you going?" They both shout after me as I open the front door.

"To find Mia!" I shout back and start running.

In a heartbeat I'm out the house, down the path and running towards Cherry Lane. Their voices calling after me fade away as I turn the corner.

I pray with everything inside of me that this is not a twisted dream, even though it's going to completely rip my family apart.

The Questions

Matt

Mia's house is staring back at me. It looks slightly different to how I remember it. The front lawn isn't freshly mowed and the flowers in the window boxes look a little thirsty. Mia's house was all about perfection. Her parents took pride in having a well presented, welcoming home. The more I look at the house in front of me the more I realise that this is far from the well presented, welcoming home I once knew.

You'd think I'd be banging on the door but I'm frozen on the path. The whiskey feels like it's left my system but there's a part of me that wishes I could have a bottle with me right now. Just to cope with this. The other part of me knows deep down that as soon as I see her nothing else will matter and I won't need anything else but her.

She could be the other side of the door, rummaging around for clues as to who I am. Yet I'm right here. I might be scared but that's because I remember. Mia is probably scared because she doesn't remember and that is worst than anything I'm feeling. It has to be. So I get the courage together and go for it, finally knocking at her door. As I wait for her to answer I only then realise how hot and sweaty I am. After all I did just run here from my house as fast as I possibly could. The first time Mia will see me in years is when I'm looking like a sweaty unattractive... *stranger*? Perfect! Before I have a chance to downplay my appearance anymore, the door opens. But it's not who I wanted it to be.

"Matt?" Liz, Mia's Mum.

She looks tired, stressed even and I'm pretty sure she's been crying. *Good, me too.* Her cheeks look just as flustered as I feel like mine are.

"Hey," I mumble flatly.

I'm not really sure how to approach this. I'm angry at her but I don't want to cause a scene. Plus, she was like a second Mum to me. I'm torn between missing her and Aaron (Mia's Dad) and disliking them all at once.

"I thought you were still in America, when did you get home?" She looks so confused but there's some sympathy to her facial expression.

"I got back today. Mum didn't call you?" I raise my eyebrow as I keep my hands in my pockets. My parents knew where I was coming, they must have given Liz a heads up.

"No? Should she have?" Liz frowns but looks worried at the same time.

Her expression makes me feel bad for her which is exactly the opposite to how I want to be feeling. My emotions are so torn right now and I hate it. I look at my shoes and remind myself why I'm here, Mia.

"Where is she? Is she home?" I finally ask.

Liz lets out a deep breath, almost a sigh. She looks heartbroken, truly heartbroken. *Stop feeling sorry for her.* I can't help but think it wasn't just me who lost Mia that day. If what they're saying is true about her memory then they lost her too. Liz doesn't respond at first and then she steps aside opening the door wide enough to let me in.

"She's not here. You better come in. I think it's about time we talked about everything," Liz tells me sadly.

I do as she says and step inside her home. The house smells of roses and apples, which is exactly how Mia used to smell. Liz always has fresh roses around the house and has never changed the smell of her cleaning products, which always smelled like apples.

Liz leaves me in the living room whilst she makes us a cup of coffee each. I take in my surroundings and look at the pictures on the wall. They're all really old pictures, nothing recent at all. They've taken down all the pictures that used to be up of Mia and I together. They've completely wiped me from their lives. Mia's house was a lot like mine with regards to pictures of us. Our parents were always so supportive of our friendship and then relationship, they'd have pictures of the two of us all over their houses. My parents haven't changed anything but Mia's have. That hurts.

I sigh and lean back on the sofa, slouching my hands down either side of me. My left hand hits something next to the sofa and curiosity gets the better of me. I lean over and take a look at what's inside the box which has been badly hidden. I open the box and see myself staring back at me. It's all the pictures of Mia and I that were once hanging around their house. Now they're tucked away in a poorly hidden box between the sofa and the wall. *Why?*

The sound of Liz leaving the kitchen makes me put the pictures back and sit as though I wasn't rummaging around, but I wasn't quick enough.

"We only took those down today, in case you were wondering," Liz explains as she places my coffee on the table in front of me. She then takes a seat in the armchair to my right.

"Why?"

"I didn't want to confuse her."

"Confuse her, it's *me*?"

"But she doesn't remember you, Matt, and that's the problem. Imagine walking into your parents home and seeing all these pictures of you with people that you don't remember."

Ok, that would be weird. But it's also something they've created.

"Maybe you shouldn't have lied to her, or me for that matter?" I scoff and immediately feel bad afterwards.

"Sorry," I mumble and run my fingers through my hair in frustration.

"No you're right, I deserved that," Liz admits. "I really am sorry, for everything."

I keep my head in my hands and try to get control of my anger.

41

They have *no* idea what I've been through these past few years and I have no idea what Mia's been through because of them.

"I'm trying really hard to hold it together right now and be polite but I'm so angry, and confused too, actually. I feel *so* much but anger tops it."

"We messed up, I see that now."

"Messed up? *Messed up*," I shout making her jump. "Why does everyone keep saying that? Messing up is not lying about your daughter *dying*, Liz! That's fucked up and nothing less."

"I know I know, you're right, Matt, I'm sorry. I'm so sorry for all of this I truly am. It was a bad choice of words," she rushes in desperation.

"You've made a lot of bad choices," I spit back.

"I know," she agrees sadly but I can't bring myself to look at her. "How did you find out?"

"Mia and I took the same taxi home from the airport and I found this on the floor," I pull out the photo of us and show Liz. "She spoke to the driver briefly, about an accident and her memory. Then my parents confirmed it and now I guess I'm here."

"She was looking for this," Liz explains as she gives the picture back to me. "When she got home she of course demanded answers and went to show us the picture but she couldn't find it. She was so angry she'd lost it."

"She probably thought she was going mad. I can't even begin to imagine what's going through her head right now."

Liz nods as looks down sadly.

"What?"

"I only wanted to protect you both. That's all I tried to do. But you're right, she thinks she's going mad. After all this time, after everything, you know her better than anyone."

"Can I ask you something?" I question.

"Of course."

"If Aaron had an accident that changed a part of him, whether that be something physically or mentally, would you walk away from him?" I ask her as calmly as possible and stare directly into her eyes.

"No, of course not," Liz answers instantly.

"So why an earth would you think that having me walk away from your daughter was something that I'd have chosen?" I can't help but slightly raise my voice.

"We *knew* you wouldn't want to walk away from her. But she wasn't supposed to survive Matt. We thought we were going to lose her and we couldn't have you just sit and wait for that to happen. You were really injured too, you were in a coma for 11 days and the longer it went on we decided you needed to focus on your own recovery and not Mia. We did what we thought was right for you both," Liz tries to reason with me, but she doesn't seem to understand that she is fighting a losing battle here.

"But that's not your choice to make! The only two people that should ever decide if they want to be apart from each other was myself and Mia! You took that from us and that was wrong. Whatever your intentions were, that was wrong."

"I will never be able to explain how sorry I am, to both of you. We all honestly thought we were doing the right thing for you both," Liz looks sad and defeated as she drops her head. "I understand now that we couldn't have been more wrong."

"Who's bright idea was it? Was it my Mum's?"

Liz shakes her head and sighs. "It was mine and your Dads decision."

"What?"

"Your Dad was holding it together better than your Mum was, she wouldn't leave your bedside. Your Dad came to see how Mia was doing just after the doctor explained the chances of Mia making it through were pretty much zero and it just sort of went from there. It felt right at the time, maybe it was just because it was something we could control. Your Mum didn't like it but eventually she agreed that it was the right thing."

My head just spins round and round as I juggle it all. There's so many lies and so much deceit, yet I'm still not with the one person that I *need* to be with.

"Where is she?" I ask after a few moments silence.

"She's upset, like you are. She doesn't trust anyone and she's confused about everything. Aaron took her out for some fresh air so she could clear her head. She didn't want to be around me," Liz explains.

"I don't blame her, I mean, I've done the same thing. I can't be around my parents right now either and if I'm really honest, being around you is just as hard."

Liz nods in agreement as if to say she understands but it still hurts her.

"Does she, um, does she really not remember me?"

Liz sighs at my question as my stomach twists in anticipation. I'm terrified to know the answer but I *have* to know.

"No she doesn't remember you. But she wants to," Liz says softly.

I close my eyes at her words and bury my head in my hands. It hurts, this all really, really hurts.

"How is it that she even knows who I am if she doesn't remember me?" I question as I try and piece everything together.

"Mia's been staying at her Grans house because the best doctor for her lives in Scotland. Before she moved there we boxed up every picture of you that my Mum had and put it in her loft so it wouldn't confuse Mia. I guess Mia went into the loft and found some things, then she came straight home. She hasn't actually been here since the accident, so we had to take everything down too. We didn't know how much she knew about you so we didn't want to make it worse. When she arrived she was so angry but when she went to show us the picture of you both and couldn't find it," Liz pauses and looks so sad. "It was just too much for her."

"When did you know she was coming home?"

"A few hours before she arrived. She's so confused right now," Liz sobs and I find myself walking toward her.

It's like my old self, the one who's not angry or hurt is back and wants to comfort the broken lady in front of me. I put my arms around her and she grips onto me so tightly as she cries.

"I'm so sorry for the hurt I've caused."

"I know you are," I reluctantly admit. "I want to help her remember and she wants to remember too. We all want the same thing, we all want our Mia back," I struggle to hold myself together as the words leave my mouth.

"I know, I just don't think that right now is the time to go barging into Mia's life. She needs to process things, as do you. She needs time, Matt. She's struggling right now more than we could ever imagine and I don't want you to add to that," Liz explains softly as I sit back down on the sofa.

"I wouldn't add to that. I can help. It's me and it's Mia. I've never done anything but make her smile and I want to do that again," I plead.

"I can't let you do that right now Matt, I'm sorry. Mia needs time,"

"With all the respect, I don't think anyone knows what Mia needs right now. What she *needed* was people she loved to be by her side and you took that from her at her most vulnerable time. I will never understand how that was the right thing to do but keeping me from her now is *not* the answer. I'm sorry Liz but you, Aaron and my parents have done all you can to keep us apart for years. That stops now. I will help her remember until the day *Mia* tells me not to."

Liz sighs and nods slowly. "On one condition."

"Which is?"

"Go home and sober up first. I could smell the alcohol on you the second you walked in."

I don't feel like I've been drinking at all, I feel completely sober since the moment I got home. But she's right, the last thing I want Mia to think when she sees me is that I'm a drunk or something, because I'm not. I've just been broken for a really long time.

"I guess it's about time we should agree on something," I mumble and she smiles.

Liz and I stand from our seats and make our way over to the front door.

"Come by tomorrow, say 9am?"

"What will you tell her?"

"I don't know yet, I need to think about it."

"Maybe try telling her the truth for once, she doesn't need anymore lies or confusion," I can't help but throw another comment at her. She gets it though, it's written all over her face. She opens the door in silence and I walk out without looking back.

The Reunion

Matt

When I got home Mum and Dad rushed out of the living room to meet me but I headed straight for my bedroom. Mum quickly asked if I'd found Mia and I simply said no before slamming my bedroom door. They'd already brought my bag up to my room for me whilst I was out and left me a bottle of water by the side of my bed. I pretty much downed the lot as I looked around my room. My bed was freshly made but everything else looked pretty bare except for the memories of Mia and I dotted around my room.

As predicted I'm sure, there are pictures of us everywhere you look. On my windowsill there's a picture of us at a concert that we saw a couple of months before the accident. It was our favourite band, Coldplay. We'd tried to see them live every time they went on tour but were never successful in getting tickets. This time though I'd somehow managed to get us meet and greet tickets which was a great experience. Next to the picture of us with the band there's our tickets with their autographs on them. Mia was so happy that night, *we* were so happy that night.

Being in this room with all these memories is so overwhelming. Everything I thought I knew has turned out to be one huge lie. I wish we could go back to how we were in these pictures before everyone started making life changing decisions on our behalf. I eventually collapsed on my bed whilst still fully clothed and just stared at the pictures, well at Mia, until I fell asleep feeling completely drained.

You know those nights where you literally close your eyes

for what feels like a second and the next thing you know it's morning? Your mind then takes a few seconds to realise where you are and what's happened? That's how this feels. My body clock is all over the place right now. It's still on American time plus pure exhaustion so I don't quite register the buzzing sound that slowly wakes me. It takes me a lot longer than it should to realise it's my phone ringing and I need to answer it. I sigh feeling exhausted as I pull my phone out of my pocket and keep my eyes closed. I just touch the screen repeatedly until the ringing stops and then balance my phone on my ear so I don't actually have to hold it there.

"What?" I groan.

"Matt? I'm sorry it's the middle of the night but,"

"Who is this?"

"It's Liz."

"Liz?" I question and then everything comes flooding back to me. I'm no longer in America I'm back in England at home in my own bed and more importantly, Mia is *alive*. In a heartbeat I'm wide awake. I sit up so quickly that my phone flies off the side of my face where it was balancing. I quickly scramble across my bed and pick it up again.

"What is it, what's wrong?" I question feeling my heartbeat quicken. *Somethings wrong, why else would she phone me in the middle of the night?*

"We can't find her. Aaron's only just got back she hasn't come home."

"Wait, what? I thought Aaron was with her? You said Aaron was with her."

"No, Mia stormed out and Aaron went after her but he couldn't catch up with her. I didn't want to worry you when you were here earlier."

"So you lied to me, again!" I snap.

"Yes but please can we not talk about that now. We need to find her," she pleads with me.

I'm so angry at her. Everyone just constantly lies and all it does is hurt myself and Mia. I take a deep breath and try to compose myself whilst ignoring the fact I want to throttle her right now. Mia needs to be my priority.

"Where have you looked?" I ask bluntly as I leave my bedroom.

"*Everywhere!* He's checked every park within a 5 mile radius, he's checked various pubs that were open and has driven down every street possible but there's no sign of her. She doesn't know anyone Matt, there's nowhere else she could possibly have gone. I've called hospitals, the police but nothing."

"Dad, I'm borrowing your car," I shout up the stairs as I grab his keys. I then realise it's 2am so he's either not heard me or I've woken him up. Either way I don't wait for a response and leave the house.

"I'm so worried, what if somethings happened to her," Liz sobs.

"Does she have her phone with her?" I ask as I unlock Dad's car and climb inside.

"It's going straight to voicemail."

Voicemail? Could it be? Could she really be at our place, at Epsom Downs? It's so high and in the middle of nowhere that we never got signal if we were at the top. If she is there then how did she know about that place? Could it be that she remembers going there?

"I think I know where she is. I'll go and check it out, phone me if you hear anything," I tell Liz before hanging up.

I haven't driven a car since the accident. But I push through how daunting that feeling is and focus on finding Mia. Thankfully the roads are completely empty so the journey doesn't take long at all. The country style roads are so dark, there's no street lights so it's just my car headlights lighting the way.

I start thinking of what I'm going to say to her if she's there. How and earth do I approach this? The thought begins to make me feel so anxious that I almost zone out and don't even realise I've parked. I turn off the engine and rest my head on the steering as I gather myself.

Think of how she's feeling.

I eventually get out the car and realise how cold it is out here. She's going to be freezing if she's been out here all this time. Dad used to keep a blanket in the boot of his car so I quickly go and check his boot. Thankfully it's still there so I grab it and knock over a flask. I can't help but laugh when I see it. Dad once broke down in the middle of nowhere during winter and ever since then he keeps a flask in the boot of his car with hot chocolate in it and a blanket. He'll change the flask every couple of days which I always thought was a waste of hot chocolate but right now, I couldn't be more thankful. I open it up just to check it's fresh first. Steam immediately comes out so I put the lid back on to keep it warm and close the boot. I throw the blanket over my shoulder and head through the darkness to what was always our spot, the highest possible view point.

The moon reflects beautifully on the small lake as I pass it and the leaves gently rustle in the breeze. I forgot how beautiful this place is. There's a bench near the top of the hill that I can just about see. On that bench is a silhouette of someone sitting on it. It's her, it has to be. Who else would come here in the middle of the night. My anxiety is through the roof as I approach because I have no idea what to say. I don't want to scare her but I almost certainly will because after all it's the middle of the night, in the middle of nowhere and as everyone keeps telling me, she doesn't know who I am. She hasn't noticed me yet, her gaze is fixed firmly on the view of London as her hair gently blows in the wind. I stand a good distance away and just watch her for a moment in complete disbelief that it's her. I'm surprised she can't hear my heartbeat. I decide that staying this far away from her at first is a good thing. She'll probably feel less worried about a man approaching her in the dark. I close my eyes for a moment and concentrate on my breathing. I count to ten, very slowly, and then finally pluck up the courage to talk.

"Mia?" I call loud enough for her to hear me in the most softest and friendly way I could possibly do.

Please be her, please be her.

The person jumps and their head whips around to the direction of my voice instantly. They scramble to their feet, grabbing their bag and take a few steps away from the bench and away from me.

"Who's there?!" Mia's panicked voice fills the silence of the night and sends shivers down my spine.

It's you, it's really you.

"Please don't be scared. I'm not going to hurt you. Your Mum, Liz, phoned me asking if I could help find you," my voice breaks as I talk, I can't control that even if I tried. I take a step closer to her but she backs away again.

Please don't do that.

"Stay where you are!" Mia's panicked voice tells me.

"Ok ok," I reply quickly and don't move as I hold my hands up in surrender. "I've brought you a blanket and some hot chocolate if you'd like it? I'll leave it here on the floor for you and I'll go back to my car so I can phone your Mum and,"

"No! Please, *please* don't call my parents," Mia interrupts with desperation in her voice.

"They're worried about you. I was just going to let them know you're ok. I won't tell them where you are," I explain calmly.

"I said no, don't call them!" She shouts but her voice breaks slightly.

Mia wipes her face and it pains me that I can't comfort her. She eventually walks back to the bench and sits back down, her shoulders slump and I can tell how tired she is even from a distance. Her outburst shocks me but I can't even begin to process how she must be feeling right now. However, with her sitting back on the bench knowing I haven't left I'm hoping it means she at the very least doesn't feel threatened by me anymore.

"Ok, I won't," I finally respond.

I debate for a few moments whether or not to leave her alone or stay. But I've been away from her for too long. My body is like a magnet to her and my legs slowly start to walk in her direction. I want her to be safe and I want to protect her. That's all I've ever wanted to do.

Starting a conversation with Mia was never hard and never an effort. Right now it feels like I have lots of doors in front of me with various options and I just don't know what one to pick. Every door has a different ending, her telling me to leave or her walking away etc. I need to get this right. Asking her if she's ok is pointless because I already know she's not. Asking her if she remembers me doesn't seem fair to her. Then I think of her parents and it's actually a good thing that she's angry at them right now because frankly, so am I. Surely that is the safest option?

"Your parents aren't really in my good books right now either and I don't want to go home. Can I sit with you for a bit?" I try to sound as causal and none desperate as possible but the truth is I'm terrified. I don't want her to tell me to go, that would hurt me on so many levels.

However, this time she doesn't jump at my voice, she just looks in my direction and studies me for a moment. I'm close enough to really see her now and I feel like my legs could buckle at any moment. Her hairs a little longer than before, she's wearing a baggy jumper that she's pulled over her hands and she has skinny jeans on. Her face is just as beautiful, but it's tired and sad. Her eyes sparkle in the moonlight but it's clear she's been crying for hours. Mia turns back to the view of London and shrugs her shoulders.

"Sure," she sighs.

I let out a breath which is thankfully disguised by the sound of the wind and I *finally* close the gap between us. I take a seat on the bench and feel like my heart is going to jump out of my chest. This is the closest I have been to Mia in over 2 years and it feels incredible as well as heartbreaking. This is the girl who I grew up with, who I'm madly in love with and yet, she has no idea who I am. I can't help but stare at her. It doesn't feel real that she's sitting next to me. Eventually she turns to face me again and we just look at each other for the longest time in complete silence.

"I recognise you, from the pictures," Mia clarifies. "Are you Matt?"

I feel a lump in my throat start to grow as I nod back at her. "Yeah, I'm Matt."

She studies every part of my face with her eyes. I can tell she's desperately trying to find something familiar about me.

"And how do we know each other?" She questions hesitantly.

"Um, well we grew up together," I do my best to word this right, she must be so overwhelmed right now.

"So we were just friends?" She frowns.

"For a long time we were best friends and then we started a relationship when we were 16 years old," I explain as my stomach drops.

She really doesn't remember.

Mia looks back at the view of London as she takes it all in. I continue to watch her almost like I'm finally feeding the craving I've spent so long trying to satisfy with alcohol.

"When did we break up?"

"We didn't," I tell her softly.

She closes her eyes at my words for a moment and then turns to face me like she's searching for something.

"I don't remember you," her voice is almost a whisper as a tear rolls down her cheek.

"I know," I reply as I wipe my eyes before the tears fall.

"I'm so sorry," Mia sobs and covers her faces with her hands.

Instinct takes over and I pull her close to me. I can't take seeing her so broken, it's killing me. I hold her so tightly whilst she cries against my chest. The feeling of her in my arms again feels like it's slowly healing this giant hole inside of me. I feel like I'm finally home.

"Mia you're frozen," I tell her. "Here, put this blanket around you."

I hold her with one arm as I reach for the blanket with the other hand and give it a flap so it opens. She grabs it with one of her hands and immediately covers her body with it and then shares the remaining bit with me. I thought she'd maybe move away but she doesn't. She lets me keep one arm around her, probably for warmth but I don't care. I'll take it.

"I don't know what's real anymore," Mia whispers to herself.

Me either.

"Why are you angry at my parents, what have they done to you?"

I huff in annoyance as I think about what they've done and what their actions have created, which is this broken girl in my arms.

"It's not just your parents, I'm not talking to mine either. They all have a big problem with telling the truth apparently," my tone is incredibly sarcastic and full of hatred as I talk. "I struggle to even look at them right now let alone be in the same place as them."

"Was it about me, their lies I mean?"

"It has *everything* to do with you," I mumble sadly as I look at her. "I don't even know where to begin."

"Well I know that night I crashed my car and,"

"Wait, what? Who told you that?" I snap feeling even more angry.

"Everybody?" She frowns sounding nervous. "Is that not how I ended up in hospital?"

I shake my head and run my fingers through my hair as I try to keep control of my anger.

Be the person she needs, control it.

"Mia, I was driving that night, not you. You were in the passenger seat."

"I don't understand, everyone told me I was driving."

"Of course they did."

Nothing surprises me anymore, they literally made sure I was wiped from her memory.

"Why would they lie about that?" Mia questions.

"Because they're arseholes!" I snap. "I don't think they know how to tell the truth anymore. They weren't expecting you to survive your injuries so when you woke up and it was confirmed you had memory loss it was easier for them to lie to you about your life in order to protect the fucking lie they told me!"

My anger is not towards her and I can tell she understands

that. She doesn't even flinch when I raise my voice, in fact she moves a little bit closer to me.

"What lie did they tell you?" She asks softly.

I close my eyes at the memory and take a deep breath before looking at her.

"They told me you died, Mia."

Her facial expression completely changes and a small laugh leaves her lips in disbelief as though I'm joking. Slowly her face turns to disgust as she realises I'm being serious.

"Oh my god, you're not joking?" She clarifies.

"No, unlike them I wouldn't lie to you about that. I wouldn't lie about that full stop."

"When did you find out the truth?"

"I'm not sure I actually know the whole truth yet," I rub my forehead before continuing. "But I found out you were alive about 12 hours ago."

"12 hours!" Her jaw drops and her lips wobble from the cold. It's like something inside of me switches and I go from being really angry to instantly wanting to take care of her again.

"You're so cold," I tell her as I reach for the flask. "There was some hot chocolate in my Dad's car that you can have, hang on."

I reach and pick up the flask to show Mia. She looks at me, then at the flask before she starts laughing.

"You do realise it's leaking don't you?"

I never thought I would hear her laugh again, at least not in person. I have videos of her where she laughs but it doesn't do it justice. Hearing it in person after all this time is one of my favourite things in the world. But the warm feeling of liquid on my skin quickly distracts me.

"What? Ah man!" I groan as I realise there's a crack in the flask. "I knocked it over earlier but I didn't realise I'd cracked it."

I quickly pull the cups off the lid and open the flask. I manage to pour us both a cup each of what's left inside, making sure hers is completely full.

"Thanks," Mia says as she takes the cup from me. She holds it for a moment to warm her hands up and then takes a sip.

"Is your Dad here?" She questions looking over my shoulder.

"No, I just borrowed his car that's all," her shoulders relax again when she's reassured it's just us.

We sit in silence again but it's a comfortable silence. I still feel like I'm going to wake up any minute and this just be a twisted dream. As much as I'm angry and confused about everything I also feel like all of my wishes have come true because Mia's here with me. And I mean actually here with me rather than my mind playing tricks on me.

"I recognise you from the pictures. My doctor is based in Scotland so for as long as I remember I've been staying at my Grans house," I just watch Mia as she talks, I can see how jumbled her head is and she just needs to get it all out. "I was having a tidy up in my room and wanted to put some of my stuff up in her loft. I'd never been up there before. It was so dark I tripped on something and ended up knocking over a box. All these pictures just spilled out on the floor around me, some in frames and some not. You were in *every* single one of the pictures with me. There were some from when we must have been maybe 6 years old. Gran wrote on the back of each picture the date, who was in it and the occasion. Time and time again I would see Matt and Mia, Mia and Matt, followed by Mia's 9th birthday, Matt's 11th birthday, Matt and Mia's graduation party. But I don't remember any of it, yet it was me in the pictures. I'm that girl and yet I don't remember *being* that girl," Mia is so confused, she sounds broken as she talks. "So I brought the box down from the loft and asked my Gran about it. She didn't know what to say or more like what she should say. She didn't give me answers so I took a picture of us, packed a suitcase and caught the first flight back to London. I thought my parents would give me answers but I couldn't find the picture of us," Mia sobs as she wipes her cheeks with the blanket. "They made me feel like I was going crazy."

"You're not crazy," I reassure her and pull the picture of us out of my back pocket, holding it out to her. "I think this belongs to you."

Mia looks at the picture and then back at me before taking it.

She stares at it for a moment and then looks at me again.

"This is the picture I lost, I don't understand? How do you have it?"

"I was at the airport today too. I thought my mind was playing tricks on me because I could have sworn I saw you there. I didn't handle it well I guess and decided to have a few drinks at the bar before going home. It turns out you and I had the same taxi driver back home from the airport. I found it on the floor in his car," I explain.

"I told him a little bit about what had happened," she says softly as she looks at the picture again. It's almost like the picture offers her reassurance in all this.

"Yeah I know, he sort of confirmed to me before anyone else that you were alive."

"I have so many questions," Mia admits.

"Me too," the problem is I don't know where to begin.

"How did you know I would be here?" Mia questions.

"Your Mum said your phone was going straight to voicemail and we never got signal here. She listed all the places your Dad checked and this wasn't one of them."

"We've been here before?"

I nod and look at her. "We called this our place. We've been coming here for years."

"Our place," Mia repeats quietly.

"It's strange isn't it, you don't remember being here but yet you naturally ended up coming here," I point out as I try to understand it all myself.

"It's like deep down I knew about this place?" She frowns in confusion and wipes her cheek again.

"It's ok to cry, don't hide how you're feeling from me. We're in this crazy situation together," I move closer and pull her tightly against me again. She cries into my chest and holds me back as I do my best to stay strong for her, but I'm feeling everything with her. The betrayal, the hurt, the confusion, the anger... I get it.

"I'm sorry," Mia sobs as she pulls away from me and wipes her face again. "I don't even know you and yet I'm crying like a baby and making your shirt all damp."

You do know me.

"You have nothing to apologise for," I tell her as she picks back up her hot chocolate. She takes another sip and then studies me again.

"I wish I could remember you," she tells me.

"I wish you could remember me too," I smile sadly.

"Were we happy?"

I nod instantly. "We really were, we were joined at the hip most of the time."

We both stay silent for a moment before Mia places her hot chocolate on the floor and then turns her body to face mine.

"Help me," she says quickly.

"What?"

"Please help me, help me to remember everything and who I am. I can't trust my parents, clearly, and it seems you and I did a lot together so if there's anyone who could help me remember, it's you right? I want to remember the life I had. I know it's a lot to ask but if you,"

"Mia, nothing you ask of me will be too much," I interrupt her whilst smiling "I will do anything I possibly can to help you remember. You have my word."

"Pinky promise?" She suggests as she holds out her pinky.

We would always use pinky promises to seal a deal, the fact she is suggesting that means that she is still in there. I smile as I reach forward to her finger and then pause.

"On one condition, even though we're really angry at your parents right now you let me take you home. If we stay here all night you'll get pneumonia," I question as I hold my finger near hers, waiting for her to agree.

She pauses and sighs before nodding and linking our pinky fingers together.

"Fine, you've got yourself a deal."

We gather our things and begin to walk back to my Dad's car. We walk in a comfortable silence through the darkness. I look at Mia as she walks with the blanket wrapped tightly around her and just can't believe she's here. I pull Dads keys out of my pocket and unlock the car as we approach.

"Go ahead and get in, I'm just going to put this flask back in the boot," Mia nods and climbs in the front seat without hesitating to get out of the cold.

Now we're at the bottom of the hill I know my signal will be back. I reluctantly pull my phone out and decide that it's the right thing to do and text Liz.

I'm with Mia, she's ok. I'm bringing her home now.

I've not even had a chance to close the boot and Liz has already text me back.

Oh thank goodness, thank you Matt! Please drive safely.

Drive safely, drive fucking safely. Is she for real? Is that a dig at me or something because it definitely feels like it. I didn't purposefully have an accident, quite the contrary.

My anger resurfaces and I instantly wish I never bothered letting her know her daughter was safe. I never used to be like this, I *never* got angry. Liz is right though, the last journey Mia and I did together was when we had the accident and it was after we left here, our place.

"Is everything ok?" Mia asks loud enough from her seat. There's concern in her voice which hurts me. She may not remember me, but the truth is I'm not the same person I was. I'm bitter, angry and just as broken as she is. I try to control my breathing before getting in the car and closing the door behind me. Mia's eyes are on me instantly, they're literally burning through my skin.

"What's wrong, has something happened?"

"Nothings wrong, everything's fine," I try to reassure her. I keep my eyes locked ahead and fumble with the keys, attempting to put them into the ignition.

"You're lying to me," she mumbles disappointingly which

makes my stomach drop. I instantly feel like an arsehole, like I'm one of *them* who just lie.

"I text your Mum just to let her know you're safe and we're on our way home. She told me to *drive safely*," I scoff and make speech marks with my hands.

"So?"

"Mia, the last time you and I were in the car together was the night of the accident," I close my eyes as I try to erase the image of that night from my mind.

"Oh," she pauses. "And you were driving?"

"I was driving," I confirm and we fall silent for a moment before I continue. "And we were driving home at night, from here."

"Can you tell me what happened?" She asks softly. She wants to know what really happened to her that night and only I can tell her. It's strange how I've tried so hard to forget it and all she wants is to remember it.

"We were driving home and were messing about with M&Ms. You dropped the bag and they went everywhere," I feel my stomach drop and the anger begin to rise. "You took your seatbelt off to pick them up. It was just for a second, and that's literally all it took," a tear falls down my face and I wipe it away quickly before clearing my throat. "The light was green, we crossed the junction and this drunk driver ran a red light. He slammed straight into your side of the car and we span into the path of another car which again hit your side, flipping us," I close my eyes and try to picture anything else other than the words that are coming out of my mouth. "Your scream is something that's replayed in my head daily. Images of your head hitting the dashboard replay over and over. Glass was everywhere, we were both cut all over and were already bleeding quite badly. But you just didn't move," Mia wipes her face as she listens to me. "It's scary how something so perfect takes seconds to completely fall apart."

I blink away the water in my eyes and face Mia again. She's watching me so carefully, studying every part of me.

"Matt, what happened to me wasn't your fault," her tone is

full of sympathy. I give her a small smile as I appreciate she's trying to make me feel better.

"I should have waited for you to put your seatbelt back on."

"Or maybe I shouldn't have taken it off? Or maybe the drunk driver shouldn't have been behind a wheel of a car?" She interrupts me. "Hindsight is a wonderful thing and a terrible thing all at the same time."

"I know you're trying to make me feel better about it all and I appreciate that I really do, but our experiences of that night and what came after are very different, Mia."

She nods and turns back to face the road ahead of us. "They are. But neither of us deserve to suffer anymore than what we already have done."

"I can't argue with that one," I give her a small laugh as I put the key into the ignition and turn the engine on. I instantly fiddle with the heaters and put them all in Mia's direction. She's still got the blanket wrapped around her but her shoulders lower as she relaxes into the heat.

"Are you sure you're ok to drive? We can walk if it makes you feel more comfortable? I don't mind," Mia asks.

I smile at her offer and shake my head. "There's no way I'm having you walk when you're as cold as you are. We used to drive home from here all the time without a problem." I tell her.

"Well show me what the drive should be like," she smiles reassuringly.

I smile back and nod. It's strange that she doesn't seem nervous about being in a car with me again. I guess it's because she doesn't actually remember the accident.

"Sure, just put your seatbelt on and don't take it off, please."

The First Day

Matt

For the first time in years I felt like my body actually slept. Last night after I dropped Mia home I laid in bed and just stared at the ceiling, processing everything before I drifted off to sleep. Although I didn't sleep for long, it was the type of sleep that is so deep it felt like I'd slept for days.

Usually I'd dream of Mia, but last night I didn't. It was as though my mind finally got the closure it needed to switch off. I didn't need to dream of her anymore, she was here.

When I woke up it felt like I was a kid again on Christmas morning. I couldn't wait for the day to begin because I was spending it with Mia which is something I thought I'd never do again. I told Mia I would pick her up at 9am and we'd start the supposedly impossible task of trying to help her remember her life before the accident, and remember me.

I haven't decided where to go yet, I think I'll wait and see what type of mood she's in first. Yesterday her emotions were all over the place, she went from angry, to laughing and then crying so quickly. I want to be careful not to push her today.

"Matt, have you got my car keys?" Dad asks from outside my bedroom door.

"Um, yeah I do," I reply as I put my shoes on. I pick up his keys and open my door to see both Mum and Dad standing there.

"Alright," I manage to acknowledge them as I hand Dad his keys.

"I've made you some breakfast," Mum tells me.

"I'm good," I dismiss her offer and walk past them both before making my way downstairs.

They follow me in silence. It's amazing how uncomfortable we all are in our own home now. I grab myself a coffee and take a seat at the dining table.

"Eat, please," Mum pleads as she places a full English breakfast in front of me. Once it's in front of me my stomach growls and I realise how hungry I actually am. Truth be told I can't even remember when I last had something to eat. My mind wants to be stubborn but my hands pick up the knife and fork without permission. Mum watches me as I start to fill my stomach with something other than whiskey for a change.

"How are you feeling?" Mum asks hesitantly.

I pause and glare at her before swallowing the piece of bacon in my mouth.

"Don't ask me that," I tell her bluntly.

She looks so sad but I try not to focus on her as she takes a seat opposite me. Dad stands next to her and places his hand on the back of her chair.

"Liz called," Dad pipes up this time.

"That's nice. Have you come up with anymore lies or are you two done with fucking up my life?" I snap and take a sip of my coffee.

"That's not fair."

"*Don't* talk to me about what's *fair*," I give my Dad probably the worst look my face has ever produced and bang the table with my fist.

Mum jumps as Dad just sighs deeply in defeat. I pull my attention away from them and back to my breakfast, filling my mouth once more.

"Liz said you found Mia last night and you brought her home," Dad tries again to start a conversation with me.

"Yep."

"Was she ok?" Mum asks.

A sarcastic laugh escapes my mouth as I shake my head. "Oh yeah she's great, she's real happy to learn everything she's been told is a lie. I can't imagine how *that* feels."

"Enough!" Dad shouts at me making Mum jump again. I shake my head at him and decide not to respond. As soon as I finish my breakfast I am out of here.

"We want to talk to you," Mum finally breaks the silence.

"So, talk," I shrug and take a bite of toast.

"How did you know where she'd be?" Mum asks softly.

"Because I *know her*," I reply instantly.

"But how did she know to go there?" Mum pushes gently.

"I don't know, maybe her memory is still in there somewhere?" I shrug.

I mean I'd like to think that's the case but I'm not sure. Silence falls between us as I carry on eating. I don't really trust myself to talk at the moment anyway so silence works for me, until Mum breaks it again.

"How did it feel being in a car with her?" She questions hesitantly.

I shrug once more as I finish the last bit of food on my plate. "Strange I guess."

"Did she say much to you?"

"About?"

"Everything, does she remember anything?" Mum pushes.

I shake my head and sigh quietly. "She wants me to help her remember stuff, us, her life, everything."

If that's even possible.

"Liz mentioned that," Mum nods.

"What time are you going over there?" Dad questions.

"Once I finish this," I indicate to my coffee. "Can I borrow your car again?"

Dad shakes his head, he actually shakes his head at me. I'm so done with them both.

"Whatever," I finish the last of my coffee and stand up. "It won't stop me from seeing her you know."

"Just wait a second," Dad begins.

"Why are you so against Mia and I being together?!" I shout as I stand up and leave the room.

"We're not!" Mum defends them both.

"Really? Could've fooled me."

"You can't take my car because we've got you your own car," Dad shouts after me.

"You what?" I question as I turn back to them.

"When we knew you were coming home we got you a car to replace your old one. We didn't tell you because we wanted it to be a surprise but then you turned up here drunk and," Mum stops herself from explaining what else happened when I got home yesterday.

"You got me a car?"

Dad opens the chest of drawers behind him and pulls out a set of keys. He throws them to me and I snap back into reality just in time to catch them.

"It's the blue Ford right outside," he tell me.

I walk over to the window and look at the shiny car staring back at me.

They bought me a car.

They're both watching me as I turn back to face them. They're giving me the smallest of smiles as they wait for me to talk.

"You know this doesn't make up for what you've done," I mumble as I fiddle with the keys.

"We know, Son," Dad's tone is sympathetic and it makes me feel bad.

I don't want to feel bad for them, I have a right to feel angry.

"You better make a move, Mia will be waiting," Mum stands as she talks and Dad wraps his arm around her.

I look at the clock and nod back at her.

"Thanks, for this," I hold up the keys and scratch the back of my head awkwardly.

"Good luck."

"I hope it goes well today."

They both say as I walk out to my new car. I meant what I said, getting me a car doesn't make up for what they've done but I am thankful for it. Having my own car will give Mia and I so much more independence whilst we try and work through this.

I check my phone and it's almost 9am so I waste no time in getting into the car and driving to her home.

As soon as I pull up outside Mia's house I honk the horn like I told her I would. I climb out of the car, which drives perfect by the way, and lean against it as I wait for Mia to come outside. Mia pulls the curtain to one side in her room and looks out at me. I give her a small wave and she indicates that she will be out in a minute. I suppose she was expecting to see my Dad's car rather than the car I have now. She was probably a little confused at first but she smiled back at me, which was exactly what I wanted to see from her.

Mia eventually walks out of her house and the sight of her in person, and in daylight, makes my heartbeat quicken rapidly. She looks stunning. She's wearing a light, colourful flower dress which has a main colour of blue and has white sandals on because it's not raining for once. I didn't realise how long her hair had gotten, it's straight, a little lighter and is pretty much touching where her belly button is. She just looks, perfect.

"Hey you," I smile as she approaches.

"Hey," she grins back shyly.

"You look beautiful," I tell her as I open the passenger door for her. Mia blushes instantly and tries to hide her face with her long hair.

"Um, thanks. You look nice too," Mia stutters nervously and climbs into the passenger side.

I close the door behind her and grin to myself. Mia was never good at taking compliments, nor giving them, so that's another thing about her that hasn't changed. I quickly run around to my side and climb in before starting the engine.

"Is this a new car or is my mind playing tricks on me. This wasn't what you had last night was it?" Mia is already doing what Mia would usually have done which is press every button and pull open every compartment on my dashboard.

"Yeah it's new. My parents insist it's a 'welcome home' gift rather than an 'I'm sorry' gift. They gave it to me this morning," I explain as she puts her seatbelt on. She smiles and looks ahead as we begin to drive away "So how are you today?"

"Good, I think, all things considering. How are you?" She questions as she keeps watching me and then the road. I wish I could watch her too, but my eyes are fixed firmly on the road ahead.

"All things considered I'm good too, better now I'm with you," I reply honestly. "Have you thought about what you'd like to do today?"

"Not really. I mean, I guess I have questions about everything and it would be nice if you could maybe answer some stuff. If that's ok?" Mia asks sounding so shy which is a totally different girl to the one I saw last night.

"Sure, that's fine by me. How about I take you to a coffee shop that we used to go to all the time and we can discuss everything there?" I suggest.

"That sounds good," she nods and relaxes into the seat as I continue to drive.

The coffee shop is only around the corner and luckily I manage to get a parking space on the street, not far from where we're going. As we walk along the pavement we just natter away together, just like we always would do.

"So our first time was here?" Mia asks as I open the door for her. She walks into the coffee shop and I follow closely behind as I explain the rest of the story to her.

"Yeah, we were 13 years old and we hated it," I laugh.

"Did you really call a latte a late-e?" She questions again as we join the queue.

"In my defence you didn't know how to pronounce it either," Mia laughs, and I mean it was a full on belly laugh. I can't help but laugh with her as we move a few steps forward in the queue. "I knew I should have missed that part of the story out."

"No, no you shouldn't have. That was too good not to mention," she tries to hide her giggling but fails in the most beautiful way.

"Yeah, yeah whatever. Now what would you like to drink?" I ask her with a smile still on my face.

"I'll have a caramel *late-e* please."

"You're really funny," I laugh sarcastically as I nudge her.

I finally turn my attention to the barrister just as she looks at us.

"Hi, what can I get... oh my god! Talk about a blast from the past! How are you? When did you get back from America?" Megan, the barrister who Mia and I met years ago still works here. She's as cheerful and friendly as always but she doesn't know about the accident. As far as she's concerned we were off to America which is why we haven't been here for so long. Mia tenses slightly next to me because of course, she doesn't remember Megan.

"It's good to see you too. We only arrived back yesterday," I smile and then change the subject. I don't want Megan asking anymore questions about us or where we've been because I can see how uncomfortable Mia is.

"So how are you?" I ask as Mia just watches, mesmerised by the whole thing.

"Good actually. I'm now the manager of this place and things are getting busy again. So what can I get you, the usual?" Megan questions.

"Yes please, vanilla latte for me and a caramel latte for Mia," I tell her just in case she's forgotten about what our usual actually was.

"Sure thing, go take a seat I'll bring it over when it's ready. This ones on me, welcome back!" Megan smiles.

"Thanks Megan."

Mia and I pick up some sugars for our coffees and take a seat by the window in the corner of the shop. Little does Mia know that this was our usual spot which we would always sit in. What I like more is that I told Mia to pick where to sit and she straight away came to this table. That has to be a good sign that she's still in there. Mia sits down and starts fiddling with her nails, then the table and then her hair. She looks really uncomfortable as she looks out the window.

"You ok over there?"

Mia nods and looks at me briefly before turning back to window. She's not ok. You don't even need to know her to know she's not ok. I learned a long time ago that when a female is silent they are *anything* but ok.

"Mia?"

"It's just," Mia fiddles with her hair again and then turns to me but doesn't actually look at me. "She's really friendly isn't she?"

"Yeah?" I can't help but frown.

"Is she your, I mean have you two," she huffs as she struggles to get the words out. I search her face and can't work her out at all.

"Have we, what?"

Mia finally looks at me and sort of widens her eyes pushing for me to catch on as she says. "You *know*."

I repeat her words under my breath quietly to myself as I try to figure out what she means. Have Megan and I, what? Then it hits me, does she think I've slept with Megan?!

"Me and Megan?" I question out loud and she gives me the smallest nod indicating I'm right.

"No, no, god no!" I rush out quickly. "Mia, she's the barrister who served us that day when we were 13 years old and then every time since then. When we actually started to like the taste of coffee we were in here every day and got to know her that's all. But never like, *that*."

"Oh."

Mia shifts uncomfortably but nods as she takes in what I've said.

Was that jealousy?

"So she knows me?"

"Yeah."

"Does she know about the accident?"

"No," I confirm. "I didn't come back in here after you, well, after the accident."

I was just about to say 'after you died' and realised how stupid that sounds when she's literally sitting opposite me.

"I don't remember her at all. She even knew what my usual

drink is but I don't even know that. I just know I like a caramel latte," Mia sighs in defeat. She's frustrated and I can understand why.

"You and I tried every drink on the menu over the years. A caramel latte was your favourite. Once we knew what we liked we'd order it daily," I explain sympathetically.

"Everyone else seems to know more about me than I do," Mia fiddles with the sugar sachets we picked up, avoiding all eye contact with me again. I hate it when she does that.

"Maybe coming here was a bad idea. I can get the coffees to go and we could go some place else if you'd feel more comfortable?" I suggest.

"No, no its ok. Sorry I was just having a moment. It can get a bit overwhelming sometimes that's all," Mia looks up and smiles at me. She looks sad but the smile appears to be genuine.

"I know you're finding this hard but we'll get there," I smile back at her.

"You don't know that," she already sounds defeated, her mood has totally changed again.

"You're right, I don't know for sure. But I *believe* we'll get there."

"How are you so confident about that?" Mia places the sugar sachets down and fiddles with her hair as she looks at me.

"Well, after we ordered our drinks I told you to take a seat anywhere you like in here, didn't I?"

"Yeah?" Mia frowns unsure of where this is going.

"You could have picked anywhere for us to sit but you chose this table which was where we would *always* sit when we'd come here."

"It was?" She questions and her voice changes a bit, almost like a little bit of hope has been included in her thoughts.

"Yep, that's not a coincidence Mia. We just have to be patient with all this," Mia studies me for a moment and then eventually nods in agreement.

Megan comes over with our drinks and places them in front of us. The coffee shop is a little busier now so she doesn't stay and chat which is probably a good thing. Mia places two sugars into her coffee and begins to stir it. I examine her every movement to be sure she is doing what I actually think she is. I watch her lips and she's counting to herself.

"8...9...10," I say out loud and laugh slightly.

"How did you know?" She stops instantly and stares at me.

"I taught you that. 10 sugar stirs,"

"Will heal your caffeine thirst," Mia finishes slowly. "Wait, you taught me that?" Her shocked expression must match mine.

How is it that she knows so much and at the same time not enough.

"Yeah, when we decided to try coffee again we had a debate about how many sugars you put in it and how many times you should stir it. That little rhyme just came out my mouth at the time and it stuck with us ever since."

"So, I just remembered something?" Mia questions hesitantly.

"I don't think you ever forgot, not properly."

Mia smiles at me and then we sit there for a while in silence, drinking our coffees.

"So um, in the car you said you had some questions you wanted to ask me?"

"Oh yeah, right. Um, well I was thinking about the whole thing with me being dead and everything," she instantly has my attention. "I'm just trying to work it all out, it doesn't make much sense to me."

"Honestly, it doesn't make much sense to me either."

"So they told you I was dead when you were in the hospital?" She questions and I nod.

"Yeah, as soon as I woke up I asked for you and they told me then."

"You asked for me?" She whispers sadly.

"Mia, you were *all* I cared about. I didn't even know what injuries I had I literally just wanted you," I admit as I think back.

"I don't understand the funeral though. Did my parents fake it or something?"

"I don't know, I didn't go to any funeral," I admit.

"You didn't?" Mia actually sounds hurt as she questions me.

"No, I didn't."

"Why? I don't want to hold anything against you but by you avoiding my funeral it probably made it easier for them to lie about it? If you actually went to it the truth may have come out a lot sooner?"

"It's not that I didn't want to go to your funeral."

"Did I not mean enough to you for you to even say goodbye?" She interrupts.

I'm stunned. I'm truly stunned and I genuinely have no idea where to start. How an earth could she think she didn't mean anything to me but also, am I really in trouble for not attending her fake funeral?

"Ok stop," I tell her as I hold a hand up.

She does as I ask and waits patiently for me to continue.

"You have always meant *everything* to me, please don't ever doubt that," I tell her bluntly but not in a nasty way.

"Then why does it feel like you gave up on me?" She asks sadly.

"I didn't give up on you!" I snap and instantly regret it. "Sorry," I sigh and run my fingers through my hair. "Mia, what have you been told about my injuries and how I found out about you supposedly dying?"

She shrugs a little. "Not much, just what you told me last night."

"Right," I shift in my seat ready to tell her what happened but then she speaks again.

"Th-they also said you didn't want to stick around after they told you I'd lost my memory," she looks *so* hurt and I'm not surprised.

"Excuse me?"

That's all I can say. My voice is full of disgust and I feel the heat slowly reach my cheeks as the rage inside of me bubbles away again.

"It's ok, I sort of understand it I guess," Mia mumbles as she looks away.

My mouth opens but nothing comes out. My knuckles turn white from where I'm squeezing my fists so tight. Anger, that's all I feel and I need to release it. Alcohol has been my release for a long time now but this is different.

The sound of the coffee shop slowly fades away and my focus turns back to the broken girl in front of me who clearly has this horrible image of me because of her parents. It's *not* ok that they've done this to her, or to me.

"Fuck this!" Falls from my mouth as I slam my hands on the table and get up.

My almost empty coffee spills it's remaining contents on the table as Mia gets ups too. I storm out the coffee shop and quicken my pace towards my car.

"Matt, Matt what are you doing?" Mia shouts after me with panic in her voice.

I hate that I've put that panic there.

"To have a little chat with your parents," I snap as I cross the road.

"Matt, slow down!" She pleads as we get to the other side of the road.

Mia grabs my hand as we reach my car and I freeze, I literally freeze. Have you ever had that feeling when someone touches you and its almost as though they sooth every bit of pain inside of you? It was like ice being poured onto a raging fire. The anger inside of me instantly starts to fizzle away as she brings me back down. I close my eyes at her touch and try to get control of my breathing. She stays behind me, still holding my hand and waits for me to compose myself.

"Please, don't let them do this," she mumbles slowly.

"They've lied so much," I sigh and turn to face her. She searches my face and waits for me to continue. "I was in a coma for 11 days Mia. When I woke up and they told me you died I still wanted to see you. I didn't realise I'd been out of it for days, I thought you'd be in a room somewhere or something. But they told me your funeral had already happened and that was that," I scoff as I explain the next bit. "They even told me your ashes were scattered in Richmond Park so I went there when I was well enough. I tried to say goodbye to you there but none of it felt real. Well, it wasn't real," I sigh and finally look at her. "I didn't question them about any of it because I didn't have a reason to. My last image of you was of you laying lifeless in the car. I didn't have a reason to doubt that you'd have survived that."

Mia squeezes my hand after I finished talking and gives me a little nod, indicating she believes me. But still, I have to make sure she understands the next bit.

"For the record, I would *never* have walked away from you. I'd have done anything to have you with me, memory or no memory it makes no difference to me, Mia. You're still *you* whether you remember it or not."

"You'd have still stayed?" She questions again.

I nod and hold her hand so tightly. "Walking away from you will never be something I'd choose to do."

"I'm sorry my parents have said all these horrible things about you."

"I'm sorry too. But I'm hoping over time we can slowly erase their lies and you'll see me for who I am rather than who they've painted me out to be."

Mia pauses and then smiles. "I already see you for who you are, Matty," she says my name playfully in an attempt to try and defuse the tension. "Are you ok now, can we go back to enjoying our day together?"

I grin back at her as I totally relax again. "Sure."

Little does she know, 'Matty' was one of her nicknames for me.

She's still in there.

The Memory

Matt

"So this is where we first met?" Mia asks as we look out the car window at what was our Primary School.

"It sure was," I nod as I think back to that day and can't help but smile.

We've spent the past few days just hanging out at Epsom Downs having picnics which has been so nice. Today Mia decided she wanted to have a trip down memory lane so our first stop of course had to be where we met.

"And we were 5 years old?"

"Yeah 5 or 6 years old. It's crazy to think that was almost 20 years ago," I can't help but think back to everything that's happened and feel my stomach drop a bit.

Mia turns away from the school and faces the road ahead of her. "You can say that again."

Her tones a little off, she sounds deflated again.

"Are you ok? If this is upsetting you or if it's too soon we can stop for today?" I suggest.

"No, no I don't want to stop. It's just," she pauses and I wait patiently for her to find the words. "It's just so hard not remembering things. I don't understand how I can just not remember someone who I have known for almost 20 years yet I remember a rhyme about stirring a drink. Do you know how frustrating that is?" She huffs in defeat as she keeps her eyes in front of her. She's snappy, really snappy actually but it's not directed at me.

"I do understand your frustration because I feel it too," I tell her and she looks at me. "Mia I was lied to by 4 people about the most important person in my life. I thought I could trust them and I clearly can't. I thought I had lost the girl that I grew up with, the girl that I had a future with," I give her a smile and take her hand in mine. There's that fire between us again, I wonder if she feels it too. "But I didn't. That girl is right here with me still. I remember exactly how it felt when I thought I'd lost you and I can only assume the loss I felt then is similar to what you're feeling now? You hear me telling you things and showing you things and it just makes you feel like you've lost her too, doesn't it?"

Mia nods slowly as a tear rolls down her cheek. "I have lost her though."

My heart breaks watching her suffer like this. I reach forward and wipe the tear away before taking her hand in mine again.

"You might have lost *part* of her, but you're still you, Mia, with or without your memories. I can see the same you that I saw every day we spent together. We will try and get you to remember her too, but if we don't it's not the end of the world. It's just the start of a new one."

Mia smiles at my words and nods slowly as she seems to come to terms with it.

"You good?"

She sniffs but smiles and says, "Yeah."

We turn and face the road as I start the engine and drive away.

"Where are we going?" Mia asks.

"You'll see," I smile as I continue to drive to our next destination with only one thing on my mind... we need to have some fun.

The problem is as I drove I kept changing my mind. I knew I wanted to do something to cheer her up but I didn't know what. Mia kept fiddling with the music and seemed happy doing so, so I left her to it as I bluffed my way through this. The good thing is that she doesn't know her way around town yet, so she didn't realise we were actually just driving around in a big circle whilst I thought of where to go.

Then it hit me, I finally decided where I was going to take her. We were going to go to London. There is always something to do in London and we used to love going there. I decided to take her to Hyde Park so we could rent out a boat on the giant lake there. I didn't tell Mia that though, I thought I'd surprise her.

I parked my car at the train station and bought us both a train ticket for the day. Mia was excited, she loved travelling which was half the reason why we wanted to go to America together. But what made this trip extra special was that Mia couldn't remember the last time she came to London, so she was really, really excited. Mia struggled to sit in her seat the entire train journey. Things only got worse as we approached London and she started seeing all the London landmarks. Every time she'd look at me I would join in in her excitement. But when she was just staring out the window I would be staring at her, admiring her every movement.

When we arrived at London Victoria, we decided to take a short walk to Hyde Park as it was a lovely day. We both got ice creams and had a slow walk to the park together, enjoying each other's company. Mia kept getting out her phone and taking pictures of everything as well as pictures of me and her which I *loved*. She said that the 'old Mia' would probably have done this due to the amount of pictures there were of us. I agreed, because that was probably true. But it was nice taking pictures with her again. Making memories with Mia is my favourite thing. Plus, if we didn't take as many pictures as we did then she'd never have found the box of everything in her Grans loft and we would almost certainly not be here today.

"So this is Hyde Park," Mia's face ignites as I stand in front of the gates presenting it to her.

"Hyde Park!" She squeals as she runs towards me.

"The one and only," I smile.

Mia wraps her arms around my neck and for the first time I get to hold her. I mean truly hold her with her holding me back and not because we're upset. I can smell the familiar smell of apples on her as I hold her tightly, favouring every, single, second. Mia pulls away after a few moments and looks slightly confused as she stares at me.

"What is it? Are you ok?" I question feeling concerned.

"I, I remember," she stutters. "Your smell, I remember that smell. It's um, it smells of mint and your aftershave is um, citrusy. But that smell reminds me of you, it's blurry but I can picture it."

A shiver literally covers my whole body with pure excitement. There's hope, so much hope.

"Picture what? Just go with it Mia, what can you remember?" I ask desperately.

She strains her face almost as though it's painful whilst she thinks. My eyes search every inch of her praying for her to say something.

"You know when you wake up from a dream and nothing makes sense, that's how this feels. I remember bits but it doesn't make sense. I can see me and you and we're in a dark blue room. It's not my room though."

"That's my room," I confirm quickly as my heart jumps. "Keep going. It doesn't matter if it doesn't add up or make sense to you, it might to me. Keep going." I encourage again.

She nods and closes her eyes as I hold her arms. It looks like I'm holding her up but truth be told I feel like my knees could buckle at any moment.

"Um, you had this new bottle of aftershave. This makes no sense at all," Mia starts laughing as she opens her eyes again. "It's a blue M&M bottle, this makes no sense."

She laughs again and shakes her head. I laugh with her as I move one hand from her arm and hold her hand in mine.

"Keep going."

"Ok, um, you sprayed it on yourself and that's what I can smell. The citrus spray from the bottle," she confirms.

"Did I say anything, can you hear, see, feel, smell anything else?" I ask her.

"What?" Mia asks as she frowns.

"Senses, it's one of the strongest triggers to remembering things. It doesn't matter how small or irrelevant you think it is, is there anything else you can picture?"

"You um," she pauses as she looks at me, looking shy again.

"Um?" I mock playfully urging her to continue.

"You told me you loved me," Mia says quietly as she blushes.

I grin at her words. "How does that make you feel?"

Mia pauses and looks at her feet before looking back at me.

"Good," she replies with her rosey blushing cheeks beaming at me.

"That was my birthday," I confirm after a few moments. "What you just described was your present to me. You managed to find an M&M blue bottle and you filled it with a really expensive aftershave. It was my 16th birthday and we were in my bedroom at the time and to be honest, I think I told you every day that I loved you."

There's those rosey cheeks again.

"I remembered something that *actually* happened?" She questions sounding so excited.

"Yeah," I smile and we embrace once more. Only this time we hold each other longer, in the middle of London ignoring the rest of the world.

Eventually we make our way through the park, we're not in any rush for the day to be over so we take our time. It's crazy, we've been apart for so long and yet the moment we are reunited she is already remember things. I was always hopeful that Mia would remember but I never expected her to remember anything this quickly.

"Ok, what's the plan batman?" Mia questions playfully.

God she sounds just like her old self.

I laugh as I stop walking and look her way. She stops and stares at me, trying to figure me out.

"I thought we could have some fun," I shrug my shoulders causally.

"What kind of fun, robbing a bank kind of fun, pranking people kind of fun or,"

"I have many things planned for us Mia but becoming criminals is not one of them," I laugh whilst shaking my head.

"So the old me wouldn't do that?" She asks jokingly sounding shocked .

"Absolutely not!" I grab her shoulders and turn her around to face the lake. "But the old you would totally be up for this. Come on then sailor, we have a boat to catch."

I walk past her to buy our tickets so we can rent a boat for an hour. It's only a small boat with a couple of ores. I sort of want to test how strong I am, or maybe how weak I've gotten. I turn around to face Mia who is still standing in the same spot as I'd left her.

"Are you coming?" I question as I hold out our tickets in my hand.

She nods excitedly and runs forward with the biggest smile on her face. She snatches her ticket out of my hand and grabs my spare hand so I move at the same pace as her, which is fast! She hands her ticket to the man at the gates of the lake and eagerly waits for me to do the same. The man leads us both to our boat as she continues to walk ahead of me whilst still holding my hand, which I *love*.

"Would you like a hand getting into the boat Miss?" The man offers Mia.

"Oh no, that won't be necessary," Mia replies confidently as she climbs into the boat with ease. Ok maybe with a slight wobble. I follow behind her as Mia picks up the two oars, taking a seat in the middle of the boat. I sit opposite her as the man gives us a push with his foot so we're away from the dock.

"Do you want me to start us off?" I ask her.

"Oh no, I'm driving or sailing or," she pauses as she struggles to find the right word.

"Rowing?"

"I'm captain, ok?" She finishes with a grin.

"Eye eye," I joke and salute her as I relax in my seat.

Mia fumbles around with the oars for a bit as she figures out how to stop us going around in the circle that we currently are. She eventually gets into a rhythm and we start covering some distance on the lake.

"This reminds me of something," Mia says as she continues

rowing the boat but her gaze is on the water.

"I hope it's not Titanic," I joke and she laughs.

Her laugh.

"Actually it is."

"Oh god, is there an iceberg behind me or something?" I joke and look behind me.

Mia giggles and shakes her head playfully. She pulls the oars into the boat so we just drift on the lake.

"I'm serious. Did we do something like this, involving Titanic? Obviously we weren't on the Titanic but," she pauses as she concentrates. "It was something *like* this, I'm sure of it."

This can't be happening. She truly is remembering things but she's doubting herself. I lean forward and take her hands in mine.

"You're making sense to me, Mia. Close your eyes and concentrate. Listen to the sound of the water, focus on the feeling of gently rocking in this boat, think of the film, think of us. Tell me what you see, what do you remember?" I encourage gently.

Mia stares at me for a moment and then does as I say. She closes her eyes and I watch her as she focuses, praying that she remembers. After a few moments she begins to talk and we both relive the memory together.

"Did you bring it?" I question as I open the door to Mia. She holds up her bag and nods looking incredibly confused.

"Yeah, but I don't understand why I had to bring my swimming costume to your house, Matt. Usually sleepovers consist of just pyjamas and a change of clothes, not swimming costumes," Mia walks into my house as causal as always. I close the door behind her and we walk into the living room to see my parents.

"Wow! Mr and Mrs Parker you look incredible!" Mia gasps.

"Thank you sweetheart." Mum kisses her on her forehead as she grabs her purse.

Both Mum and Dad are going to celebrate their anniversary together tonight. Mia often sleeps over but tonight we actually have the house all to ourselves. Once my parents have had dinner they're going to stay in a hotel in London. They'll be back tomorrow so it's just one night, but that's fine by us.

"Right guys, have fun tonight but behave," Mum looks at both of us sternly.

"We will Mum," I moan. "Go and have fun, we'll see you in the morning."

"Come on love, we're going to be late," Dad nudges Mum, trying to get her out the house.

"Ok, any problems give us a call and we can be home in," Mum begins but I interrupt her.

"Mum, stop it. I'm 16 years old and you're leaving for 1 night. I will be ok, we will be ok," I gesture to Mia and I.

Reluctantly Mum eventually leaves with Dad, leaving just Mia and I alone. Mia picks up her bags from the floor and begins to take them upstairs when I stop her.

"Get changed into your swimming costume and meet me in the garden," I grin.

Mia pauses and stares at me looking really confused.

"Ok," she studies me for a moment as she tries to figure out what's going on. Then she runs upstairs excitedly to do as I say.

I laugh as I take my shirt off and go into the garden. I turn the outside lights on, which are small colourful little bulbs dotted around the garden giving it a little bit of light. I make sure everything is set up and perfect before I wait for Mia to finally come into the garden.

"Ok Matty, I'm here and in my costume. What's going on?" She shouts as she walks through the backdoors to meet me.

"Oh my god!" She gasps as she looks around.

I watch her as she slowly takes everything in. The lights, the food, the swimming pool, the giant TV screen and then she looks back at me excitedly.

"What is this?" She questions.

"Remember you saw that thing on the internet about that place in London where they were doing screenings of Titanic in a swimming pool and you could watch it all whilst sitting in a boat on the water?"

"Yeah, yeah I remember," she answers quickly.

"Well I tried to get us tickets but they were sold out. So I thought

I'd make our own. Dad and I went and got the swimming pool today. Mum spent all afternoon blowing up the inflatable boats for us to lay on in the pool whilst Dad and I set up the TV for us out here. It's not quite the same but it's as close I could get it," I explain proudly.

"You did all this for me?" Mia questions shocked.

"Well yeah, I'd do anything for you Mia, you know that."

Mia wastes no time in rushing over and kissing me. She doesn't rush our kiss even though I know she is excited to watch the movie. She takes her time and the kiss lasts until I feel like I can't breathe anymore.

"Matthew Parker, I love you," she whispers.

"I love you too," I whisper back as our foreheads rest against each other. "Are you ready to get this movie started?"

"Yes!" Mia squeals as she runs over to the pool.

I watch as she jumps in, totally ignoring the fact that the water is freezing and climbs into her inflatable boat. I press play on the TV and run over to my side of the pool. I hand Mia some popcorn and a couple of Pepsi cans before climbing into my own boat.

"This is amazing, thank you for this. I would be totally lost without you," she smiles as she puts a handful of popcorn in her mouth.

"I would totally be lost without you too," I reply "Now stop talking, the movie is about to start."

We both laugh and she throws some popcorn at me. Mia then reaches for my hand as we sit back and watch Titanic in our boats.

"Wow, I can't believe you remembered all that," I gasp in disbelief as we both finish putting the memory together. Mia slowly opens her eyes and looks into mine as we drift quietly on the lake.

"I know. All of this time I've not remembered anything but then you come along and everything changes," she tightly holds my hand in hers and bites the bottom of her lip.

I can tell she's contemplating about whether or not to mention something to me. Mia pulls her hand away from mine and grabs hold of the oars again. As she begins rowing she keeps her head down and I can tell she is still thinking. I hate how she shuts down so quickly, she never use to.

"What's on your mind, Mia?"

Mia keeps her head down and rows a little more before stopping. She looks up at me and huffs slightly before taking a breath.

"You're going to think I'm crazy."

I smile at her comment and shake my head. "Try me."

She drops the oars completely and rests her hands on her legs as she leans closer to me.

"I don't want to go home," she almost whispers as though she doesn't want anyone to hear her.

"We don't have to go home yet, we can do something else afterward this if you,"

"No you don't understand. I *don't want* to go home, Matt. I don't want to live with my parents right now," Mia explains. "I can't understand why they'd keep me from you," she mumbles sadly.

"I don't understand that bit either. But you can stay at mine if you want? You can have my room, I'll kip on the sofa it's no big deal," I shrug doing my best to try and solve how she's feeling.

"No offence, but I don't want to stay there either. I don't want to be around those that lied to me, or to us. Not for a while at least anyways," Mia mumbles.

"So what are you saying, where will you go?" I question feeling a little nervous.

"I've got some compensation from the accident, a lot of compensation actually. I think I'm going to stay in a hotel for a while," Mia explains and I nod indicating that I understand. But truth be told I'm worried. I'm worried that this hotel will create distance between us.

"I was hoping that, maybe, you would think about staying with me?" She finally says.

I lift my head up and our eyes meet, she looks so nervous and shy and just… *perfect.*

"Please don't feel like you have to. It's just you're helping me, like, *really* helping me and I don't want to be away from you right now but I also don't want to be around our parents. If you don't want to then can you please continue to help me through this," Mia rambles on so fast it's hard to take everything in. She doesn't stop for air so I have no option but to interrupt her.

"Of course I'll stay with you, Mia," I confirm before adding. "Just to be clear, even if I didn't stay in the hotel with you, you have to understand and believe me when I say I am *not* going anywhere. I will help you through this Mia," she grins happily and nods. "Right, it's my turn to row, swap."

We both stand up and the boat rocks as it tries to balance itself. Our instincts kick in and we grab onto each other laughing the whole time as try to find our balance. Once we steady ourselves we both take our seats and I begin rowing as Mia stretches out to enjoy the sun.

"So, I'm going to text my parents and tell them that they have to meet us at your house. Then we can tell our parents together about our plan, deal?" Mia asks as she gets her phone out.

"Sure. I mean, they can't stop us anyways we're not kids but yeah, we should tell them together. We should also tell them about your little flashbacks today," I nudge her with my feet and she smiles but looks a little nervous at the same time.

"It's because of you, I hope you know that," Mia smiles as she playfully nudges me back with her foot back.

She taps away on her phone as I continue rowing us around on the lake. Mia puts her phone away and starts to relax in her seat again. In the corner of my eye I can see that she's staring at me and I can't help wondering, what is she thinking about?

The Showdown

Matt

"Are you sure this is what you want to do?" I ask Mia.

Mia keeps her face down staring at the doorstep as I fumble with my door keys. We know both our parents are behind my front door waiting for us just like Mia asked them to be. Our parents have no idea what we want to talk to them about, but they agreed to meet because let's face it, they're in no position to say no to us about anything right now.

"If you've changed your mind it's okay you know," I nudge Mia gently to try and help her relax. She lifts her head up and nudges me back, smiling.

That smile.

"No, no I want to do this still. It's just," she says almost like she's convincing herself to go through with it. "It doesn't matter let's just go inside."

Mia shrugs off what's on her mind and takes a step forward, indicating for me to hurry up and open the door. I decide not to do that yet and gently pull her arm so she faces me once more. She's shut down again, I need her to know she doesn't have to do that with me.

"Whatever is on your mind does matter, Mia. Talk to me, please," I tell her gently.

Mia sighs and fiddles with her hair whilst keeping her head down.

"Promise you won't laugh."

"I promise."

"I'm nervous," she mumbles.

"What are you nervous about?" I ask but she stays silent so I continue. "If it makes you feel better I can do the talking or you can wait in the car," I ramble on trying to come up with a solution to make Mia feel more comfortable but she interrupts me.

"I'm not nervous to tell them I want us to move into a hotel for a while. I'm nervous about meeting your parents," Mia finally admits as those rosey cheeks of hers return.

I try my best to hide it but I can't help smiling a little bit. This whole thing means something to her and I *love* that.

"But Mia, you have met them before."

"I know I have, but I don't remember that. So even though it isn't, it feels like the first time for me. I just, I want them to like me," she explains although the last sentence is quieter.

"Are you kidding? How could they not like you?" I question in disbelief that the thought would even enter her mind.

"Well they did tell you I'd died to keep us apart. Maybe they hated me and you never knew or,"

"Mia, stop."

I pull her close to my chest and hold her tightly against me. She wraps her arms around my neck and holds me back. She finally stops talking and buries her head into my chest. She relaxes as I stroke her hair and I rest my chin on the top of her head.

Seeing her this way makes me so angry. The four people inside my home did this to her and she doesn't deserve that. But holding her like this, it means everything.

"My parents loved you, you were like the daughter they never had. Don't ever think for one second that you're not good enough, because you have *always* been more than enough," I tell her.

We hold each other a little longer and it takes everything inside of me to stop myself from kissing her, even just her forehead. I feel like there's still a line between us, despite everything, and I can't cross that yet. I have to push my own feelings to the side for her sake. But I don't think I can hide how loud my heart is beating against my chest even if I tried.

Can she hear it?

When we eventually pull apart Mia takes a moment to open her eyes, almost as though she is repeating my words in her head and composing herself. She then looks at me and smiles whilst nodding her head slowly.

"Ok, let's do this," she says with a bit more confidence this time.

"Yes ma'am," I nod and unlock my front door.

We can hear our parents chatting in the living room but the sound of the door closing behind us quickly draws a silence from them all. Mia looks back at me for reassurance and holds out her hand. Once I realise she is indicating for me to hold it I don't hesitate and reach forward, threading my fingers through hers. Her hands are so cold even though it's summer. Thinking back she'd often have cold hands but she was always oblivious to it. The warmth from my hands would always remind her that she was actually cold and then she'd hold onto me tighter and steal my body heat.

"Your hands are so warm," she whispers as we walk towards the living room.

Mia then grips tighter to my hand, just like she always used to do to steal my warmth. I can't help but smile. It's the little things that truly matter and make a person who they. This is just another reminder that she is still in there which feels my heart with such hope.

We enter the living room and face our parents together for the first time in years. My body tenses as I feel my anger towards them all surface but I know I need to control it. If I snap I might push Mia away and I can't let that happen. I won't let that happen. Mia gives my hand a gentle squeeze. I can't work out if she's felt my body tense or whether it's because she's nervous. But just like that, she's brought my anger back down to a level where I feel in control again because *she* is my focus.

Our parents look at me, then to Mia and then collectively look at our hands, noting that they are locked firmly together. Mum gives a soft smile which she tries to hide, but all four of them look so nervous.

Mum then looks at Mia again and studies her. She studies her in a similar way to what I did when I first saw her again. She looks her up and down slowly, admiring Mia's long hair, her effortless beauty and then breaks the silence in the room. She lets out this really awkward sob and covers her mouth. I can't lie, hearing that hurt me. Mia's head quickly turns to face me, her face is full of concern and I can see that she once again feels the way she did on my door step. Without her saying it, I know that she's asking if she's good enough. I squeeze Mia's hand again to try and reassure her but we're distracted by my Mum who stands up from the sofa.

Mum wipes underneath her eyes and walks forward towards Mia. Before we have a chance to process what's happening my Mum wraps her arms around Mia in the tightest embrace I think I have ever witnessed. She didn't even hug me like that! The force of my Mum crashing into Mia pulls our hands apart as she has no choice but to take a few steps backwards to prevent them from falling over. Mum holds Mia and sobs into her as we all watch, saying nothing. Eventually Mia raises her arms and wraps them around my Mum too. Her face is partly covered but I see her smile in relief.

"Oh sweetheart, I've missed you so much," Mum manages to say.

Mia doesn't respond and I don't blame her. I understand that for Mia this is really weird because my Mum is a stranger to her now.

"Mum, Mia needs to breathe you know," I remind her as I tap her shoulder.

"Sorry, I'm sorry," Mum sniffs as she takes a step back and holds onto Mia's hands whilst she admires her again. "You're even more beautiful than I remember."

Mia blushes in the most adorable way and smiles.

"Thank you Mrs Parker."

Mum gives a little chuckle as she continues to hold Mia's hands.

"You always insisted on calling us Mr and Mrs Parker even though we told you time and time again to call us John and Debbie."

"I did?" Mia questions and Mum nods back at her.

"Uh-huh, some things will never change. I've missed being called Mrs Parker."

Dad gets up from the sofa to join them both. Mia takes her eyes off Mum and looks at him. Mum finally lets go of Mia's hands and steps back next to Dad.

"Look at her John," Mum gushes in admiration.

"I *am* looking at her," Dad laughs as he steps forward. "It's really good to see you again, M," he wraps his huge arms around Mia for a moment before stepping away from her.

"M?"

"I'd always call you M, very rarely called you Mia," Dad clarifies.

Mia nods and watches Dad guide my Mum back to the sofa. Mia steps closer to me again and threads her fingers through mine once more as everyone positions themselves on the sofa. We decide to stay standing.

"Are you ok?" I whisper loud enough for only Mia to hear me.

"Yeah, I think so," she responds quietly. "I guess I was good enough."

"I told you that you had nothing to worry about."

I'm aware that everything is so uncertain for her at the moment but I know that piece by piece I'm proving to her that I can be trusted. At least I hope so.

"So, what did you both want to talk to us about?" Aaron asks hesitantly.

I haven't seen him yet, not since before America. He hasn't changed at all, except for his hairline reducing slightly.

Probably all the stress from lying.

Mia and I stay quiet for a moment as we both try and find the right words. Mia looks at her parents, to the floor, then to me, then to the floor again. She's shutting down I can tell. I decide to take the plunge and tell them what Mia told me but she beats me to it.

"I can't live with you anymore," Mia blurts out.

I personally wouldn't have been so blunt, I'd have tried to soften the blow a little bit but here we are diving into the deep end together.

"I'm sorry Mum, Dad, but I don't think being around you right now is the best thing for me."

"You've only just come home," Aaron begins but Mia interrupts him.

"Well if everyone was honest from the beginning I would never have stayed away for so long, would I?" Mia snaps which takes me by surprise too.

Shes not really shown this side to me yet, as in her anger side. I've seen her upset, hurt, confused and then today she was happy. But I've not seen any anger from her, until now apparently.

Both our parents shift in their seats uncomfortably as they know Mia's right. This is on them, although in their heads they had good intentions it still doesn't make this any easier.

"So where do you intend on going?" Liz questions sounding a little annoyed.

"Matt and I are going to stay in a hotel for a while."

"A hotel?" Aaron frowns.

"You're welcome to stay here with us, sweetheart. You don't have to stay in a hotel," Mum tells her softly.

Mia goes from looking angrily at her parents to looking sadly at mine.

"I just don't want to be around those who lied to me, well us. The only person who knows how I feel is Matt. He was lied to in such a horrible way by all of you."

She's defending me.

I'm so focused on her I have totally lost my voice. I thought this was about her but she's making it about us and I love that.

"But leaving doesn't change that," Liz tells her and I frown at her comment.

"You're right, nothing any of you do can change that. But Matt can change me. He's the only one who is truly helping me at the moment. I need to stay with him and away from all of you, at least for a little bit," Mia sounds uncomfortable but I think it's more because she doesn't want to come across as rude to my parents rather than her doubting her decision.

"I'm not comfortable with this. I want you to stay home with us Mia. We're your parents we can also help you too," Aaron tells her.

Mia laughs but it's not a happy laugh. It's full of sarcasm and anger.

"Right. So you truly think the best place for me is surrounded by those who lied about me *dying* and then told me that the the reason the guy in the picture hasn't been around since the accident was because he didn't want to be burdened with someone like me!" Mia's voice raises as she talks but she just sounds so broken by the end.

"What?" Mum questions and looks at Liz.

"You didn't know that bit?" I frown.

"No," Dad says bluntly as he looks at Liz too.

Confusion fills the room mixed with anger and just pure, 'what the hell' if that's even a feeling.

"I had to say something to shut her down. I didn't even know Matt was back from America," Liz sighs in frustration.

"You could have said something else other than that."

Mums pissed. Ironic really considering this is all down to them regardless of what Liz said yesterday.

"Don't worry though Mum, he told me the truth which is something that you don't seem to remember how to do anymore."

"Mia," Aaron warns.

"Don't 'Mia' me! Answer me this, should I be worried about Matt, is he going to put me at risk?"

"No," Aaron and Liz sigh in defeat and shake their head.

"Then what's the problem? You had a lot of time to help me, Matt didn't and I want to stay with him. It's that simple," Mia says a little more calmly now although very stern.

"We did what we could with what we were faced with. You were in hospital for *months* Mia, the majority of which you were sedated for. Once they finally discharged you we followed the doctors advice which was not to push you or overwhelmed you! We then moved you to Scotland so you could have specialist treatment for your memory followed by therapy and physio. You've come a long way Mia you really have, but physically rather than your memory. You couldn't walk, you couldn't talk, you couldn't even feed yourself so don't say we haven't helped you because you can now do all of those things!" Liz raises her voice slightly and Mum wipes a tear from her face as she talks.

I didn't know this, I didn't know *any* of this.

We've not really talked about what happened after the crash. I just assumed she woke up without her memory and then was sent to Scotland to live with her Gran. I thought she was doing just that, living. Not learning to talk, walk or feed herself again.

"What?" I blurt out.

The mood in the room shifts as my head spins. Everyone's gone from looking at each other to me, only me, including Mia. She looks terrified.

"Is that true?" I ask her and only her.

"She didn't tell you?" Liz questions sounding uncomfortable.

"Mia?" I push for her to respond.

"I didn't know how," she mumbles quietly and then turns back to Liz. "You told me he didn't want to stay because I was like that. Why *would* I tell him?!"

It feels like someone's punched me in my gut, pierced my skin and then they're using my insides as some kind of squeeze toy. The sound of Mia and Liz arguing fades away, I have no idea what they're screaming at each other. All I can think of is firstly what an earth has Mia gone through, secondly what must she think of me for not being around and thirdly, thirdly, I'm going to be sick.

I let go of Mia's hand and thankfully my legs get me to the downstairs bathroom just in time before I spill my guts into the toilet.

"Matt," I hear my name but I can't focus enough on who it is.

I lean away from the toilet and place my back against the wall to try and steady myself. Everything's spinning so I hold my head in my hands and try to gather myself. It feels like I've been drinking way to much and in a way I wish I was. It would numb some of how I'm feeling right now.

"The colour has drained from his face," that's Mums panicked voice in the doorway of the bathroom.

"Do you need some fresh air?" That's Dad, he must be next to her.

No, I don't need air. I need to numb how I'm feeling and there's only one way I've learned how to do that.

Alcohol.

I manage to stand and push past my parents avoiding all eye contact. I don't want to talk, I can't talk. I just need this to stop. My legs manage to carry me into the kitchen but I hear footsteps behind me. I open one cupboard, nope not there. I open another, not there either.

"What are you doing?" That's Mum again.

I ignore her and carry on searching. *Where is it?* They always move stuff around from cupboard to cupboard it drives me mad. I swing open the last cupboard and almost take it off it's hinges, but I don't care as I finally see what I'm looking for. I grab the whiskey bottle out and slam it on the kitchen side. My breathing is all over the place as I wrestle with the lid.

"Son, you don't need that."

I do, you have no idea how much I do. I feel their eyes on me, watching, waiting. I place my hands flat on the counter and lean over the bottle breathing deeply. I close my eyes and replay everything over and over. Mia couldn't walk. Mia couldn't talk. Mia couldn't even feed herself. She had to learn *everything* from scratch. This goes way beyond just losing her memory, this is so much more than that.

Then I think of how Liz made me out to be such a horrible person. The anger boils up again, the hate I feel for everyone takes over and I can't hold back anymore. I grab the whiskey bottle and just as the lid touches my lips it's like the spell around me is broken when I hear her say my name.

"Matt, please," Mia's voice is quiet but there's a sense of desperation in it.

For the first time I look in the direction of where the voices have been coming from. Everyone is standing around the door looking at me. Mia must have pushed through everyone because she's at the front. She's crying and I realise I am too. She looks so worried, they all do as my tears blur them out. I blink away the glaze that's covered my eyes and realise Mia is coming towards me. She's hesitant. She's moving slowly.

Wait, is she scared of me?

Mia gets close enough for me to smell her and not the whiskey seeping out of the bottle. She searches my face for a moment and then slowly reaches for the bottle in my hand. She keeps her eyes on me as she pulls it away and to my surprise, I let her. Mia puts the bottle on the kitchen side behind me and waits to see what I do or even how I'll react. But I just stare at her and do nothing.

A tear falls down her cheek as she reaches up and wraps her arms around my neck, burying her face into me. My arms instantly wrap around her waist as I hold her back, breathing every ounce of her in. Once again she puts out the fire inside of me with her touch. The rage melts away and I no longer need or want to numb what I'm feeling anymore.

"I'm sorry, I should have told you," Mia sobs.

"I'm sorry you had to go through that," I tell her as my voice breaks.

We lean apart so we can see each other's faces but we still hold each other tightly.

"You really wouldn't have left me," Mia says almost to herself rather than me.

"Never in a million years."

"I shouldn't have said that to her about you, Matt. I'm really sorry," Liz's voice takes our attention away from each other.

We reluctantly turn our bodies to face our parents again but still keep one arm around each other.

"No you shouldn't have," Mum snaps. "What were you thinking, look what we've turned him into."

"Turned me into?"

"You've turned to alcohol to cope with it all, haven't you?" Mum sobs and looks at Dad then back to me. "Is this what you've done whilst you've been in America?"

"It's not a big deal," I try to brush it off because they're making me sound like a damn alcoholic and I'm not!

"Son, you turned up from America drunk. You then started drinking whilst arguing with us before running off to Mia's and now this. I've never seen you this way." Dad tells me.

"*We've* never seen you like this." Aaron corrects and looks at me. "You never used to drink or anything."

"Yeah, well," I stop myself because I don't really know what to say.

"Is this how you've coped, with alcohol?" Mum pushes desperately.

"Yes, ok, yes!" I snap but Mia gives me a gentle squeeze. I squeeze her back letting her know I'm good.

"How often did you turn to alcohol?" Dad asks.

"A lot." I mumble.

"It's ok, we can get you some help for this," Dad begins but I cut him off.

"I don't need help! When are any of you going to understand that the only thing I've ever needed is right here next to me!" Mia's gaze is on me and I turn my attention to her as I continue. "Alcohol helped numb the pain of losing her but she's back now. If I had to choose between Mia and alcohol it's Mia, every time it's Mia."

Her eyes fill up with water and she smiles at me. She hears me, she sees me, she knows I'm telling the truth.

"It doesn't always work like that though," Aaron begins but I cut him off.

"Right, and Mia wasn't supposed to survive or get her memory back was she?" I snap.

"No, no she wasn't."

"And yet here we are, all in the same room," I huff sarcastically.

"Yes but her memory may still never come back," Liz adds.

"Wrong," I scoff.

"What do you mean?" Mum questions quickly.

Mia and I look at each other and smile before we turn back to face everyone again.

"I'm remembering things," Mia confirms.

The room is filled with gasps of disbelief from our parents. Aaron and Liz's mouths are pretty much hitting the floor.

"What do you mean you remember things, what is it you remember?" Liz asks quickly as she tries to process everything.

"Today Matt and I hired a boat in Hyde Park. I told him it reminded me of the film Titanic and something to do with a swimming pool. If wasn't clear at first, it felt like a confusing dream that made no sense. But Matt helped me focus on what I could remember and guided me through the story, helping me remember it by using my senses and stuff. I remember it now, clearer than earlier too. I was staying at Matt's house for the night as Mr and Mrs Parker were going to London to celebrate their wedding anniversary. Matt arranged for us to watch Titanic in his garden whilst laying in inflatable boats in a swimming pool," Mia says proudly.

"That's right, that did happen," Mum confirms in disbelief.

"And I remember for Matt's birthday I got him aftershave but I put it in a blue M&M bottle. I remembered his blue room and everything," Mia adds.

"This is unbelievable," Liz's shakes her head as Mia talks.

"It happened Mum, I know it sounds stupid but that's what I got him," Mia protests as she tenses.

"I know you did because I helped you transfer the aftershave into the bottle," Liz slowly reassures her. "I just mean *this* is unbelievable, you, you remembering things. It's almost impossible to believe."

"Do you remember anything else?" Aaron asks and Mia nods.

"We went to a coffee shop the other day and I picked what was our usual spot to sit at which can't just be a coincidence. Then Matt counted how many times I stirred my coffee and it turns out that the reason I stir my coffee that many times is because of a rhyme Matt told me years ago."

"Oh my god," Mum gasps as Dad places his hand on her shoulder.

"10 sugar stirs will heal your caffeine thirst," Dad says.

"Yeah that's it," Mia says excitedly and Dad laughs.

"You both used to drive me mad with that, you'd say it all the time."

"This makes no sense," Aaron mumbles.

"I'm not saying it makes sense, Dad. I agree it doesn't make any sense at all. I don't understand this anymore than you do but I do know that if I have any chance of remembering *anything* I have to have Matt with me."

Her words make me smile, although I try my best to hide it. She needs me, Mia needs me. I have needed her since the day we met but to know that after everything we've been through she still needs me in return is the best feeling.

"The reason I remember things is all because of Matt,. It's not because of treatment I've had and definitely not because of anything anyone else has done," Mia finishes.

"I don't see why you need to go and live in a hotel though. Matt can come over anytime we won't keep you two apart anymore. You don't need to spend money staying at a hotel," Aaron doesn't seem impressed at all. It's not that he wants to keep Mia and I apart which is good, he just doesn't like the idea of a hotel I suppose.

"Dad, I'm sorry but the four of you lied to Matt and I for too long," Mia explains bluntly as she looks at our parents. "Whether you understand it or not, I find it very hard being around you right now. The only person who I feel like I can trust is Matt."

Aaron sighs in defeat and looks at Liz. It's clear that they don't like the idea of this but that they also understand. They know that there is nothing they can do anyway considering we're both adults. But I suppose no matter what age you are you always want your parents approval.

"If this is what you want then I guess it's ok," Aaron mumbles.

Mia squeezes me tightly and once again I find myself trying to hide the smile that's crept onto my face.

"If you want to stay in a hotel then that's fine, but you could always stay at our lake house instead?" Mum suggests. She looks uncomfortable, almost like she doesn't want to offend anyone by her suggestion but the thought of the lake house does sound good.

"The lake house?" Mia looks confused and turns to me for answers.

"My parents have a lake house, we used to go there every summer with my parents until we were old enough to go by ourselves. It's nice, it's out of the way and I suppose it wouldn't cost us anything to stay there," I tell Mia quietly as our parents discuss everything in the background.

They're basically talking about how it's a better idea than a hotel and that they would be happier if we went there. Personally I think its probably because at least they would know where we were rather than all the possible hotels we might be staying at.

"Do you think we should stay there?" Mia asks.

"We could try it out and see how you feel? It is a nice place and we have lots of memories there," I shrug letting her know I don't mind either way.

Mia nods and turns back to our parents who happen to finish their conversation at the same time.

"So, lake house?" Mum says cheerfully.

"Sure," I confirm.

"Brilliant. I'll go and get you the keys," Mum runs off happily that we have accepted her offer. Everyone else in the room looks more relaxed, including Mia which is my main concern. Mum comes back over to us and hands me the keys smiling.

"That place is yours for as long as you want. Get to know each other again and just have fun. Even if your memory doesn't return its not the end of the world... it's just the beginning of a new one," Mum whispers to both of us and she's right.

Of course I want Mia to remember everything, but if she doesn't it's not the end. It's the beginning of something new which might be even more exciting.

The Lake House

Matt

We've been driving for a little over an hour now and aren't too far away from my parents lake house. Once everyone agreed to us coming here, we wasted no time in packing and getting on the road. Half way through the journey we picked up a few necessities at the supermarket to keep us going and then continued the journey. It's almost 9pm and the sun has only recently set due to the summer nights. We turned off the motorway a while ago now and are currently making our way through country lanes at the slowest speed known to man due to Mia's poor map reading skills.

"Tell me again why we can't use a Satnav?" Mia moans as she unfolds the map.

"Because the Satnav doesn't get signal this far out, we're literally in the middle of nowhere," I laugh as we get to the end of the road. "Ok map girl, am I going left or right?"

Mia stares at the map for a few seconds, turns it to one side and then to another. She frowns and throws her hands up in defeat.

"It all looks the same to me, I have no idea."

We both laugh as I rub my temples. Mia looks back at the map and then looks left and right, staring down each possible route for us.

"Ok I'll be honest, we're lost. I think we were meant to take a turn a few miles back and then I got confused and… anyway, when in doubt go left because it will always be right," Mia says proudly as she signals for me to turn left.

I don't move at first. I just repeat what she said a few times in my head. I taught her that saying years ago when we were lost in the woods near the lake house.

"Earth to Matt," Mia clicks her fingers around my head playfully. "Did you not hear what I just said? Let's go left."

"I heard you alright," I smile and turn to face her. "When we were about 11 years old we got lost in the woods near the lake house and that's when I first said that to you, go left because it will always be right."

"Really? So I remembered something else?"

I turn left down the road and continue driving.

"Is that something you'd usually say?"

Mia shakes her head next to me as she keeps her eyes on the road ahead.

"No, I don't ever remember saying that before now."

"Maybe these roads have just subconsciously triggered something?" I question and Mia shrugs. "Either way, I love how you're remembering things when we're together."

Mia doesn't say anything, it's just a comfortable silence as we continue down the country roads.

"So what happened the day we got lost?" Mia asks.

"It was nothing exciting really. We got lost for only about 10 minutes and you were freaking out. You kept saying *no-one will find us* and *we're in the middle of nowhere.* Oh and the best one was *we're going to die out here,*" we both laugh as I explain the story to her.

"I did *not* say that," Mia hides her face in embarrassment as she laughs at herself.

"I promise that you did. So I had to try and calm you down because you were going all loopy on me," I joke although it's kind of true.

"Hey!" Mia punches my leg playfully.

"So we found a pathway and we had the choice of going either left or right. The pathway seemed to panic you more because you kept saying *if we take the wrong direction we'll be even further away from the house and we have no water* etc."

"Oh god, that's so embarrassing," Mia laughs.

"I had to try and calm you down, so I randomly just thought of the lets go left because it's always right thing and it made you laugh. You seemed to relax and we went left which eventually turned out to be the right direction. Then the saying just stuck I suppose. We'd always use it if we got lost or couldn't decide where to go and I'd say about 90% of the time it worked," I finish as we approach a familiar dirt track. "Once again it seems to have worked, I know where we are," I smile proudly.

Mia sits forward in her seat eagerly as she realises that we have arrived. We reach the end of the dirt track and finally the lake house becomes visible through the trees. The house is made out of wood and is much bigger than my actual home. I haven't seen this place in years and I cannot begin to explain how good it feels to be back here. The house looks exactly the same, the decking around the front of the house is smothered in solar lights which makes the place look so magical and welcoming.

I park my car right outside the front of the house. When Mia and I get out of the car our eyes are locked firmly on the house in front of us. I'm overwhelmed with the smell of the wonderful outdoors. All you can hear are the faint sounds of birds in the trees and the gentle wind blowing the leaves around. Then of course there's the best bit which is the soothing sound of the water from the lake which is directly in front of the house.

"Wow! This place is incredible," Mia gasps.

"Uh-huh," I mumble as I pull the house keys out of my pocket. "Here, go open up the front door while I get our bags from the car."

"Ok!" Mia looks so excited as she takes the keys from my hand and runs up to the front door. She fumbles with the lock for a moment and then manages to open the door. Mia wastes no time and runs inside as she starts to explore.

I laugh at her reaction and grab our bags from the car plus the necessities we bought earlier. Once I lock my car and look back at the house I notice that most of the lights are already turned on. She seems to have been in every room already! The sound of her footsteps running around upstairs going from room to room is all I can hear when I finally enter the house. I close the front door behind me and drop all the bags on the floor.

"Mia?" I shout as I try to work out where in the house she actually is.

"Oh my god, this house is amazing!" Mia screams as she finally becomes visible to me again. She hangs over the balcony upstairs with pure delight over her face.

"Are you glad that we didn't stay in a hotel now?" I ask smiling at her.

Mia makes her way quickly down the stairs as she nods.

"Are you kidding? This is *so* much better than a hotel. Have you seen the size of the bedrooms?" She shrieks.

"Once or twice," I joke as Mia stands next to me.

"Sorry. I know I've been here before but it feels like the first time," Mia suddenly looks shy as though she is embarrassed by her reaction.

"Hey, don't apologise," I hold her hand reassuringly and she seems to relax at my touch. "Do you want to see something really cool?"

"Sure!" Mia nods and follows me.

I lead her through the lobby, through living room which connects to the kitchen and then out the back door. The garden is once again covered in solar lights which makes everything sparkle.

"The garden is so pretty!" Mia admires her surroundings and then looks at me. She smiles and then her eyes look behind me. Her face lights up even more and I laugh at her reaction. "Oh my god, is that,?"

"A hot tub? Yes, it is," I confirm.

Mia runs past me and over to the hot tub. I help her remove the lid from the top and then turn the pump on. Mia puts her hand in and splashes the water a little bit as it begins to bubble and fizzle away. We watch it for a moment and then the steam from the water slowly starts to rise. Mia wastes no more time and jumps straight into the hot tub, fully clothed.

"Mia!" I laugh as she dunks herself completed under the water.

When she comes back up she wipes her face and then moves closer to the edge getting comfortable.

"What are you waiting for, get in!"

I debate for what feels like a second and then jump straight into the hot tub with her. Mia laughs, I laugh, Mia splashes me, I splash her, Mia looks happy... I *am* happy.

A few moments pass without us saying much, it's a comfortable silence as I watch Mia play with the bubbles all around her.

"Can you remember being in a hot tub before?" I ask and she shakes her head.

"No," she bits her lip looking nervous and then continues to speak. "When I was having all the therapy, they put me in a swimming pool to help the muscles in my legs start working again. I'd have a person either side of me and I had to hold these bars that were in the water for support and try to hold myself up whilst making my legs move. Outside of the pool there was a jacuzzi. I remember thinking, one day I want to be able to go into one of those without someone helping me in or out."

Mia instantly has my attention. I've wanted to know more about what she's actually gone through since Liz blurted it out earlier but I didn't want to ask. Now she's choosing to open up to me about what she's been through. I need to know more. I want to know everything.

What did my girl go through?

"How long did you have to have that for?"

She shrugs causally. "A few months or so. I wasn't paralysed or anything and it wasn't that I didn't know or remember how to do those things. I'd been in a bed for so long that they basically described it to me as though my muscles had fallen asleep and just needed to wake up again."

There's me galavanting around America and she's going through all this, without me. I'd have been in that pool with her every day if I knew.

"What about the eating and talking that your Mum mentioned?"

"Similar with the eating I'd been fed by a tube for so long and then of course I didn't have the muscle strength to lift a spoon or cut anything so I physically couldn't feed myself at first. Mum sort of exaggerated the talking thing. My throat just hurt from all the tubes that had been shoved down there for so long. I guess I took a little while to properly pronounce stuff again. But just like with the walking, it wasn't that I couldn't remember I just had to re-train my body on how to do things."

"God Mia, that sounds so tough," I mumble.

Her eyes meet mine and she looks a little sad as she thinks about it all.

"It was, I guess," she barely even says it loud enough for me to hear. But I hear her alright.

"How long were you sedated for?" I can't help but ask more questions now she's planted the seed.

She sighs and leans forward a bit and then straightens her back just enough so the bubbles don't hit her in the face.

"Months," she finally says.

"Months?" I gasp and she nods.

"The accident was in July wasn't it?"

"Yeah, July 4th," I confirm.

"The first proper memory I have after the accident isn't until February, the following year," Mia hesitantly confirms.

"What?!" I lean forward and count the months out on my hand in front of her quickly. July, August, September, October, November, December, January, February, "8 months?! You were sedated for 8 months!"

I feel like all the air has left my lungs. How is that possible? Why her, why couldn't it be me? She didn't deserve to go through that. I *hate* that she's gone through that.

"There or there abouts. I do sort of remember waking up every now and then. But it's really fuzzy and so unclear. Mum said they tried a few times to bring me round earlier than when I properly remember but I'd just freak out and it wasn't safe for me to be that worked up, so they'd just sedate me again. I sort of remember machines bleeping and just really bright lights. But that's it really, it's so strange."

I struggle to find any words for a moment. I'm in disbelief about what she's telling me. I feel like I'm just staring at her for the longest time before I finally snap out of it. I rub my face with my wet hands and then run my fingers through my hair.

"Did you remember your parents when you woke up?" I ask eventually.

"Not at first," Mia replies instantly. It's almost like she wants to give me all the answers I'm craving to try and make me feel better whilst taking it all in. "It took maybe a few days or so. I remembered my Gran, my parents and a few other family members but that's literally it. Any memories of my life or the people that were in it just vanished. Something to do with the part of my brain that was damaged. I sort of accepted that things weren't going to change so I just switched off at my doctors appointments and then stopped going altogether."

"I had no idea it was that bad," I tell her.

"If it helps, I have no idea about most of it either. Memory loss and all that," she jokes. She actually jokes and then smiles at me. *This girl.*

I can't help but laugh with her even though nothing about this is even the slightest bit funny.

"How do you do it?" I gaze at her, totally and completely lost in her beauty.

"Do what?"

"You just have this control over me. You're the only one who can literally change how I'm feeling in a heartbeat."

Those damn rosey cheeks will be the death of me.

"I don't know," Mia blushes, failing miserably at hiding the grin on her face.

We both stare at each other and I wonder what she's thinking. Her smile slowly fades away but she doesn't look sad, she looks content. Eventually she leans back against the side and closes her eyes as she relaxes. I find myself copying her somehow feeling relaxed too despite everything she's just told me.

After a good 20 minutes in the hot tub Mia and I decide to go and get changed out of our wet clothes. We run back into the house together on our tip toes, laughing as though we are school children again. I do my best to ignore how her shirt has sucked in against her skin from being wet so I keep my back to her as much as possible. There's towels in the downstairs bathroom so I grab one each and place her towel around her shoulders, covering her body. I rub her arms for a moment whilst she gently shivers. She then holds on tightly to her own towel as I wrap my own towel around me. The water was so hot that the chilly night air makes us instantly feel so cold.

"I know it's summer but I could put the fire on in the living room if you like?" I suggest.

"That sounds like a great idea."

"Ok, stay in the bathroom and I'll go grab your bag for you," I tell Mia as I quickly run into the hallway to grab it for her. Mia takes the bag from me and then she closes the door so she can get changed.

"I'll meet you in the living room once I've changed," Mia shouts through the door.

I pick up my bag from the hallway and go into the living room to get changed myself. My clothes are completely saturated and stick to my skin as I remove them from my body. There's a pair of grey jogging bottoms in my bag which I change into before hanging my clothes to dry near the fireplace. Mum always leaves fresh wood in the fireplace for 'decoration' as she thinks it looks nice. Dad and I never thought it looked nice but I'm thankful for my Mum and her ways today as it saves me having to set it all up tonight. There's a small box of matches on the fireplace which I use to light the fire. It takes a few seconds to catch but eventually the fire spreads properly and I begin to feel the heat. Whilst Mia is still in the bathroom I decide to take advantage of that and sit directly in front of the fireplace, making sure all the heat is going onto me.

Most people don't like the smell of fireplaces, but I love it.

The smell reminds me of my childhood when I'd have holidays down here with my Mum, Dad and Mia. It was such a fun part of my life which was another thing that just stopped after the accident. We'd come here every summer and sometimes we would treat ourselves to a long weekend away. There's only ever been happy memories at the lake house. I'm glad that I have the opportunity to create more with Mia. That's something I thought would never happen again.

"Look at you stealing all the heat," Mia laughs as she walks into the living room. Mia's changed into her pyjamas and is holding her wet clothes in her hands.

"Sorry," I laugh as I get up to meet her. "Here, let me take those from you; go make yourself comfortable in front of the fire."

Mia pauses for a moment and just stares at me. Well, when I say stares at me I mean she's actually staring at my bare chest. I totally forgot I wasn't wearing a shirt and suddenly feel like I've made everything awkward. I can't make out Mia's expression, have I offended her or does she, maybe, (hopefully) like it.

"Do you work out?" Mia manages to ask once she realises that she has been staring for a while. Her question makes me smile, it almost makes me laugh but I hold it in and make sure it is just a smile on my face that Mia can see.

"Not really, not anymore," I answer her as she tucks her wet hair behind her ear and quickly goes to sit in front of the fire.

"It doesn't look like it," Mia tells me as I hang up her wet clothes to dry.

"So are you trying to tell me that I look good?" I smile playfully as I pause what I'm doing and face her.

Mia laughs hiding her face and then looks up at me again.

"I'm saying that you're pretty toned for someone who doesn't work out."

"I'll take that as a compliment," I laugh as I finish hanging up her clothes.

Mia hold her hands out closer to the fire, warming herself up as I walk over to the chest of drawers in the corner of the room.

I pull out two larges blankets for us and make my way back to Mia.

"Here you go," I hand her the blanket which she gladly takes from me. I throw a few cushions from the sofa onto the floor for us to sit on and then settle down in front of the fire next to Mia.

"You've literally thought of everything," Mia tells me.

"When we were younger we would often go for a swim in the lake and then come back in here freezing. So believe it or not, sitting in front of the fire wrapped in blankets was sort of our thing," I explain to her.

"Oh," Mia pauses. "Well thank you anyway, for all of this."

"You don't need to thank me. I want to be around you, I *love* being around you actually. I just want to do all I can to help you remember these things. So stop thanking me," I nudge her playfully and she laughs.

"Were we the type of people who hung out at the gym or something?" Mia asks.

I turn to her and raise my eyebrows. Mia sees that I don't understand what she's getting at so she decides to elaborate.

"You said you used to work out, so did we use to work out together or something? We weren't one of those who were like 'a couple that trains together, stays together' were we? Because if we were I definitely don't want to remember that," Mia cringes and we laugh together. She couldn't be more wrong.

"We were definitely *not* that type of couple so don't worry. I actually started working out once I was in America. After the accident and everything I was really angry. I never really coped with the idea of losing you and had a lot of guilt and anger built up inside of me. So one day I decided to join a gym out there. It turned out to be a really good way to get the anger out of my system. For a while anyway. Then I obviously turned to alcohol," I explain.

"Guilt? I understand the anger but why the guilt?" Mia questions softly as she turns to face me.

I keep my eyes locked on the fire and watch the flames rise and listen to the gentle sound of cracking from the burning wood. I think back to how I felt and the pain hits me just as hard as it did back then. I fight to keep the lump in my throat away as I picture the night in my head, just like I have done countless times before. The sound of her scream, the way her head hit the dashboard and the feeling that she died all because of one thing which simply was...

"I was driving, wasn't I?" I manage to say as I turn my face to meet hers.

Mia looks sad, she looks really sad and also concerned. I suppose my face isn't that good at hiding how I'm feeling anymore. No matter how strong I try to be for her there are just some things that I cannot hide.

"It wasn't your fault, I've told you this," Mia says softly as she places her hand onto mine.

"It will always feel like it. Especially after hearing what you've actually gone through, that guilt has just multiplied. I should have been more careful. I should have swerved to avoid that driver or do more to prevent you from hitting your head. I tried Mia, I *really* tried to grab you as the car flipped but it just wasn't enough," I reply feeling emotional.

I take a few moments to compose myself before I continue to talk to her calmly.

"I can still picture the moment the car hit us when I close my eyes. Seconds earlier we were so happy, we were laughing and joking about damn M&M's and then suddenly both our worlds were destroyed. Our laughter was replaced with the sound of your scream and the grinding of metal and glass smashing around us. The moment your head hit the dashboard Mia is an image I will *never* be able to forget and the silence that followed haunts me. Moments earlier you were laughing and then your lifeless body was in front of me and there was absolutely *nothing* I could do about it... all because *I* was driving."

Mia blinks her tears away and turns her body to face me. I try my best to hold back my tears too but my eyes glaze over no matter how much I try to fight it. Mia strokes the side of my face gently and then takes my hand in hers.

"Matt, please listen to me. What happened that night was not your fault. The drunk driver is to blame, not you."

"Alcohol helped me forget," I continue, dismissing her words. "I couldn't sleep without picturing everything so one night whilst in Las Vegas I got really, really drunk to the point where I passed out. I'd still dream about the accident but when I woke I was so hungover the dream was fuzzier than usual and truth be told, being hungover made me feel pain. Whether that was a headache, sickness or sometimes even feeling delirious if I was still drunk, I actually *felt* something. I craved to feel pain, I wanted to hurt and physically feel like I was being punished for losing you."

I've never tried to put how I'm feeling into words before. It feels weird but as I talk it also makes so much sense. I've bottled everything up for so long. I didn't talk to anyone about anything I just carried on punishing myself because it's what I deserve.

"Matt, for years you were led to believe that what happened that night killed me and I absolutely *hate* that our parents did that to you. But I didn't die, and even if I did die that night, it was still *not* your fault. I will tell you that every single day if I have to, but you should never carry any guilt with you for what happened," Mia's voice is genuine and full of concern but she's also being stern with me. I can't tell she truly means what she's saying which I can't lie, it does gives me a bit of comfort.

"I just can't shake that feeling of being responsible for everything you've gone through and are still going through. I have only ever wanted to protect you."

"So are you telling me that I was the only one that was hurt that night?" Mia asks.

"Yes!"

"No, Matt, you're wrong. I may have lost my memory but other than that I'm ok now. You were hurt too in many ways and your way of dealing with everything was to blame yourself which is *so* wrong. You've spent 2 years physically and mentally hurting yourself because of something someone else caused. The *only* person to blame is the guy who drove into your car.

That's it!" Mia is blunt but sympathetic as she talks to me.

"I understand what you're saying, but,"

"No buts Matthew Parker, I won't hear it."

Just like that, the mood has shifted. I turn to face her and she's grinning but her eyes are fixed firmly on the fire that's burning in front of us.

"Matthew?" I frown. "*Never* call me Matthew again."

"Sorry, *Matthew*."

Mia looks proud as she deliberately says my name again and nudges me playfully. I reach forward and begin to tickle her as she screams whilst trying to fight me off. We roll around on the cushions as the room is filled with the sound of our laughter, just like it always was years ago. We both give up after a while and lay on the cushions together after behaving once again like teenagers.

Mia leans into me, resting her head on my chest and wraps one arm around me. To say my heart feels likes it could jump out of my chest is an understatement. I feel so complete when she's in my arms, it's still hard to believe she's actually alive let alone here with me like this. I eventually compose myself enough and start fiddling with her hair. I feel her breath on my skin as she sighs, finally relaxing into me like she always used to.

"I can understand how I loved you," Mia mumbles tiredly against my chest. "You're a pretty cool guy."

Did she just says that?

I don't think I can hide the fact goosebumps cover what feels like my whole body as I repeat her words.

"And you're a pretty cool girl," I manage to reply and she chuckles quietly into me.

I don't remember being awake for much longer. I just remember holding Mia and finally feeling like my missing puzzle piece has returned.

The Kiss

Matt

Mia and I spent the first couple of days in the lake house just enjoying the space and each other's company. We'd watch movies, sit in the garden and talk, of course enjoy the hot tub and would experiment in the kitchen every evening together cooking dinner.

During the day though Mia would always disappear for a nap in the afternoon. She seems to get tired easily which I'm guessing is something to do with her head injury. I don't want to ask and she doesn't talk about it so whilst she naps I usually clean up after lunch. What I have noticed though is her looking at me sometimes. When I catch her she always looks away, almost like she's embarrassed. I wish I knew what was going through her mind.

Most evenings end the same, the fire goes on, the blankets come out and the cushions go onto the floor. Mia lays on my chest and we both fall asleep in each other's arms, it's perfect. Sometimes though, to give our backs a break from the sofa cushions, we do sleep in our own bedrooms, although not often.

This morning I'm woken up by the sun beaming through the windows shining directly on my face. I suddenly realise just how hot and sticky I am as I untangle myself from the blankets. Every morning the same thing happens, I wake up alone. Mia is never next to me and it always messes with my head. Those first few seconds when I wake up I forget I'm no longer in America, I forget Mia is alive and I feel as though everything that's happened over the past couple of weeks is a twisted dream. This morning for some reason just hits harder than usual and it takes me longer to snap back to reality. *She's still here,* I tell myself over and over.

I lay there for a few moments and then decide to get up. I fold away our blankets and place the cushions back on the sofa before heading towards the kitchen. As I approach I can hear that's where Mia is and I feel my shoulders relax a bit.

"He's awake!" Mia says cheerfully as I walk in. "Be honest, was it the smell of the food cooking that woke you up? It was wasn't it?"

I laugh as I make my way over to the breakfast bar and take a seat on one of the stools. Mia has already set two cups out for us and has freshly brewed coffee ready and waiting for me. I don't hesitate in pouring myself a cup as well as topping hers back up.

"Everything ok over there?" Mia asks sounding a little concerned as she turns her back to the stove and faces me.

"Yeah, yeah sorry. I guess the mind wondered off a bit when I woke up and you weren't there. I don't think my mind fully accepts that you're actually here with me and it's not my imagination or something playing games," I explain as I stir my coffee.

Mia puts down the spatula next to the stove and walks over to me with a face full of sympathy. She places her hand on my arm and rubs up and down gently.

I love it when you touch me.

"I'm not going anywhere. So tomorrow when you wake up, and the next day and the next day, I'll still be here," Mia tells me with a smile on her face.

"The next day and the next day?" I question raising my eyebrow.

"Yep, until you get bored of me of course," Mia nudges me playfully and walks back over to the stove.

"Of course," I laugh and begin to relax. The power of this woman is incredible.

"So what's for breakfast?"

"Pancakes," Mia says proudly as she turns around with the frying pan in her hand. She empties the pancake on a plate and presents it in front of me.

"I had mine about half an hour ago whilst you were getting your beauty sleep."

"Beauty sleep? Judging by your 'do you work out comment' the other night I don't think I need any beauty sleep," my tone is full of confidence as I tuck into the pancake.

Mia blushes and spins around to the sink.

"Ugh! You're not going to let me forget that are you?" She moans but I can tell even though her backs to me there's a smile on her face.

I love this side of her. It's so fun tormenting her about it so I decide to play on it a bit more, especially as I'm still shirtless. I place the cutlery on my plate and flex my arm muscles whilst pretending to stretch.

"Forget what, Mia?" I joke and she turns around.

Mia laughs at me but she can't help herself from staring at my muscles. Once I've finished my 'stretch' I carry on eating.

"You're such a dork do you know that?" Mia tells me as she takes a sip of her coffee. "So, I was thinking today we could have a walk around the lake?"

"Fine by me. But do me a favour and wear your swimming costume," I tell her as I finish the remainder of my pancake.

"You want me to walk around in just a swimming costume?" She raises her eyebrow at me, "I may have lost a lot of my memory but even *I* know that's a little weird," Mia takes my plate away and puts it in the dishwasher for me.

"I didn't mean it like that," I laugh feeling a little awkward. "We built something, years ago and if it's still here then you'd need a swimming costume or whatever. You only ever get into the hot tub fully clothed so I thought you might want to actually wear a swimming costume today," I point out.

"True. Ok, I'll wear the appropriate clothing."

"Great."

"Did you say we built something?" Mia questions.

"Uh-huh," I reply as I have a mouthful of coffee.

"Oh, the rope swing?" Mia asks casually as she closes the dishwasher.

I literally choke on my coffee as she hits the nail right on the head. She's not meant to know about the rope swing, she isn't even meant to remember the rope swing. Mia whips around to face me as I cough and splutter from choking on the coffee.

"You, you remember?" I eventually ask.

Mia looks just as stunned as I do as she pauses. She closes her eyes for a moment but when she opens them her expression is strange, she almost looks worried.

"I, um," Mia stutters and her cheeks go red.

I get up from my seat and walk over to her. She doesn't flinch when I gently place my hands on her arms even though she looks scared.

"It's ok, Mia. How long have you known about the rope swing? When did you remember it?" I ask her calmly as I gently rub my hands up and down her arms to try and reassure her.

"Um, I don't know. I thought it was a dream. We'd built a rope swing together and, and we didn't tell your parents about it for years because you fell off of it and broke your arm," Mia pauses before continuing. "We lied about how you actually broke it, we said you tripped over a log instead. But that was a dream, wasn't it?"

I'm completely gobsmacked. Mia may have dreamt about it but she is absolutely correct. I thought she would only remember things whilst being awake but I suppose it doesn't matter if she's awake or sleeping, her brain is always working.

"This is amazing. You're right, you're absolutely right. That wasn't a dream Mia that happened," I tell her excitedly as I give her a massive hug.

This time she doesn't look as excited about her remembering something which I can't understand.

"What's wrong?" I ask.

Mia shrugs sadly. "I don't know. I just, it still feels like a dream I suppose. Sometimes it's hard to believe that all of this is real, it's so confusing for me."

I pull her in for another hug and hold her tightly. This time she holds me back and buries her head into my chest.

"Do you know the best way of making you realise that this isn't just a dream?" I ask her quietly.

"No," she mumbles.

"By going out and experiencing it together. So go get ready and I'll take you to where the rope swing was. You'll then notice that your dreams are not just dreams, they're the missing parts of the puzzle that we're trying to fix together."

Mia lets out a deep breath into my chest and we pull away from each other. She gives me a smile and eventually nods her head in agreement. She looks much calmer than before, she's no longer looking panicked or confused.

We stare at each other and for a moment we just seem to totally zone out. I stare into her beautiful green eyes and have this overwhelming feeling to kiss her. I want to, more than ever before, but I can't help feeling like it would ruin everything. I don't want to misread anything and then push her away completely. We've been playfully flirting with each other for a while now but its never been anything more than that. However, the way she's looking at me now makes me feel like she wants to kiss me as much as I want to kiss her. She hasn't turned away, she's not even broken eye contact with me and she looks as though she's craving my touch just as much as I'm craving hers. I'm *so* tempted to lean down and just see if she'll meet me half way. But I can't, I can't push her if she's not ready. If Mia want's to kiss me then she needs to make the first move or make it absolutely clear it's what she wants.

"Shower," I suddenly blurt out.

Brilliant, Matt. Well done.

Mia blinks and she appears to completely snap out of whatever was going through her head. She frowns as she repeats what I said.

"Shower?" She questions.

"Um, yeah. I'm going to take a shower upstairs and then get ready. Be ready in like, 20 minutes?" I ask her as I force myself to walk away.

"Ye-yeah sure," Mia replies with a tone that sounds almost disappointed, at least I think so.

I don't look back. I just walk out the kitchen quickly, but I feel her eyes watching me until I'm out of sight. I run up the stairs 3 at a time and pass the room my parents gave Mia when we were younger and head to mine. We both have our names painted on our bedroom doors in blue paint. We did that one summer together, I think it was the first time we ever came down here on holiday with my parents so we were no older than 7 years old. Both of our bedrooms have an en-suite so we can still have complete privacy from each other.

I waste no time in entering my room, closing the door behind me and climbing into a cold shower. Yes, a cold shower for obvious reasons. I probably could have handled that situation a bit better. It's just so hard being around her and not being able to act on the feelings I have. I wish I had the guts to just kiss her and more importantly, I wish me kissing her was what she actually wanted.

After my shower I quickly get changed into my blue swimming shorts. The sun is shinning brightly outside so I decide to not bother with a shirt as I'd quite like to top up my tan. At the bottom of my bag I find some shoes which are easy to slip on and off so decide to wear them. As I leave my room I hear Mia's door open. She steps out and has a blue and white striped swimming costume on with denim shorts and white sandals. Her hair is in long French plats and she just looks, *perfect.*

"Ready?" I ask her cheerfully.

"Sure am," she smiles.

We make our way down the stairs and out the lake house together. Thankfully it seems that we have both managed to put aside the awkward moment in the kitchen and just act normal again. Whatever normal is for us now.

"So, I have a question for you," Mia breaks the silence as we walk next to the lake together.

"Ok, shoot."

"Are you planning on wearing a shirt at all whilst we're staying here?" Mia grins playfully when I look at her.

"It's summer, I want to get a tan," I laugh. "If you'd prefer I could go and grab a t-shirt quickly," I tease and pretend to walk back to the house. She doesn't hesitate in grabbing my hand, pulling me back to the direction we were walking.

"No no, there's no need for that," Mia giggles and threads her fingers through mine. I look down at our hands that are entwined together and realise she's smiling although she's not looking at me. This has got to be a good sign. We usually only touch if we're comforting each other but this is different, this *feels* different.

"So how far away is this famous rope swing?" Mia asks snapping me back from my thoughts.

"Not far. You look nice today by the way," I try to sound causal and cool but I'm pretty sure I sound the complete opposite. Mia blushes all the same.

"Thanks," she grins and then bites her lip. I've noticed she does this when she's thinking about something or wants to ask me something. I'm right as always.

"Did we ever argue, when we were together?"

"Where's this come from?" I frown. I wasn't expecting that sort of question from her.

"It's just I cant find, I mean, I haven't remembered anything yet that was bad regarding us. Everything is always so nice but surely we must have argued or one of us did something horrible at least once?" She questions in disbelief.

"Honestly, we were best friends a long time before we started a relationship with each other. We knew each other inside out and spent all of our time together. Of course we would bicker every now and then but it would be over silly things like eating the last M&M, which you would *always* do by the way," I explain and Mia laughs at my comment.

"That's really the worst it got with us, we'd argue over an M&M?" Mia questions. "That can't be true!"

"Sounds crazy doesn't it, but it's true. We really were one of a kind, I've never known anyone else to have what we had. We didn't argue, we never gave each other a reason to," I tell her honestly as I think back.

Mia nods and we carry on walking. Even though I'm not looking at her, I can tell that she hasn't finished asking questions. There's something else she wants to ask me but she doesn't know how to.

"Ask, whatever it is just ask me," I encourage.

"How did you know I have a question?" She sounds shocked that I can figure her out.

"Because I know *you*, Mia. You might think you have changed but you haven't, you're the same old Mia you were before the accident. So come on, what is it?"

"I was just wondering, it's fine if you have because you thought I was dead and all that. But, over the past few years, was there ever a time that you thought about moving on with someone else? Or did you ever actually move on with someone else?"

I can hear a sense of sadness in Mia's voice as she asks me. I think it's one of those questions where she wants to know the answer but also doesn't at the same time, in case it's something she doesn't want to hear. Selfishly I can't help but love the question because it just gives me hope that she still has feelings for me otherwise she wouldn't be this interested in the answer.

I stop us from walking and turn to look at her but she keeps her eyes locked firmly in front. I put my spare hand on her shoulder and turn her gently to face me. She looks at me with a bit of sadness in her eyes and I give her hand a little reassuring squeeze.

How could she even think I'd ever want anyone else?

"You have to understand that you were my everything. There was never anyone else that caught my attention or crossed my mind whilst we were together. When I was told you'd died I did some stupid things, a lot of stupid things actually and I'm not talking about all the alcohol I drank. I'm talking about things like, refusing to eat M&M's again," I explain and Mia can't help herself from laughing.

"You gave up M&M's?" She raises her eyebrows at me.

"Yes," I confirm. "Eating M&Ms was our thing so seeing a packet of them just reminded me that you weren't here anymore. I spent most of my time in Las Vegas whilst I was in America. Did you know on The Strip they have a massive M&M store, similar to what's in London. It's called M&M World?"

"No, I didn't know that."

"Well I didn't either, so when I saw it I had a bit of meltdown. Actually it was a *massive* meltdown," I scoff in disbelief as I think back. "Which ended up with me having a talking to by the police."

"What?! What happened?" Mia gasps. I have her full attention now.

"I was drunk because, well that's what I'd do most days and I went for a walk on the first or second day that I got to Las Vegas. When I saw the M&M store staring back at me I marched inside and might have destroyed a few things in there," I down play what happened purely because Mia looks really shocked. "The shop owner called the police and I was so close to being arrested, but I just completely broke down. I sat on the floor and literally had a complete and utter breakdown in front of the owner, the police and the shoppers who stuck around to watch. If you look hard enough it's probably on the internet somewhere. I told everyone about you, well, I sort of screamed at them about you because I was so upset. The shop owner felt bad and told the police he wasn't going to press chargers and then offered me a job there to work off the damage I'd done."

"I, I didn't know that," Mia eventually says.

No one knows that.

"Yeah, that's just one of the many breakdowns I had over you," I mumble a little sarcastically as I think about it.

"But, but what does that have to do with what I asked?" Mia pushes gently and I smile.

"Mia, if I couldn't even eat a damn M&M because I couldn't get you out of my head, do you really think I'd be able to be with anyone else? It's only ever been you or no one."

"Really?" Mia questions sounding much happier than before.

"Really," I confirm.

The smile on her face is so big I'm sure you would be able to see it all the way from the tops of the trees around us. She then steps forward and wraps her arms around me, giving me the tightest hug. I close my eyes and savour the moment. Thinking about what happened in Las Vegas just reminded me of how dark my world was without her in it.

"It's you or no one," Mia whispers quietly.

Is she repeating my words or is that her saying the same thing about me? I pull away from our embrace to look at her but her expression gives very little away. Her eyes are locked on mine and her hands are still wrapped around me, but she does say anything else.

Don't over think this, you'll ruin it.

Confusion kicks in and I panic because I just don't know how to approach anything with her at the moment. Is she giving me a sign or am I just wishing she was giving me a sign? I blink and snap myself out of it, breaking the trance between us. She almost looks disappointed, at least I think she does.

I look away from her momentarily seeing the rope swing behind her and do the first thing that comes into my head. I place my hands on her shoulders, turn her around and then point in front of her to the rope swing.

"We're here!" I tell her, totally dismissing any feelings that I have trying to surface.

I give her a gentle nudge with my hands still on her shoulders so she begins walking forwards.

"I can't believe it's still here, it might be a bit fragile so let me go first as I weigh more. If it can hold me then it will definitely hold you," I tell her.

Mia says nothing and just watches me. The rope is tightly wrapped around a branch which after what feel like forever I manage to unwrap it, setting it free for us to use. I kick off my shoes and walk up the small hill with the rope in my hand preparing to swing down into the water. I tug the rope a bit, testing to see if it's loose but it stays in place. I step back and make a run for it.

"Wait, before you," Mia begins but its too late.

I've already jumped on the swing and fly past Mia as she watches. I let go of the rope once I'm over the water and land in the lake below. The water is cold but refreshing as it completely swallows me up. I swim back up to the surface of the water and take a deep breath. My eyes sting a little from the mucky water but once they refocus I notice that Mia isn't standing where the swing was anymore. She's actually not in sight at all. I can't even hear her.

"Mia?" I shout as I do a full 360 spin in the water looking for her.

There's no response.

Wait, what was it she was going to tell me before I swung in to the lake? Maybe she wasn't feeling well or maybe she saw something that scared her? Every possible scenario starts flowing through my head as the panic sets in.

"Mia! Mia talk to me!" I scream as this suddenly feels more serious. I begin to swim back towards the trees where I last saw her as quick as possible.

"To infinity, and beyond!"

Mia's voice stops me from swimming and I look around for her. I finally see Mia just in time before she jumps out of a tree that's above me. She screams all the way down until she hits the water which splashes *everywhere*. Relief washes over me and I can't help but smile when I see her. She comes to the surface and laughs whilst wiping her eyes.

"You're face, you should have seen your face!" She laughs as she swims over to me.

"That wasn't funny!" I splash her playfully as she approaches.

"Oh relax, *Matthew*," She teases.

She called me Matthew again.

That's it.

I don't respond to her comment; I decide to scare her back instead. I take a deep breath and go under the water, swimming in her direction. She was so busy splashing me that she couldn't see me go under the water. I can hear her calling my name and saying that she's sorry whilst laughing. I reach her foot and grab it, dragging her backwards. Mia screams at the thought of something touching her leg. I could continue playing around but I decide to put her out of her misery. I come to the surface and her panicked face turns to an irritated one.

"That's not funny!" She screams as she hits me playfully.

"Neither was climbing in a damn tree," I nudge her back laughing. "Even?"

"Fine, even," she laughs.

She dips back under the water and then wipes her face.

"The water feels so good."

"It does now you're not splashing it at me," I joke and she giggles. "What were you going to say before I jumped in the lake?"

"Um," Mia bites her lip and comes a little closer to me. "I meant what I said, its you or no one."

"I thought you were just repeating what I'd said?" I need her to confirm that she wasn't just doing that. I think I always knew, but I *need* to hear it from her.

"No, it's you or no one," she confirms.

"I meant what I said too," I tell her honestly.

"Good," Mia smiles and closes the gap between us completely, wrapping her arms around my shoulders. I look from her eyes to her lips and want nothing more than to just kiss her but I feel like I need permission.

"Mia,"

"Shh," Mia places her finger on my lips. "Don't say anything," she whispers.

I do as she says and she slowly removes her finger only to replace it with her lips.

Finally.

I just needed her to make the first move, that's *all* I needed from her and then I will gladly take over. I wrap my arms around her, holding her closely against me as we both get completely lost in the moment. Mia opens her mouth slightly giving me access which I gladly take. She moans at our contact and threads her fingers through the back of my hair giving it a little tug.

I love it when she does that.

My hands travel up and down her back as I feel every dimple and curve her body has and then hold her body against my chest. Another moan escapes her mouth before we eventually pull apart. We rest our foreheads against each other and slowly open our eyes at the same time.

"That was better than I remember."

"That was better than I imagined."

The M&Ms

Matt

"Are you sure you don't want me to come with you?" I ask.

"Uh-huh. I have my phone with me," Mia opens up her locations app and slowly turns in the direction of where it's telling her to go, well almost. "I need to go this way."

I look at the app and realise she's 90 degrees off, I grab her shoulders and turn her left slightly and she giggles.

"You need to go that way," I confirm.

"I know, I was just testing you."

"Sure."

Mia spent the evening looking at places that were nearby to the lake house. Well when I say nearby I mean at least a few miles walk. She found our local town which has a hair salon, a mini supermarket, a pizza place, a pharmacy and a charity shop.

Mia said the last time she got her hair done was almost over a year ago so she wanted to treat herself. I offered to go with her but she declined telling me I'd find it boring. She's right, I would have found it boring.

This will be the first time we've been apart since we got to the lake house over 2 weeks ago now. The thought feels a little strange but I keep telling myself it's ok because she will be coming back. She will.

"Be back before it gets dark," I'm semi serious here which she catches onto.

"I will, I will."

Mia takes one step outside and then turns back to face me.

She walks forward and places a gentle kiss on my lips which is long enough to still take my breath away. She holds the top of my shirt in her hands and breathes deeply, staring directly into my eyes. Mia then leans forward again and gently rubs her nose against mine.

"I like this," Mia tells me.

Her voice is so content, she feels so relaxed against me.

"Me too," but this time I plant a kiss on her forehead and she smiles. "Go, enjoy your pamper session and I'll see you in a bit."

Mia nods and turns away from me, making her way down the porch steps. I lean against the wooden posts and watch her as she walks. She has her phone in her hand and looks at it, then back in front of her, then back to the phone before turning to face me.

"The shops are left," Mia shouts.

"Yeah?" I frown back at her.

"Left is always right," Mia says proudly.

I laugh and nod back at her.

"I told you."

Mia slowly turns away and carries on walking. She looks back every now and then just to check I'm still there. She'll give me a little wave each time and I'm sure I can hear her laughter through the trees. Mia naturally puts me in such a calm, settled place. She's always had the power to do that. So I stand and watch her until she's completely out of sight and then go back into the lake house.

Although I did get used to my own company whilst in America it was mainly because I was either drunk or I was too miserable for anyone to stick around and tolerate me. People avoided me like I was The Plague and to be honest I don't blame them, I was miserable. But now, it's different. I'm just, happy, in every way. However, now she's gone I feel a little lost in how to fill my time without her with me.

I decide to once again pack away the bed we made in the living room last night. As much as I love sleeping like this I don't think my back can tolerate sofa cushions on a wooden floor for much longer. I have thought about suggesting to Mia that we do exactly the same each night just either in her bed or my bed, but I'm worried that she'll misunderstand me and think I want *that*. I'd be lying to myself and her if I said I didn't want to, because *of course* I want to, but I decided long along not to push or suggest anything like that to her. I know her, she will let me know when she's ready and I'm more than ok with that.

Once the living room is all packed away I then decide to tidy up after breakfast. We had pancakes again, Mia's favourite thing to cook apparently. Every morning it's a different piece of fruit in it, today was blueberry and it was actually probably the best one she's done so far. She always looks so proud when she gives me something that she's cooked and I enjoy it. I think there's still a lot of self doubt in her head about being able to do things so it's like a reassurance for her that she can still do them.

After the kitchen is all sorted I check my phone and see a text from Mum.

I hope you're both ok darling, I love you x

Before I even realise it my phone is calling her. Neither of us have spoken to our parents since we left over 2 weeks ago now. I get the odd text from Mum every now and then but I never respond, until now that is.

"Matt?" Mum answers immediately.

Her voice is sort of mixed with excitement and concern. Excitement because she's hearing from me and concern because she hasn't heard from me for so long.

Does she think something is wrong?

"Hi Mum," I sigh, barely even a mumble comes out.

"Hang on, let me put you on loud speaker so Dad can hear you too."

The sound of her fiddling with her phone rustles in my ear. Dad tells her to press a button and the line goes quiet. She's put me on hold instead. I can't help but smile as I picture them eagerly trying to work it out. I take a seat at the breakfast bar and lean on one arm as I wait for them to sort themselves out.

"Matt are you still there?" Mum says as she manages to take me off hold.

"Yep."

"Right, now press that button there and not that one this time," Dad instructs her.

"Can you hear us?" Mum asks me.

"Loud and clear."

"There we go," Mum says to herself as they finally manages to put me on loud speaker.

"Hi Son."

"Alright."

There's a moment of silence and to be honest I don't quite know what to say or even why I called.

"So how are you both?" Mum asks.

"We're good, things are good," I confirm.

"Has she remembered anything else?" Mum pushes, she sounds desperate to know everything.

"Yeah, bits and pieces. It's still a bit fuzzy for her but she's making progress."

"She is?" Mum sounds *so* happy.

"Uh-huh."

"What seems to trigger her memory?" Dad questions causally.

"Sometimes just seeing familiar things and then sometimes she'll dream stuff instead. It's sort of just happening I suppose without us really pushing it."

"That's amazing," Mum gushes.

"She, um, she told me about her recovery."

Why am I telling them this.

"She did? What does she remember?"

"Did you know she didn't properly wake up until February?"

There's an awkward silence. I'm not angry as such I just want to know everything. But I sense they don't want me to get angry at their answer.

"Yes love, we knew," Mum eventually confirms.

"Did you know about all the therapy she had to have?"

"We knew all of it, Son."

"Right."

"Does she remember anything else? Mum questions.

"Like what?" I frown.

"Nothing in particular, I'm just interested in how much progress she's making," Mum clarifies but her tone is a little off.

"Well no, not really. She mentioned that they tried to wake her up a few times but she didn't handle it well so they had to sedate her again."

"I remember when that would happen," Mum mumbles sadly.

"It just seems so harsh, rather than comfort her they'd just put her to sleep. That doesn't sound right."

There's silence again. I'm still feeling relatively calm and in control of my feelings which is almost foreign to me.

"It was the right thing to do at the time, for her," Dad eventually confirms.

"Did you ever go and see her?" I question and then there's silence, again.

So that's a yes.

"We did, a few times but she was never awake. We would talk to her about you, mostly."

"You did?"

"Always," Mum says sadly.

"If we didn't find out about each other the way we did, would you ever have told me?" I can't hide the pain in my voice as I ask them.

"One day, yes, once we figured out how. We always knew we'd have to tell you the truth," Dad explains.

"Yeah," I sigh.

"Is she there?" Mum asks, changing the subject.

"No, she went to get her hair done."

"By herself?" Mum questions sounding shocked which irritates me.

"Yes Mum, she's not incapable of doing things for herself or going places alone. She has her phone, she'll be fine," I can't help but snap at her a bit. Her tone made me feel as though they think I'd put Mia at risk. I'd *never* do that.

"I just meant it's good you're able to have time apart too," Mum mumbles and I instantly feel like a dick.

I rub my temples with my free hand as Dad talks.

"So you said that seeing familiar things has helped her remember sometimes?"

"Yeah."

"Have you gone through any of the pictures yet from our holidays at the lake house?" He asks encouragingly.

"No we haven't done that actually."

"Try it, Son, the photo albums are in the chest of drawers in the lobby."

"Ok I will, thanks Dad."

There's that feeling bubbling up inside of me again.

Hope.

"Has there been any progress with you both, you know, feelings wise?" Mum asks hesitantly.

My mind goes to us in the lake and I can't wipe the smile from my face. Ever since then we've been affectionate with each other just like before the accident. She'd randomly kiss me, I'd random kiss her, she'd come and wrap her arms around me and I'd do the same to her. It just feels so natural between us, I guess it always has done.

"Yeah, a bit."

"A bit?" Mums excited, she can't hide that even if she tried.

"Uh-huh, she kissed me the other day," I tell her cringing a little inside.

"She kissed you?"

"Yes Mum. Calm down would you," I laugh and they do too.

This feels nice, this feels normal and I don't mean normal from when I was in America. I mean normal from before the accident. My parents were always like my friends rather than my superiors. I could tell them anything and there would never be any judgment from them.

"Sorry love, I'm just excited for you that's all. You deserve this, you both do."

"I know, thanks Mum."

"Thanks for calling, it's really nice to hear this side of you again," there's some sense of relief in Mums voice.

"This side?" I question.

"Yeah, the side of you that only she's able to bring out of you."

Her, only ever her.

"Stay in touch, Son."

We say our goodbyes and it feels good to actually talk to them again. We've never not spoken for so long nor have we argued like this before. The divide between us might have closed a little, although it's still very much there. But as long as I have Mia by my side and she's happy then I'm willing to try and move past everything, with *both* our parents.

I check the time and Mia's already been gone an hour. She should be in the middle of getting her hair done now and be enjoying her little pamper session. I decide to spend a bit of time doing what Dad suggested and dig out the old photo albums. They're exactly where he said they'd be but they're covered in dust. I wipe each album down before placing them on the coffee table in the living room. Then I decide to pick out a few movies too in case Mia doesn't want to go through the albums yet. I wonder what film genre she'd like now? Will it be the same? I decide to go for an old favourite of hers, well ours, and grab all of the Harry Potter films. I set them all out on the table for her, that way if she remembers them she can pick the one she wants to watch and if not, we can start at the beginning.

I put my feet up on the sofa and start flicking through the sports channels. I eventually let my mind focus on the football results. I'd always enjoyed watching Soccer Saturday. I haven't watched it in years as they don't play it over in America because of the time difference. Or maybe I was too drunk to notice.

Another hour has almost passed when I hear footsteps on the porch.

She's home.

I turn the TV down and get up from the sofa as the front door opens. Mia walks in causally with a carrier bag in her hand and smiles when she sees me. I'd never say this to her, but her hair looks *exactly* the same as when she left. That's an easy £50 in the back of some lame hairdressers pocket!

"Hey you."

"Hey."

"Your hair looks nice, did you enjoy yourself?" I mean, her hair still looks nice so I'm not entirely lying.

Mia laughs back at me. "Really?"

"Yeah, why?" I frown smiling back at her.

"You're too polite for your own good. I didn't get my hair done," Mia laughs and walks over to the sofa. She sits down and puts her bag on the floor still giggling away.

"You didn't?" I question as I go and sit next to her. Well that explains why it looks the same I suppose.

"Nope!" Mia seems so happy and I can't work out why.

"What have you been up to then?" I question.

Mia turns to me with the biggest grin on her face. She reaches for the carrier bag and tips the entire contents onto the coffee table in front of us.

"I was getting these," Mia says proudly.

I look at her and then to the table again which is now covered in different sized packets of M&Ms, some of which have fallen on the floor around us. There are *so* many packets.

"I don't understand."

"I wanted to surprise you. I said I was getting my hair done because I knew you wouldn't come with me. I actually went to the little supermarket in town and bought every packet of M&Ms they sold."

"Why?" I laugh quietly and look to her again.

Mia's eyes meet mine and she's still smiling.

This woman.

"When you told me about what happened at the M&M store in Las Vegas it made me feel really sad. You stopped eating these because I wasn't around and from what I can tell you loved them. So I thought it's time we stop punishing ourselves for things we can't change and do what we once loved to do."

My insides twist at how thoughtful she is and how much she cares for me. I suddenly feel really warm inside as I stare into her beautiful eyes. I'm so in love with every inch of her.

"Mia," I want to tell her I love her but I manage to stop myself. Just. "I love that you've done this for me."

Mia reaches across and grabs a packet from the table. She opens it and picks out a blue one.

"Open up," Mia tells me and I oblige.

Mia pops the M&M in my mouth and then gives herself one too. We crunch it in silence and she nods.

"That's good," Mia tells herself more than me. She then reaches forward and pushes some of the packets off the Harry Potter DVDs.

"What's that?" She asks.

"It's a film series called Harry Potter. Do you remember them?"

Mia shakes her head and pops another M&M in her mouth.

"Nope. What's it about?"

"Magic, wizards, witches, goodies, baddies," I summarise playfully. "We saw every film in the cinema when they were released."

"We did? How many films are there?"

"There were 8 films in total. They were a book series first but the last book is so long they made that one into two films with a part 1 and part 2."

"Oh wow, that's a lot. Can we watch the first one now."

"Absolutely," I grin.

Mia gets comfy on the sofa as I get up. I grab the first film from the table and set it all up for us. All I can hear behind me is the rustling from the packets as Mia munches away on the M&Ms. I put the DVD on and then go back to the sofa. Mia looks at me and I raise my arm up, indicating for her to come closer. She doesn't hesitate and shuffles closer, resting herself against me as I put my arm around her shoulder. Every now and then she'll reach up and feed me an M&M, just like she always used to.

The Joke

Matt

After we watched the first Harry Potter movie, which Mia loved, we turned our attention to the photo albums. We're currently going through the third album now which is the one that has the most recent photos in it. Mia is still resting against me as I balance the album across our legs whilst flicking through it.

"What are we doing?" Mia laughs and points to a photo.

"Ah," I begin. "That was another one of your bright ideas. You insisted on us both having a face mask one night. We took the picture and sent it to our parents. However, the picture doesn't show that I had a reaction to whatever rubbish was in the face mask and my whole face turned red for a couple of hours afterwards." I laugh as I think back.

"It didn't!?" Mia gasps trying to hold back her laugh.

"Oh it did," I confirm and turn the page.

There's a picture of us in the hot tub holding up some champagne flutes. I explain to her that was after we graduated from university. We had a family holiday with both our parents to the lake house and they'd planned us a surprise party to celebrate. The other page is just a candid one of us in the garden. We're talking to Liz and I have my arm around Mia's waist. She has one hand on my chest, leaning into me, and we're both really laughing at something Liz said. I can't remember what.

"I like that one," Mia tells me and points to it.

I turn the page again and there's one of me carrying her bridal style out of the lake. Once again, we're laughing and are completely unaware that the picture was being taken.

"What's the story behind this one?" She questions.

"You were being you," I laugh.

"What does that mean?"

"Apparently something touched your foot in the water and you totally freaked out. I then had to carry you out to safety of course," my tone is sarcastic as we laugh together.

On the next page there's one of us sitting on the porch during a sunset. We're cuddled up together on the same sun lounger with a blanket wrapped around us. Underneath that picture there's another one in the same position only this time we're kissing.

"That's cute," Mia says quiet.

"Uh-huh," I agree. It is.

Mia let's out a deep breath into my chest and gives me a little squeeze. She seems relaxed against me as we continue to flick through the album.

"We really were happy, weren't we?" She questions as we reach the last page.

I don't say anything, I just hold her tightly and kiss the top of her head. She holds me back and we stay there for a moment, almost like we're holding onto the memories of us by holding onto each other.

"Are you hungry?" Mia questions and then looks up at the clock. "It's late, we should have something for dinner."

"What do you fancy?" I question as we reposition ourselves and sit up a bit.

"Pasta, I'll make a nice sauce to go with it," Mia grins and gets up.

"I can cook if you want?"

"No it's ok, I like to cook."

Mia walks off into the kitchen and I tidy the living room up. I can hear her pottering around in the kitchen. The house fills with the sound of pots and pans clanging together and cupboard doors opening and closing as she gets started.

I grab all the photo albums together and walk over to the chest of drawers to put them away. It's a shame it hasn't triggered any memories like I hoped it would, but it was nice to look through them all the same. As I walk back into the living room to pick up the M&M wrappers I'm quickly snapped out of my thoughts.

"Ow!" Mia screeches.

I drop the wrappers and dash into the kitchen quicker than I think even she thought was possible.

"What is it, what happened?" I question as I approach her.

"The knife slipped as I was cutting the onion," Mia has her eyes closed and holds her finger up to me. "Is it bad, is it really bad?"

"Ok, let me have a look," I gently take her hand in mine as she keeps moving it around. She's sort of bobbing on the spot but still refuses to open her eyes. Her finger is covered in blood to the point where I can't tell what the damage is.

"Come to sink we need to wash the blood away so I can see it better," I tell her.

Mia does I say, still with her eyes closed and I shove her hand under the cold tap. The blood washes away long enough for me to see it's a deep cut just before her nail starts. But it's not too bad.

"Well?" She questions.

"You might need stitches, I better call 999," I joke.

Only Mia doesn't sense it's a joke *at all*.

"No!" She screams and pulls away from me.

Mia walks backwards and looks absolutely terrified. Her eyes are wide and she's shaking her head frantically at me. Mia knocks into one of the saucepans on the stove and water spills all over the floor.

"Wow, Mia, calm down," I plead and walk closer to her with my arms out.

"Don't make me go back there!" Mia sobs and hits another kitchen side as she continues to walk backwards away from me. She's backed herself into a corner and her legs buckle from underneath her. She slides down to the floor and then wraps her arms around her legs, burying her head.

"Mia it's ok. *You're* ok. I was just joking, it was just a joke," I tell her desperately as I crouch down beside her.

"I can't go back there!" She cries and my insides twist with guilt. "Please don't make me go back there!"

"Look at me," I tell her and place a hand either side of her face, forcing her to look at me.

Tears are running down her face as she finally brings her eyes to mine.

Well done, Matt!

"I was joking, your finger will be totally fine. It was just a really bad joke. I didn't realise, I'm so sorry."

Mia sobs a couple of times as she gains control of her breathing. She's doubting me, I can tell she doesn't trust me. There is so much trauma behind her beautiful eyes that I don't think even she understands.

"Look for yourself," I tell her and hold her finger up for her to see. "It's just a small cut, we'll put a plaster on it and by the morning it will be fine."

Mia studies her hand for a moment and her shoulders start to relax as she realises it's not as bad as I joked it was. She wipes under her eyes and finally looks like she's back in the room with me. Her eyes then scan the room as she looks behind me and she looks horrified.

"I've made so much mess!" She gasps referring to the water on the floor.

"Don't worry about it," I reassure her quickly.

"But there's water everywhere!"

"I don't care," I tell her honestly as I continue to hold her.

Her eyes meet mine and for the first time she gives me a small smile.

There she is.

"I'm so sorry I joked about that, I didn't think."

"It's ok."

"No it's not, I should have been more considerate to what you've been through,"

Mia cuts me off by kissing me. It takes me a second to realise what's happening and then I'm right there with her. Her kiss feels desperate tonight unlike the one in the lake. Her hands grip around my neck pulling me closer to her and she slowly starts to lean back onto the floor, taking me with her. Her lips vibrate against mine as she moans against them, giving me access to slip my tongue inside. Her hands explore my body and grab the back of my shirt. She begins to pull it off me and we break momentarily so I can lift it off over my head. Mia wraps her legs around my back, pulling me closer to her as we reconnect our lips once more.

Can she feel me against her?

Does she want us to have sex like this on the kitchen floor? Is that what she really wants, because I don't want that for her.

"Mia," I say against her lips.

"What?" There's a sense of frustration in her voice as we continue to kiss.

I pull away from her lips and gently leave kisses down her neck. Her breathing is completely over the place but I can't tell if it's from pleasure or frustration.

"We need to stop," I manage to breathe out.

My body is doing the exact opposite of what my mouth is saying.

"Why?"

"Because," I leave her neck and plant one more kiss on her lips as I hover over her. "You deserve better than a kitchen floor."

Mia laughs and closes her eyes before eventually nodding in agreement. My body absolutely screams at me as we pull apart. I help Mia off the floor and realise her clothes are wet from laying in the water that she spilled.

"Go and get changed, I'll clean this up," I tell her.

Mia smiles back at me looking a little shy and does as I ask.

I should get a medal for that!

The Moon

Matt

Mia and I decided to go for a walk after I'd finished cleaning the kitchen up. We could both do with some fresh air after our moment in the kitchen to just regain our composure again. We didn't walk far, we walked to the rope swing and sat down against a tree to watch the sunset. We didn't talk, we just relaxed in each other's company and breathed in our surroundings. The sky slowly started to change from an orange sunset to dark grey colour. Clouds that were clearly full of rain started to grow and make their way over to us. The temperate began to drop and suddenly it didn't feel very warm anymore.

"Did you feel that?" Mia asks as she turns her face around to look at me.

"No?" Just as the words leave my mouth a giant rain drop hits my cheek. "Yes," I correct and Mia laughs.

"Come on!" Mia gets up first and pulls me to my feet.

We jog back towards the lake house as the chunky drops of rain start to become more frequent. The moment we step onto the porch the rain releases from the sky with a vengeance. The drops we felt moments earlier are multiplied and the speed they fall down washes the summer day away in seconds. I've always enjoyed the sound of rain and the wet smell in produces, especially when you're outside surrounded by nature. The smell of damp wood from the porch and all the different plants that surround us is so strong. We watch the rain together whilst being sheltered by the porch.

"I've never seen rain like this before!" Mia shrieks next to me.

"Look at it, it's hitting the ground so hard that it's pretty much bouncing back up to the sky!"

"The sky?" I raise my eyebrow.

"Maybe I exaggerated a little bit," Mia grins.

"Maybe," I joke and put my arm around her shoulder.

We watch the rain for a few minutes until there's a flash of lightening followed by a giant grumble of thunder immediately afterwards. Mia jumps and grabs hold of me.

"Wanna go inside now?" I ask and she nods instantly.

Mia leads the way back inside and I close the door behind us, once more shutting us away from the world outside.

"I think I'll attempt to finish cooking us dinner again," Mia says as she walks into the living room.

"Finish? You barely even got started, you only peeled an onion," I point out and we both laugh. "How about I order us a pizza instead?"

"Yes, I haven't had one in so long!" Mia replies excitedly as she turns to face me. "Can I get a thin crust pizza with,"

"Pineapple, sweetcorn and extra cheese?" I interrupt. I'll never forget what her favourite pizza is.

Mia's mouth drops as she walks over.

"No way, you like the same pizza as me?" Mia asks sounding shocked.

I instantly shake my head and give her the straightest unimpressed expression I could possibly do.

"No, because those toppings are *disgusting* and shouldn't be allowed on pizzas," I reply honestly. "I'll order my own, *normal*, pizza and you can stick to your weird yellow toppings."

"You remember my favourite pizza?"

"It's impossible to forget something so ridiculous like that," I tell her. Which is true, because it is ridiculous.

"I bet you haven't even tried it before!" Mia protests as she follows me to phone.

"Oh I bet I have," I turn to face her whilst dialling the number. "I'll even bet that every time you'd ordered this stupid pizza you'd make me have a bite just incase I changed my mind, which

I never did by the way."

"You're lying, I'd never make you do that," Mia laughs as she tries to hide the fact that deep down she knows that's exactly what she'd do.

"Oh really?" I frown.

"Ok, that *does* sound like something I'd do," Mia gives in laughing. "I think you should have a bite of my pizza tonight for old times sake."

"And I think you should learn to eat a normal pizza," I gently nudge her as a man picks up the phone. Mia runs upstairs to her room to get changed whilst I place our orders.

Afterwards I decide to make both Mia and I some hot chocolate. Whilst the milk heats up on the stove I quickly run upstairs to get changed myself. I can hear Mia in her room as I enter my own. I just throw on a pair of jogging bottoms and a shirt, something to lounge in. Once I'm changed I head straight back downstairs and realise Mia's door is open indicating that she's already downstairs.

When I enter the kitchen I see Mia has taken over making our hot chocolates, which I'm secretly pleased about. Mia was always better than me at making hot chocolate. Whenever I make it there would always be lumps in it and it just didn't taste as good. Mia's however was always the right temperature, lump free and beautifully warm.

"I figured you were making hot chocolate rather than tea or coffee?" Mia asks as she places a full steamy cup in front of me. "I hope you don't mind that I took over."

"Not at all, yours always tasted much better than mine ever did," I tell her honestly.

"Of course it would," Mia jokes.

We both take a seat at the breakfast bar and hold our cups so they warm our hands up. The rain is still very heavy outside as it violently bashes against the windows.

"So," Mia begins breaking the silence. "Can I ask you some stuff?"

"Sure."

"Ok, so we were 16 years old when we started dating, is that right?"

"That's right," I nod trying to work out where this is going.

"How long had you liked me for, before we actually started dating?" She questions.

"Um," I think for a moment before I answer. "Honestly, I'd always liked you. But I think when we started high school things started to change. It confused me a lot and I didn't know how to address it, so I hid how I was feeling from you."

"Why would you hide something like that?" Mia asks and takes a sip of her hot chocolate.

"For you," I tell her softly. "I was so afraid you didn't feel the same way and that by me telling you how I felt it would ruin what we had. You were my best friend before anything else and I couldn't risk losing you over it."

Mia looks back at me as she holds her drink still.

"Did you ever think about me being with someone else and me just never knowing how you felt?"

"Rightly or wrongly, I've always put your happiness above my own. Seeing you with someone else would have destroyed me, I won't lie about that. But if you were happy then I'd just find a way to deal with it I suppose."

Luckily for me no one ever paid any attention to either of us. They left us alone and we left everyone else alone. I think people thought we were always together anyways because of how close we were.

"You'd put my happiness before your own?" She questions quietly.

"Well, yeah. It's all I've ever done."

Mia searches my face for a moment as though she's looking for the right words. She'll ask, I know she will. I just wait patiently and watch her as she takes another sip of her drink.

"You know earlier in the kitchen, when we were on the floor?" There's those rosey cheeks again.

"Yeah," I nod.

"Did you really want to stop?"

Mia watches me as I think of how to word it, she looks really nervous as she waits for me to answer her.

"I'm very aware that just because you loved me once it doesn't mean you still could again. All of this must be really confusing for you and I don't want to do something that ruins the progress we've built over the last few weeks," I tell her as her eyes are fixed on me. "Did I want to stop it? No, absolutely *not*," we both can't help but laugh a little. "But I want you to be absolutely sure that it's what you want to do. You'd just hurt yourself and although I really, *really* wanted to. I just didn't think it was the right time, for you."

Mia nods and places her hand on my cheek gently. She leans forward and replaces her hand with a kiss.

"You really are something," Mia whispers against me and stands.

She walks over to the kitchen sink and watches the rain against the windows. She drinks her hot chocolate and stares at the water trickling down the glass.

"Do you still love her, I mean the person I was before the accident," Mia asks as she turns to face me. She looks sad, she's doubting herself and I can't figure out why.

"Of course," I reply instantly.

I thought that would help reassure her but it doesn't seem to, not in the way I hoped it would. She almost looks sadder as she turns back to the window.

"But I'm not her anymore," Mia mumbles.

"Yes you are."

I get up from my seat and walk over to the window where she is.

"I'm not, how can I be someone that I don't even remember," Mia questions.

I take her hands in mine and she turns to face me again.

"Of course you're still *you*, Mia."

Mia closes her eyes and looks uncomfortable. I can't work out if she's trying to remember something or if there's something else that's bothering her that she's not told me yet. Her mouth stays closed and she doesn't say anything, it's almost like she's scared to say something.

"Mia?" I push softly.

She opens her eyes and looks at me sadly as if to say she's sorry.

"It's ok," I reassure her.

"What if I never remember who I was, is that going to be enough for you?"

Mia's question catches me off guard and I can see the panic in her eyes. The atmosphere in the room has completely changed, the air around us suddenly feels so thick. She's doubting *everything* and it's killing me.

"Going to be enough for me?" I repeat as I look at her.

"I'm not the same girl you fell in love with, Matt. I can't be if I don't remember her. You have so many memories of me, but it's not me. It's a different version of me that you love," Mia sounds panicked and sad when she talks which breaks my heart.

"But you are remembering, Mia. Some things you have remembered perfectly, others have been a little fuzzy, but in the short time that we've been together you have remembered bits of you!" I reassure her, trying to sound positive.

"But if I don't keep remembering things, is that going to be enough for you?" Mia's tone is scarred but she keeps her eyes locked on mine.

Why does she keep asking if she's enough for me? How can she not tell that she's always been more than enough for me.

"I don't want you to love who I was. I want you to love the girl who's in front of you now."

Mia's voice is almost a whisper as she finishes. I don't for one second want her to think that I'm only here with her now because she's remembered things. I keep pushing her to remember our past because that was what *she* wanted. But if she doesn't want that anymore, or doesn't remember anything else, that is also fine with me. Mia is still Mia, past or present she is and always will be the same person to me. She is the girl I fell in love with when I was child and the girl I will continue to love as an adult. With or without her memory.

"Come with me," I grab her hand without saying anything else and walk us out the kitchen.

I don't feel like I can say anything that will help reassure her. Her mind is fixed on feeling like she's not good enough. But I hope that by showing her an example of how I see her now it will help her understand. She holds my hand tightly as I walk us towards the front door. I can almost picture her frown when I open it.

"What are you doing, it's still raining outside!" Mia shrieks as we walking onto the porch.

I don't answer her. I don't want to say anything else until I can show her an example of how I see her. We walk down the steps of the porch and the heavy rain attacks our bodies instantly. Mia's shoulders dip as the cold water hits her. Her eyes are on me, but I'm looking elsewhere.

Where are you?

"There!" I point up with my hand and stand behind her. I place my hands on her shoulders and she shudders from my warmth.

"What?" Mia asks as she looks up to where I've pointed.

"Just look, what do you see?" I ask her as she catches on.

"The moon?" She answers.

I place my chin on the top of her head and do my best to use my body to shield her from the rain as we stare at it together. The rain pours down around us as the bright moon shines through a gap in the clouds. The light reflects beautifully on the lake in front of us. With the help from the rain, the light from the moon almost makes it glitter. It looks amazing.

"Describe it to me," I tell her.

"What?" Mia laughs as though she thinks I'm going mad.

"Describe it," I laugh and tell her again. "What do you see when you look at the moon?"

"Um, ok," Mia pauses. "It's bright, it's white, and it only comes out at night."

We both laugh at her answer and I shake my head smiling. I

can see that she is *totally* not following me here. She probably thinks this is me getting out of answering her question but she couldn't be more wrong. I lift my chin off of her head and turn her around to face me as the moon stays to our side.

"Do you want to know what I see?" I ask her seriously.

Mia stops giggling and nods before turning her head back to face the moon.

"I see something that as you've quite rightly pointed out as being bright which if you look at the lake, it creates a beautiful sparkle. Is the moon doing anything in particular? Nope, its just floating around being all moony in the sky," I joke and she giggles. "The thing is, that moon will disappear in a few hours. If you look hard enough though, when its daylight you can still see it. It's *always* there. Only tomorrow night when it reappears the moon will look different. It will have changed slightly. Sometimes the height is different, the moon may be closer or further away. Sometimes the shape even changes, but it still does the same thing. It comes out at night and shines, the way it *always* has done."

I turn to face Mia. She looks at the moon a few seconds more and then stares at me.

"Just because something goes away and changes, it doesn't mean it's less beautiful," I lean forward and stroke the side of her face gently with my hand. Mia closes her eyes at my touch and gives me a small smile.

I have a short conversation with myself about my next words. The example of the moon seems to have worked. Mia seems more relaxed and I think now she understands how I see things and more importantly how I see *her*. She knows already, I'm sure she does. But now is the time to tell her something I have told her a thousand times before, but only this time, to her, it will feel like the first time.

"Mia, I love you," I tell her softly. "Every version of you, every inch if you, every part of you. I'm completely in love with all of you. I always have been and I always will be."

Mia opens her eyes the moment the words leave my mouth.

All I hear is the rain. She doesn't say anything.

"You love me?" Mia finally whispers.

"Of course I do."

Mia's smile get bigger as she walks forward, wrapping her arms around me tightly. I'm sure I can hear her repeating 'you love me' as the rain comes down. Mia then leans back and places her forehead against mine.

"It's you or no one," Mia says.

"It's you or no one," I confirm.

I tilt her chin up slightly and place my lips on hers. She melts completely at my touch. Her arms wrap around my neck as she pulls me down closer to her.

"I love you," Mia whispers against my lips, instantly squashing any doubt I had about her feelings towards me.

The First Time

Matt

"What's been your favourite film so far?" I ask Mia as she lays across me on the sofa.

We've watched a Harry Potter film every evening for almost a week now. The credits of The Deathly Hallows Part 1 have just started as Mia sits up. She shoves an M&M in her mouth and shakes her head.

"Not that one, the ending was so sad. I don't like it when good characters die," Mia pouts her lip and reaches forward, giving me an M&M.

"Right, well you probably won't like the last one then," I laugh and crunch away.

"Why? Who dies?" She asks eagerly as I get up.

"The question is more, who doesn't die, Mia," I tease and turn the TV off.

"What? You're lying!" She gasps and her eyes follow me whilst I walk around the room.

"Am I? I guess you'll find out tomorrow," I laugh and turn the radio on. I skip through the different stations until I find something that's calm and relaxing for us to have playing in the background. When I look back at Mia she's watching me but is clearly still thinking about the film.

"Well Harry doesn't die, they wouldn't kill him after everything would they? Or would they?" Mia questions as I sit back down next to her.

"But would they kill Voldemort after everything?"
I love teasing her.

Mia frowns as she thinks and then throws a cushion at me that I only just manage to block.

"Stop confusing me!" She laughs and then snuggles back into my side.

I love how we have just moulded back into the way we once were. It's almost like all of the time we've had apart never happened. I drop my arm around her shoulder and Mia fiddles with my fingers as we listen to the music that's playing in the background.

"Can I ask you something?"

"You don't need to ask for permission every time you want to know something, just ask me."

She keeps on fiddling with my fingers and I wait patiently for her to talk. Sometimes she takes so long to figure out how to word things, but she'll always say it eventually.

"What was our first time like?" Mia asks quietly.

"Our first time?" I frown and then the penny drops. That's why she's a little nervous again.

"Oh, right, our first time," I clarify and she nods.

"Yeah," she giggles softly into my chest.

"Ok, so what exactly do you want to know about it?" I ask.

"Let's start with how old were we?" Mia replied.

"We were 18 years old."

"18? We waited until then?" Mia sounds shocked as she tilts her head up to face me.

"Yep. We were always just content with how things were, we didn't feel pressure from anyone around us nor did we pressure each other to do anything."

"So we did nothing sexual until we were 18 years old?" She raises her eyebrow at me.

"I didn't say *that*, we just didn't slept together until we were 18," we both laugh and Mia nods her head before settling back down next to me.

"Was that all you wanted to know, just how old we were?" I raise my eyebrow back at her. Although she's not looking at me she can tell by my tone that I know she wants to know more.

"Well, no," Mia laughs uncomfortably again. "I want to know things like when, where, how etc."

"Are you sure you don't want to watch the last Harry Potter film?" I joke and reach for the TV remote control.

"Matt, come on," she moans playfully.

"Ok, ok," I settle back down and put my feet on the coffee table and begin. "So we were 18 years old, it was on our 2 year anniversary and it was actually here at the lake house."

"It was?"

"Uh-huh, and as for *how*… I know you don't remember much but I'm sure you remember the birds and bees so I don't need to explain that part."

We laugh again and she nudges me gently. I look down at her and see those rosey cheeks of hers again staring back at me.

"What's with all the questions about it?" I ask her gently.

Mia shrugs causally next to me. "I just wanted to know. Everyone should be able to remember something like that and I don't. It's quite a big deal for a girl, you know? I just wish I could remember some of the things from my past that are kind of, important to me I guess."

"It's quite a big deal for a guy too, you know," Mia smiles at my words and silence falls around us.

Although I can't fully relate to what she's feeling, I understand where she's coming from. I can only imagine what it's like for her and I suppose with certain situations only *I* can give her the answers she needs.

"Ok, so we were 18 years old and it was our 2nd anniversary," I begin again. Mia's head quickly turns to face me as I speak and I can see by the expression on her face that she was thanking me for continuing.

"It was actually our first time down here alone without my parents. I'd planned to take you away for our anniversary and wanted to make it as romantic as possible for you, well for us. On the day of our anniversary we didn't do anything during the day that was special. We just chilled by the lake and occasionally messed around in the water. Then that night whilst you were in the shower I snuck into your room. Your Mum had previously helped me pick out a dress for you to wear that evening which I'd packed for you. You had no idea. I put the dress on your bed and left you a note."

"What did the note say?"

"It said something along the lines of *'You have one hour to get ready for our date, I'll pick you up at 7pm. I hope you like the dress!'* or something like that. The dress was a present you see it wasn't one you already owned. Although I never got to see your face I wish I'd have known what your reaction was when you saw it. The dress was dark blue with a sort of shiny effect to it so it sparkled when the light caught it. It was really nice."

"It sounds it," Mia smiles at me.

"I made us pasta for dinner that night. It was nothing special as I was very new to this whole cooking thing. Mum gave me a lesson or two before that weekend so I sort of knew what I was doing. I dished up the pasta into this massive bowl so we could just help ourselves. I then ran back upstairs and got myself ready literally within 5 minutes."

"What did you wear?" Mia asks eagerly.

"Something I shouldn't have," I laugh and shake my head. "I'll get to that bit though. So, I finished getting ready and then knocked on your bedroom door right at 7pm on the dot. I'm not kidding when I say this Mia, but you looked incredible. I've never shopped for a girl before but I definitely picked well with that dress. You looked so excited too as you had no idea I had this planned. The smile on your face made me instantly relax."

"You were nervous?" Mia looks at me sounding shocked.

"Well yeah. I'd put a lot of effort into planning the evening and I wanted everything to run smoothly, for you," I explain and she nods.

"I took your hand and we walked downstairs together. You kept saying you couldn't believe how you didn't know I had this planned and stuff, you were so happy. Anyway, I sat you down at the table and lit the candle that was in between us. You dished your pasta up and then I dished mine up. Everything was going well, *really well* actually."

"But?" Mia smiles as she waits for me to continue.

"I spilt a load of pasta, which was in tomato sauce by the way, down my white shirt which Dad *insisted* I wore," I laugh.

"Oh Matt, you didn't," Mia laughs with me and covers her mouth. "Why would you wear a white shirt when you knew you were making a tomato pasta sauce?"

"I thought I could eat without spilling it all down me considering I was 18 years old!" I protest.

Mia chuckles in the most beautiful way next to me. I get lost in her beauty for a moment until she breaks the spell.

"So then what happened?"

"Well, you jumped up and went into 'I can fix this' mode and tried to clean it off me. You picked up my napkin and wiped my shirt but all it did was smudge the stain."

"I would never do that," Mia sounds embarrassed at herself as she tries to hide her laughter.

"Oh you did! You panicked at how big you'd made the stain so you dragged me upstairs to my bathroom to try and clean it. We were both laughing the whole way to my room. You just kept saying 'I can fix this' whereas I only really wanted to eat the rest of my dinner," Mia nudges me playfully as I talk. "What? I'm not being big headed or anything but it was *so* good, Mia. I'll have to cook it for you some time."

"I'd like that."

I give her a gentle squeeze and continue. "But yeah, back to that night. We got to my room and you took me straight into the bathroom and splashed water all over the stain but you wasn't concentrating and actually splashed boiling hot water over me instead."

"Oh god! This is just brilliant, it's literally going from bad to worst," Mia shakes her head in amazement as she proper belly laughs.

"You kept saying 'I'm so sorry' as we went back into my bedroom but I found the whole thing hilarious by that point. You didn't at first, you were too worried about all the hot water you'd splashed at me so your instinct was to unbuttoned my shirt and get it off me. As soon as it hit the floor you sort of checked me over with your hands and then stood back. You just stared at me and then suddenly I felt really nervous."

"Nervous? Why?" Mia frowns.

"Well we were in my room, you looked amazing and you'd just taken my shirt off. The situation made me a little nervous with how you were staring at me at first. I couldn't work you out," I shrug causally against her. "I turned away from you and walked over to my suitcase which was on the floor. The idea at the time was to get another shirt out to wear so we could continue the evening, but as I flipped open the lid of the suitcase a pack of condoms flew out. They literally skidded along the wooden floor and landed pretty much at your feet."

Mia seems to find this hilarious and bursts out laughing.

"No way, that is *not* what happened?"

"It is!" I confirm laughing with her. "I was *so* embarrassed!"

"But you packed them?" She manages to point out whilst still laughing.

"No, no I did *not* pack them. I had *no* idea they were in there. Good old Dad took it upon himself to pack them for me 'just in case' but he didn't seem to think it was necessary to actually *tell* me."

"What?" Mia gasps.

"Yes, I was just as shocked as you were at the time. You literally stood there staring at them. I attempted to explain the situation but I was so nervous the words that came out of my mouth were gibberish. Nothing I said made any sense and you just stared at me with the strangest look on your face. I literally wanted the ground to open up and swallow me whole."

"Oh Matt!" Mia grins as she places her hand on mine.

"Eventually I was able to explain to you that I had no idea they were there and that the whole reason I brought you here wasn't to have sex with you," I told her.

"Did I believe you?" She asks.

"Yes. I think just because you saw how panicked I was you

realised there was no way in hell I had planned the whole thing," Mia laughs as she realises that actually makes sense.

"I went to pick up the box, mentally cussing my Dad in my head and was about to throw them in the bin. But you grabbed my hand and pulled me so I was facing you. You gave me that beautiful smile of yours and took the box from me. You then opened it and pulled a condom out. You dropped the box and kissed me. The rest just sort of fell into place I suppose," I can't help but smile as I think back.

"Were you still nervous?" Mia questions.

"I was at first, more down to the confusion of it all. I genuinely had no idea anything like that was going to happen. But as soon as you kissed me and I knew what was going to happen, I realised just how simple it all was," I tell her honestly.

"Was I nervous?" Mia asks as she looks up at me.

"If you were you didn't show it at all," I pause as I think about it. "I guess when you're in love with someone you have nothing to worry about. That's what made it so special. Leading up to it, it was just a disaster but everything else was just, simple. You and me, me and you, it always just, worked."

Mia stares at me for a moment and it feels like she's scanning every inch of my face with her eyes. She gives me a small smile and places her hands against my cheek.

"Thank you for telling me the truth," Mia whispers just loud enough for me to hear.

I lean down and place my lips against hers. It's only for a moment, but it still takes me breath away.

The song on the radio changes in the background to something that couldn't be more perfect for us, it's a song by Tom Baxter called Better. The lyrics are just *us*. So I reach for her hand, giving her a gentle tug and she looks back at me confused.

"What are you doing?" She giggles.

"Dance with me," I tell her as we get to our feet.

Mia continues to giggle nervously and wraps her hands around my neck. I slide my hands around her waist, pulling her closer to me. She's reluctant at first but then listens to the lyrics and rests her forehead against mine.

"This song," Mia mumbles in amazement.

"Uh-huh," I agree as we slowly sway together.

Mia holds me tightly as she pulls her body away. Her eyes pierce straight through me, deep into my soul. She's looking at me with an expression I haven't seen from her in years.

"Matt," is all that comes out of her mouth in the smallest of whispers. Her eyes tell me everything else.

She's ready.

I don't wait a moment longer before leaning down and closing the gap between us, placing my lips against hers. Mia does what she always does and threads her fingers through the back of my hair. My hands travel down her back and I have to bend slightly as I get to her thighs. Mia jumps up and I catch her, holding her in place as she wraps her legs tightly around my waist. Our lips stay connected as I walk us through the living room and up the stairs.

There's no way the first time she will remember of us being together will be on the sofa. She deserves, actually *we* deserve, to do this properly in my bed. Mia pulls away from my lips half way up the stairs and turns her affection to my jawline, kissing down it softly before she starts kissing my neck. I'm thankful she's done this as I can now actually see where I'm walking!

The floorboards creak underneath my feet as I walk us into my bedroom. Mia stays wrapped around me when I lower us onto the bed and straight away she starts lifting up my shirt. We pull apart for a moment as I tug it over my head. I immediately start to unbutton her shorts as I lean back down to kiss her.

"Wait, wait. I have scars," Mia pants against my lips.

"Huh?" I pull apart from her momentarily as I manage to undo the button but she places her hands on mine.

"From the accident, they had to operate a few times and I have some scars on my stomach," Mia sounds panicked, almost self conscious which she *never* used to be.

"Mia, I don't care," I reassure her and place my lips back on hers.

"But they're really bad," she continues against my lips.

I pull apart from her again and cup her face in my hands as I stare directly into her eyes.

"Mia, I *don't* care," I repeat.

Mia pauses and then shifts from underneath me slightly. She sits up just enough to make me sit back on my knees. Mia keeps her eyes on me as she slowly starts to unbutton her shirt. She looks so nervous however I can't help but find this so sexy and almost seductive, even though that's the exact opposite of what she's intending to do. I swallow the lump in my throat and just watch as she finishes the last button. Mia takes a breath and slowly pushes the shirt over both of her shoulders, revealing herself to me. Her shirt drapes over her elbows before she lets it fall off completely. Mia then shuffles a bit to pull her shorts off until she's sitting in front of me with just her blue laced underwear on. Her long hair slightly covers her chest as her whole body posture changes. She's tense and her face looks so vulnerable. Mia indicates with her eyes for me to look at her body, and so I do. She has a scar to the side of her bellybutton, maybe 3 or 4 inches long and then a longer one on her lower stomach, just above her underwear.

"I had some internal bleeding and they had to remove my spleen too but there were complications and they had to operate again. I don't remember it but,"

"You're even more beautiful than I remember."

Mia stops talking and searches my face to see if I'm lying, which I am *absolutely* not. Is she different visually? Yes. Does it make me want or love her any less? Never. My body is like a magnet to hers, it always has been. I can't control that part of me even if I wanted to. Which I don't. I crave her touch, I crave her body, I crave *everything* this woman has to offer. Mia gives me a small smile and her shoulders relax. I lean forward and we reconnect our lips once more only this time she's completely with me.

Mia's hands explore my chest as she runs her fingers over every muscle which makes my skin shiver in the *best* way. Her hands reach the waistline of my grey jogging bottoms and she pushes them down as far as her hands will let her. She then brings up her foot, puts it on the waistline and pushes them down the rest of the way with it, giggling against my lips as she does it.

"Is that how you're meant to do that?" She asks playfully as she pulls away.

"It worked either way."

I hover over her for a moment and think about what my next move should be. She doesn't know what to do, she doesn't remember anything about what she used to do or what *we* used to do. Mia's eyes follow my hand as I gently trace my fingers over her stomach. I start at her bellybutton, just next to one of her scars and bring my fingertips up to the bottom of her bra. My stomach flips with nerves as I follow the line of her bra to the side. She arches her back allowing me to get my hand underneath her. When I get to the back of her bra I feel around for the clasp.

Don't make this look difficult.

To my amazement and I think to hers too, her bra unclips instantly as I pinch it. Immediately the bra becomes lose around her body and the strap drops down her arms. Mia follows my eyes again and watches me pull down the straps completely before I throw her bra to the floor. My eyes visually attack her body and I swear I can feel my pupils dilate as I take her in. She watches as I trace my fingers gently over her chest before I cup each of her breasts in my hand. A soft moan escapes her lips as she watches my every touch so closely. I bring my lips back to hers as my hands continue exploring her chest. Her back arches at my touch and then she takes one of my hands. She starts to slowly drag it down her chest, over her bellybutton and stops at her underwear. Her hand lets go of mine once she's positioned it where she wants it to be and then she wraps her hand around my neck again to deepen our kiss. I do as she asks even though she's not said a word, and let my hand go into her underwear. She moans as I do so and I can't hide how eager I am to be inside her once more. As one finger enters her the rhythm to our kiss changes slightly as she adjusts to this new feeling. Her body slowly relaxes to my touch and she begins to deepen the kiss again just as I enter a second finger. Mia opens her legs a little bit, widening the entrance to make it easier for me to get to her. I curl my fingers inside of her and a few more moans escape her mouth before she pulls apart from me.

"Are you okay?" I ask.

Mia nods instantly as she traces her finger over my lips.

"I want you," she whispers.

She is so turned on, her eyes are wild.

As I lift myself up from her, I pull her underwear down completely and throw them on the floor. Mia watches as I remove my boxers and throw them onto the floor too. I would like to think that I was a little more subtle when I scanned her body than what she's doing to me right now. Her eyes are fixed firmly on what's just sprung free from my boxers. She then looks at me and giggles slightly as she realises that she was staring.

I hover back over her again and don't hesitate in reconnecting our lips. Mia explores my body slowly before grabbing me in her hand. I take a sharp breath at her touch, a touch I've craved for so long. Her body just knows what to do and her hand slowly pumps me up and down. I already feel like I could explode at any moment which is when it hits me.

"Shit, I don't have a condom," I breathe against her lips.

"You don't?" She pants as she lets go of me.

"No, I didn't think we'd need one because I didn't come here with that in mind. Fuck!"

This is the worst sexual torture I have ever given to myself and I'm completely to blame. I rest my forehead against her chest as she holds me. Our breathing is all over the place from pure sexual frustration.

"What about your Dad, will he have some in his room?" Mia suggests eagerly.

"Ew Mia, don't mention my Dad right now."

Mia giggles underneath me and I can't help but smile even

though the comment of my Dad just makes this even more annoying. As tempting as it can be sometimes, we've always been really careful. I would always make sure I had one in my wallet but when she wasn't around anymore I no longer had to be prepared. Annoyingly, I know there's some condoms in the chest of drawers by my bed at home although they're probably out of date now. Hang on, chest of drawers? *Please* say there's still some here too.

"Let me just check in here," I tell her as I lift my head and reach across to the chest of drawers next to my bed. I yank it open probably a little too aggressively and see a couple of blue shiny wrappers in the corner.

Please be in date.

"Have you got one?" Mia asks as I pull one out the drawer. I turn it over and see the expiration date on the back.

"Thank god, we have a month left before it expires!" If it was out of date that would have been even more torturous.

"Can I?" Mia asks as she places her hand on mine and takes the condom from me. She doesn't remember doing this before, it's like she wants to know what it's like to do everything.

"Shall we do it together?" I offer and she nods sitting up slightly.

I sit back on my knees again and take the condom from her. I tear it open and hold it out to her. Mia pulls the condom out of the wrapper and pinches it with her fingers.

"It's so slippery," she says to herself as she moves closer to me. "So what do I do?"

"Come here."

I place my hand on hers and make sure she pinches the top of the condom. I hold the base of my erection with my free hand as she looks at me and then back to our hands. We position the condom on to the tip of my erection and then I relax my hand from hers slightly.

"Now just roll it down," I tell her.

Mia follows my instructions and rolls it down all the way to the base.

"Oh."

I smile at her as she stares at the condom she's just put on me, admiring her handy work.

She's so perfect.

I cup her face in my hand and gently brush my thumb up and down her cheek. Mia closes her eyes as I touch her and she relaxes into me. She reaches for my spare hand and pulls me closer to her as our lips reconnect. We slowly lean back down against the bedsheets and her hands start to explore my back again. I return the favour and gently caress her breasts in my hand which earns me a moan from her.

"Are you ready?" I whisper.

I can't wait anymore, I *need* her. I've needed her since the last time I had her which was too long ago.

Mia opens her eyes and gives me a small nod before pulling me back down to her, kissing me softly.

I don't break our contact as I put all my weight on one arm and lean to one side slightly as I position myself against her with my free hand. The rhythm of our kiss is broken as she waits for me to continue. I take one of her hands in mine, threading our fingers together, before placing it slightly above her head.

"If you need me to stop just say," I tell her and she nods instantly.

I then lower myself down to her completely so our chests are touching and slowly push inside of her.

Finally.

She takes in a slow, deep breath as I kiss down her neck. Every part of my body wants to move but I wait for her body to adjust to me again and just keep kissing her neck instead.

"Are you ok?" I ask in between kisses.

"Yeah," Mia pants.

With her reassurance I slowly begin to move my hips again. Mia shuffles underneath me a little as she gets comfortable. I pull away from her neck and take a moment to just look at her. Our eyes lock and I can't believe this is finally happening again. After years of being apart we're finally together in every way I'd dreamed of since we were torn apart. Her eyes still manage to sparkly in the darkness as a small moan escapes her lips.

"This, this feels," Mia can't find her words as she closes her eyes.

"Good?"

"More than good," she breathes and opens her eyes again.

Mia wraps her hand around my neck and pulls me closer to her, connecting our lips again. She opens her mouth, giving me access to slide my tongue inside which I do instantly. Her hand grips me tightly as she moans into my lips. I start to quicken my pace but feel the ache in the bottom of my spine begin to form almost straight away.

Not yet!

I mentally curse myself as I don't want this moment to end. I've waited for what feels like a lifetime to have this connection with her again. Mia moans against me but louder than before. Her head tips back slightly against the pillow and her eyes squeeze shut. I know her, I know her body and I *know* what this means.

"Go with it, Mia," I manage to say as she tenses slightly almost as though she's uncertain of what she's feeling. She listens to me though and relaxes as she completely lets go. I feel her tighten around me as she arches her back, finally hitting her climax. Watching her completely come undone underneath me ruins any focus I had in trying to prolong my own release. I feel the pressure begin to rise until I can't hold on anymore. I lose myself completely as my thrusts become sloppy. Mia kisses me once again and then I let go, filling the condom completely.

Our breathing is so erratic as we both come down from our highs. I hover over her probably longer than I've ever done before as I take everything in. This isn't a dream, she's really here and after everything we've been through we still find ourselves in moments that are just so special. Like this one.

"Are you ok?" Mia questions as her breathing steadies.

I nod and lean down to give her a small kiss.

"Are you?"

Mia bites her lip with a mischievous look on her face.

"I want to do that again."

We both laugh as I pull out of her. I discard the used condom into the bin and lay down next to her again. She nestles into my chest as I wrap my arm around her.

"Just give me a bit of time to recharge and then I'm all yours."

My tone is playful but she and I both know I mean *exactly* what I say.

The Secret

Matt

It's the middle of the night when Mia decides she wants to have a shower before we actually go to sleep. We've been lost in each other for a few hours. I feel like I've explored every inch of her body and she's certainly had all of mine.

Typical Mia ran into my shower and only once she got under the water she realised she needed her toiletries from her room. My jogging bottoms are in the pile of clothes on the floor, so I grab them quickly and put them on before making my way into Mia's room, grabbing was she needs.

Her room is so neat and tidy, her bed is freshly made and her dressing table is all in order with various products on it. I pick up her deodorant, a hair brush for her and then go over to the bed. Mia always used to fold her pyjamas neatly underneath her pillow. I can't help but smile as I pull back the pillow and see them there just like before. When I pick them up they reveal a book hiding under them. Curiosity takes over and I can't seem to stop myself from sitting on her bed and having a little nosey.

Once I open the book I realise it's actually some sort of scrapbook, from years ago and way before the accident. How does she have this? *Why* does she have this? I feel like I'm invading her privacy but I can't help it. I skim through the pages and see it's filled with special occasions that we shared or just memories of us in general. It's full of different colours, quotes from days out, pictures and her attempts at drawing things that we've shared over the years. It talks about our first coffee trip, her birthday present to me, the night we watched the film Titanic in my garden, our first time, graduation, she's literally included *every-thing* that was important to us. The last entry is July 3rd, the day before the accident. Mia wrote how we'd planned to go to our place to celebrate our anniversary and that it was almost time for us to leave for America. The next page says 'our next chapter' and then that's it. Theres *nothing* else in the book.

I'm so engrossed in flicking through the pages that I don't even notice the water from the shower has stopped. The creak of the floorboards tell me she's here. As I look up I see Mia in one of my shirts that covers her body to the top of thighs. Her hair is dripping wet down her and she looks as nervous as hell.

"What are you doing?" Mia's voice is panicked as she stays frozen in the doorway.

I look at her and then hold the book in my hands as I stand from the bed.

"What is this?"

"It depends, how much of it have you read?" Mia mumbles.

"Mia," I say sternly, urging her to explain.

She sighs deeply and lowers her head. My stomach drops at the way she's behaving. This isn't her at all. We've gone from such a perfect moment to whatever *this* is.

"Can you just do me one more thing first?" Mia asks sadly as she walks towards me.

"What?"

"Kiss me," Mia stops in front of me with such sadness in her eyes. "Please?" She whispers.

I don't move at first as my mind races to try and work out what's going on. However Mia slowly leans in and I find myself doing this same, meeting her half way. The magnet thats always been between us springs to life once more as our lips collide. Mia is different, everything about this is different, it's desperate and it almost feels like *goodbye*.

Why does it feel like a goodbye?

When we pull apart Mia places her forehead against mine and keeps her eyes closed. Her hands grip tightly on my shoulders as though she's holding on.

"What was that for?" I ask and she opens her eyes.

Sadness, all I see is sadness.

Mia reluctantly loosens her grip on me and takes a small step backwards.

"Because I don't think I'm going to get the chance to do that again."

My stomach drops and I feel the lump in my throat return which is filled with absolute dread. Don't ruin this, don't ruin *us*.

My feet are glued to the floor as she battles in her head with how to word it, just like she always does. I have no choice but to wait and watch her which feels like a twisted type of torture. It's like she's standing there with my heart on a string in front of me that's hanging over a bed of nails. She's swinging it from side to side and with each swing, with each second that passes, her grip on the string slowly loosens and my heart gets lower, and lower, and..

"I've been lying to you."

...and then it drops right onto the bed of nails.

"About what?" The words only just manage to leave my mouth.

Mia fiddles with the bottom of my shirt that she's wearing and keeps her head down as she speaks.

"I haven't remembered anything, Matt, nothing at all."

I blink at her words and I feel my eyebrows raise. Mia lifts her head up and meets my eyes for the first time.

"Yes you have," I protest.

Hasn't she?

"No, I haven't," her voice is soft almost as though if she says it quietly it won't hurt me as much. But she's wrong.

"I don't understand."

Mia's eyes are on me, piercing through me actually, as she finally starts to explain. "The day I came home from my Gran's, I argued with my parents and then went to my room and just destroyed it. I was looking for another clue that you existed. My parents made out you didn't and then said all these horrible things about you. It made me feel like I was going crazy."

"Your room was full of pictures of us."

"No it wasn't, they removed them when they found out I was coming back home, but they forgot about my hospital bag. It was tucked away in the back of my wardrobe and it had all my belongings from the night of the accident. In that bag was that book."

Mia points to the book in my hands and I look at it too. I turn it around and look at her, shaking my head.

"You didn't have this with you that night."

"I must have, it was inside a small blue handbag that had my purse and phone in it."

Did she have it with her that night? No, we had a picnic and then we set off some fireworks. She did have her bag with her but that's normal.

"Well I didn't see it."

Mia looks confused and then nods. "That book was all I had to prove that you existed. So I took it and left my parents house. I read through it at the place where you found me until it got dark and then I put it back in my bag. I knew I wasn't going crazy, but I felt like I was. I just sat there and cried until you came."

"I don't understand," my legs can't hold my weight anymore so I sit on the edge of her bed as she talks.

"Didn't you find it weird how I didn't run away from you that night? I knew it was you straight away, I just knew. Not because I remembered you but because I'd *read* about you," Mia's voice sounds desperate as she talks.

"I just thought, I thought that,"

What the hell did I think that night?

She's right, why didn't I question it at the time. It's not normal to not panic when a stranger approaches you in the middle of the night in a dark, wooded area.

"Mum made out you didn't care but the person I read about seemed the complete opposite. I just didn't understand why you'd leave me. Your absence made me angry, bitter even. I guess I held it against you."

"My absence, Mia I didn't know!" My voice is louder than I intended and she jumps slightly.

"I know that now!" Mia reassures. "I didn't know that at the time though did I? I felt like I couldn't trust anyone. Then when I realised you were telling the truth of course I felt awful for you, but," she pauses.

"But?" I push as I feel the anger in me begin to rise.

Mia bites her lip and as the words leave her mouth it's almost like they're causing her pain. "But, I hated you for not putting it all together and figuring everything out."

"Are you fucking kidding me?" I snap and stand up from the bed.

I throw the book across the room and then run my fingers through my hair in frustration, turning my back to her. Mia sniffs behind me and for the first time I don't want to comfort her. Instead I shout at her which is something I'd *never* have done before.

"Let me just make sure I'm hearing this right, *you* hated *me* for something our *parents* created?"

"Yes, at first," she sobs desperately behind me. "But I don't now, I haven't for a long time."

"Oh great, that makes it *so* much better," I scoff and turn to face her. "Is that why you've pretended to remember things, to try and hurt me?"

Mia wipes a tear from her cheek and nods slowly.

"At first I did. But then I got to know you and I realised that you weren't the bad guy. Far from it actually."

"When, when did you realise that? How long did it take for you to realise that?"

I'm so angry, I feel myself shaking as the words leave my mouth.

"It was when I saw your reaction to what Mum said about what I'd been through after the accident. The day we went to Hyde Park. The day we came here. I realised you really were hurting."

Ah yes, the day I chucked my guts up after hearing that she

had to learn to walk, talk and feed herself again. Then I went for the whiskey and only she could stop me.

Whiskey.

"It took you *that* long?" I scoff and she eventually nods. "Wait, you just said you were pretending to remember things to punish me, up until the day we left to come here," I frown and she nods again. "So why have you still been pretending to remember things whilst we've been here then?" My voice raises again and I can see it's scaring her but I can't help myself.

"I thought that you'd only want to stick around if I was remembering things," Mia mumbles.

As she says the words a tear falls from her eye. She sounds broken and so vulnerable as she fiddles with the bottom of my shirt. But the slight sympathy I feel towards her disappears as I repeat her words in my head.

"Have I *ever* made you feel like that?" I shout at her.

Mia says nothing, she keeps her focus on the floor and continues fiddling.

Have I made her feel like that?

"You told me it was what *you* wanted, you said you wanted me to help you remember things. That's why I've pushed so hard with it because it's what you said you wanted. All I ever do is what I think *you* fucking want!" How *dare* she turn this on me.

Mia looks up at me as I swear and for the first time I can see anger on her face.

"You don't see what I see!" Mia shouts and points her finger at me. "You don't see the hope all over your face when I lie to you about a memory. You don't hear the excitement in your voice. You don't feel how your body trembles against mine when you hold me. You don't feel none of that! So don't tell me you've done this because it's what I've fucking wanted when it's clearly something that *you* want."

"You are unbelievable," my words are full of venom as I walk past her.

Mia's chest is rising heavily from anger as she watches me leave. I walk into my bedroom and see the tangled bedsheets, our clothes on the floor and all I smell is her, *us*. I can't stay in this room, not tonight. I turn around and see Mia standing in her bedroom doorway, watching my every movement as I walk to the stairs.

"Where are you going?"

I don't reply.

"Matt!"

Mia calls after me again and chases me down the stairs. I still don't reply. Nothing I say will be nice so I choose not to say anything at all. The floor creaks as we walk, my heavy stomps mixed with her frantic quick steps fills the silence. I walk into the living room and there's just essence of 'us' everywhere. The sofa we've laid on, the blankets we had around us, M&M wrappers everywhere, unopened packets on the table, the Harry Potter DVDs... she's *everywhere*.

Anger slowly bubbles inside of me as I stare at everything. It's rising, every second it's rising, higher, higher, and then...

"I'm sorry," Mia sobs behind me.

Snap.

"You're not sorry, you *meant* to hurt me!" I shout and run forward into the living room, lifting the coffee table up with ease and tipping it onto the floor. "And you did just that, hurt me!"

Mia covers her mouth as she cries, she stands back and watches me as I tear the living room apart. I step on an unopened packet of M&Ms and reach down to pick them up.

"None of it was real!" I shout and open the packet. I then whip my hand around and spill the contents of the M&Ms everywhere. The room fills with the sound of them flying through the air and crashing against things. I grab the sofa cushions and throw them all the way into the kitchen before reaching down and lifting the sofa up so it falls onto it's back. I then grab one of the blankets and manage to rip it in half and then toss it to the side. There's a large bookcase in the corner and that's my next plan of attack. I clear a shelf of books in a heartbeat, watching them crash to the floor. The destruction I'm creating somehow helps the pain I feel inside. It's releasing something that's been building for years. I clear another shelf and then reach for the top of the book case and pull it down to the floor completely causing an almighty thud. My eyes scan the damage in the room that I've created. Destruction is everywhere around me. Then my eyes fall on *her*.

Mia's face is full of horror but also guilt, definitely guilt. She's played a massive part in this and she knows it.

"You used me," I pant and she shakes her head. "You did, you used me for you own sick, twisted, revenge for everything that's happened to you."

"No, I didn't," Mia sobs.

I walk over to where she's standing as her eyes stay firmly on mine. When I reach her the sound of her breathing is loud and erratic, almost like she's terrified. But she doesn't move, she stands her ground in front of me.

"I've spent so long trying to convince you that you're still the same person whether you remember it or not. But you were right all along. You *have* changed, you're not the same person you once were," I watch as a tear falls from her eye, but I feel nothing, absolutely nothing. "I guess a part of you really did die in the accident."

Mia takes a sharpe intake of air at my words. I can see that I've hurt her and I don't care. The anger inside seems to turn me into either a raging alcoholic or a viscous destructive man.

I don't want to be either of these things.

Losing her made me one way and having her back has made me the other.

I hate them both.

Mia watches as I step to the side of her and walk back into the lobby. I grab my car keys from the side and the sound of them jingle in my hand makes her turn around.

"What are you doing?" Mia's panicked voice fills the lobby.

I open the front door and pause. I can't stay here if she's here. I can't be around her. She's bringing out this side of me that just hurts us both and I need to get as far away from the whiskey as possible, it's like I can hear it screaming for me from the kitchen.

"Do me a favour, don't be here when I get back," I mumble and walk out, slamming the door behind me.

I pretty much run down the porch steps and unlock my car as I approach it. The front door frantically opens behind me just as I open my car door. Mia appears, running through the darkness towards my car.

"Matt!" She screams as I close my door. I drown her voice out by quickly turning on my car engine. When she gets to my car she slams her hands on the car bonnet, holding herself up. I turn the headlights on and she squints at the brightness.

"Move!" I shout at her but she doesn't budge.

I check my rearview mirror and then shove the car into reverse. Mia's hands fly off the bonnet as I speed backwards in the opposite direction to where she's standing. I quickly change gears and turn away from her, driving off into the night. I look in my rearview mirror once more and she eventually gives up chasing after me before she disappears into the darkness.

The Acceptance

Matt

When I open my eyes it's daylight again. I don't even remember falling asleep. I was too angry to drive last night and had nowhere to drive to. So I parked up on the side of the road, about a mile from the lake house and then I just remember breaking down, completely. The anger inside of me eventually softened and began to turn into sadness as the reality of everything hit me. Everyone I thought I was close to has lied to me in the worst possible way. But I didn't expect that from her, never from her. My eyes feel so heavy from crying, my body aches from the pain and my mind is tired from all the hurt. Mia made me feel so complete. She made me think she loved me again. How could *anyone* do what she's done, but especially *her*. That's not the Mia I knew.

I hate myself for what she's done but I hate myself for how I handled it. I don't recognise the person I've become, with her or without her. The drinking, the violence, that's not me. I totally destroyed that room last night but that wasn't just aimed at her, that was aimed at everything that's happened since the accident. Drinking numbed the pain but that's not what I needed. I needed to let it out, I get that now. I never grieved for her, I didn't let myself. Then all the lies slowly wore me down and boom, I exploded last night. I hate to admit it but I feel better for getting it all out, finally. But now I have to deal with the aftermath of everything and I don't know how I can do that. I told her to leave and for the sake of both of us, I hope she actually did.

The sound of my engine starting breaks the silence of the

quiet, empty country road. Driving back to the lake house takes minutes and before I know it, I'm standing outside the front door.

I can't hear her and she must have heard the sound of my car if she was still here. It's so quiet out here that there's no way she couldn't have heard it. As I walk inside the house it's quiet. There's no sound of a TV. No sound of her in the kitchen and I can't hear the shower or any floor boards creaking.

"Mia?" I shout out.

Silence.

She's not here.

I toss my keys on the side and walk through the lobby towards the living room, bracing myself to see the destruction from last night. But I see nothing.

The sofa is back in it's place and the cushions are ontop of it again as normal. The blankets are folded neatly to the side and the coffee table is back in its upright position. The empty M&M wrappers have gone, there's not even a stray M&M on the floor. The Harry Potter DVDs are stacked in a neat pile, although cracked, and the bookcase is standing in the corner again with ever book back in its original position.

Mia tided away every visible broken part of me from last night.

My stomach drops and I can't work out why. I shouldn't feel guilty. She caused this. She caused me to break. But I already miss her. I know she's hurting, her guilt made her try to fix the destruction I left. Did it make her feel better? I'm not sure if it's made me feel better.

As I walk through the house I see that everything is immaculate. Mia must have spent the rest of the night cleaning and tidying up. It's like there's no trace of us living here left. Everything looks like it's not been touched.

The floor creaks as I make my way up the stairs. I first go to my room and she's made my bed for me. Her clothes are gone from the pile that was on the floor and anything of mine that was on the floor is now in the washing basket. I turn and look towards her room, her doors open and it's almost calling me inside. My legs walk me to her room and as I stand in her doorway I see that all of her belongings have gone. Her toiletries, her clothes, everything. Except something left on her freshly made bed. I frown and walk over to see that she's left me a note and a book, no it's a diary.

I don't know if I'm ready to read this yet. I don't think I can handle feeling any worse than I do right now. There's nothing she can say to make this better, her actions have spoken louder than any words that she could ever write. Yet here I am, sitting myself down on the edge of her bed and opening the letter. My hands tremble as I pull out the folded paper. I sigh and close my eyes for a moment.

Just read the damn letter.

And eventually, I do.

Matt,

I know that nothing I write can make up for what I've done, I see that now. But I hope you believe me when I say that I'm sorry for everything, because I truly am. Yes, my intentions at the beginning were horrible and unforgivable. You didn't deserve to be mislead like that. My anger towards you was misplaced and I realised that as soon as I let myself get to know you. I saw how much you've been torturing yourself since the accident and I'll never forgive myself for adding to that. I know everything I told you tonight hurt, but I couldn't lie to you anymore I had to tell you the truth, no matter how bad it was.

I didn't expect to fall in love with you, but I did and I'm so thankful for that. I'm thankful for you. The way I feel about you is all true, please don't doubt that for a second.

I've left you my diary. I started writing in it the day after we met that night, the day I came home. I wrote down all of my thoughts and feelings that I felt at the time after spending each day with you. Read it, please.

More than anything, I wish we could start over. It's you, or no one.

I love you,

Mia x

A tear drops on her letter and that's when I realise I'm crying. I quickly wipe it away and push the letter to the side, knocking the diary with my hand. I pick it up and start to flick through the pages, just as she asked me too.

The first page is after the night we met. Mia writes about how confused she was and how angry she was at her parents and me. She couldn't understand why we'd lied to her and she writes about how she's not good enough for anyone if someone like me can walk away from her.

Fucking Liz and her shitty comment.

I force myself to keep reading so I can try to understand her side.

Mia writes about how she hated being at home and hated being around her parents.

So that bit was true.

She writes about our coffee trip and how she loved rowing the boat in Hyde Park. That's the first time she writes about feeling bad about lying to me, referring to the Titanic story.

The tone of her writing changes on the next page. It's after the confrontation with our parents. Mia's words hit me, she writes, *'I saw his pain, I felt his pain and that's when I realised he's not the person I should be angry at. I just want to take all of his pain away.'* I swallow the lump in my throat as I re-read her words before turning the page.

Mia writes about how I make her nervous because she's never felt like this about anyone. She says she feels safe when she's next to me and sleeps better when we're together. Mia mentions her insecurities about her scars and likes how I'd just let her get in the hot tub time and time again without asking any questions.

She explains how she doubted my feelings towards her because I never made the first move. She mentions her walk to the shops to get the M&Ms and that she got lost at one point.

I didn't know that.

She writes once more that she's worried I don't feel the same way about her and then the next page is after the night I told her I loved her. Mia writes, *'he made me feel like I'm the only one that matters to him, like I'm good enough just the way I am.'*

How an earth had I made her feel anything other than her being good enough for me.

I'm starting to think I didn't know Mia at all and she certainly didn't know me.

The Guilt

Mia

The taxi ride home felt like such a blur, as did the night before. Matt made my first time so special. He was so gentle, so reassuring and so understanding. Just like he always is. Until he wasn't, and I don't blame him for it. Not even a little bit. I broke him, I actually broke him. Matt was the one person who seems to only have ever done right by me but I let him down and I can't take that back. I can't take any of it back. He took away my pain and in return I gave him pain. He didn't deserve that.

When Mum opens her front door she looks just as shocked as when I came back from Grans.

"Mia, what are you doing home? Where's Matt?" Mum asks but looks behind me looking for him.

"I've ruined everything," my voice breaks as I talk.

It's the first time I've said it out loud and it hits home.

Mum doesn't say anything, she just pulls me inside and closes the door. Dad appears in the doorway of our living room with concern on his face.

"What's happened?" He asks Mum rather than me.

"Take her inside, I'll put the kettle on," Mum tells him.

Dad puts his arm around my shoulder and pulls me close to him as we walk into the living room. I sit on the edge of the sofa as Dad goes back to his armchair.

"You look like you haven't slept."

"I haven't."

We say nothing else until Mum comes back into the room carrying a tray. She has a pot of tea on it and three cups. She pours me a cup first, handing it to me carefully and then does the same for her and Dad.

"Have you eaten?" Mum questions.

"I'm not hungry."

"You need to eat something," Mum goes to get up again and I feel irritated immediately.

"I said I'm not hungry!"

Mum stops and sits back down.

"What happened, have you remembered something?" Dad questions hesitantly.

I can't bring myself to look at them as I talk so I look out of the window instead.

"I lied to him," the words hurt when they leave my mouth. I can still picture his broken face when I told him the truth.

"About what?" Mum pushes.

"About everything. I made him think I was remembering things but I haven't remembered anything," I finally admit and my stomach turns.

"You haven't?"

"No," my voice is almost a whisper now.

"Why would you lie about that?"

"Because I was angry at him for walking away from me! But when I found out that wasn't true I just got mad that he didn't figure it all out. I misplaced my anger towards you all on him," my voice raises as I talk.

All I'm doing is trying to push the blame onto them. But it's me who chose to do what I did to Matt, no one else.

"Oh Mia, why would you do that," Mums voice is sad as she moves over to me and places her hand on my knee.

"I was so confused," I cry into my hands as they watch me.

"Are you still angry at him?" Mum asks softly.

"No, I'm angry at myself," I pause and look at her. "I love him, Mum, I really love him and I've been so horrible to him," I cry out as they can do nothing but watch.

"What did he say when you told him the truth?" Dads eyes are watching me closely.

I picture Matt's face when I told him and I can still hear the sound of him destroying the living room.

"Nothing that I didn't deserve," I mumble honestly and hear Dad sigh.

"I'm confused though, the things that you said you remembered actually happened?" Mum frowns next to me as she tries to make sense of it all.

They both watch me as I put my tea down on the side and grab my bag. Their eyes follow my movements before I pull out the scrapbook I found.

"Where did you find that?" Mum gasps.

"In my room the day I came home. It was in a bag full of my belongings from the accident at the back of my wardrobe," I explain.

Mum takes the scrapbook from me and quickly scans through it. She gets to the last page and looks at Dad briefly. Their expressions are strange, I don't understand them. It's like they're having a conversation with each other about the book.

"So you read things in here and then pretended you remembered them?" Dad questions.

I nod as I hear the disappointment in his voice.

"You really don't remember anything? Nothing in that scrapbook triggered anything at all?" He pushes.

"No Dad, I've lied the entire time!" I snap.

"Did Matt see this?" She holds the scrapbook up again.

I nod and wipe my nose with my sleeve. "He found it and then I told him everything."

"Did he recognise the scrapbook, had he seen it before?" Mum pushes again.

"No," I shake my head at them. "He said I didn't have that with me on the night of the accident."

Mum looks back at Dad and they start to make me feel uncomfortable. It's like there's a giant elephant in the room.

"Did I have it with me?" I frown.

Mum pulls her head away from Dads again and stares back at me. Her expression is strange, is it sympathy? I can't tell, but it's not relaxed.

"Yes love. We made a lot of this scrapbook together. You weren't sure whether to give it to him that night or wait until you got to America. You obviously decided on America," Mums voice is quiet, its gentle, it's *different*.

I take the scrapbook back from Mum and flick through the pages again. Everyone knows so much about my life and I hate it. It's like everyone has a puzzle piece to me and I always just feel, incomplete.

"We made this?"

Mum nods. "I just helped print some of the pictures for you really, you did the rest," she clarifies.

We're silent for a moment as I skim through each page with a bit more understanding as to how it was made. But why didn't I give it to him?

"What else was in the bag you found?" Dad asks me.

Mum gives him what looks like her stern face, she's not happy he asked that. I think she can tell I'm tired and mostly, I just want Matt.

"Um, my purse, my old phone and just my handbag. This scrapbook was inside that," I tell him and wipe my face again as I sit back against the sofa for the first time. My eyes feel so heavy.

"Are you ok?" Mum leans back against the sofa with me.

I go to talk but no words come out. Am I ok, physically yes. But in every other way I'm not. I'm far from ok. My stomach twists when I think of what I've done and how I've treated him. Mum puts her hand back on my knee and rubs gently.

"He'll come around," she says softly.

"You didn't see him, Mum," my voice cracks and Mum wraps her arms around me, holding me tightly as I cry into her chest.

I think back to his reaction when I told him the truth. I think of how he destroyed everything in his path, everything. I think of how he drove away into the night, leaving me alone. Then I think of his words, he referred to the part of me that he loved as being dead and he meant that.

It's over, it really is over.

The Break

Mia

Day 1

I called his phone but it just rang for what felt like forever and then went to his voicemail. I heard his voice, all it said was 'Hey it's Matt, leave a message and I'll call you back.'
But he didn't call me back.

Day 2

I sent Matt a text today. It's not even been opened. I called him again too, but he didn't answer.

Day 5

I went through the scrapbook again, I cried. Mum held me until I fell back to sleep again. I don't sleep very well anymore, I've only ever truly slept when Matt was next to me.

Day 7

Mum made me leave the house today so I went to our place. I waited there all day, until it got dark, just like last time. But Matt never came for me this time.

Day 10

I called Matt again today. His phone didn't ring for as long this time, I think he cancelled the call.

Day 12

I left the house again today and went to Matt's parents house. I knocked but no one answered. I looked through the living room window and I'm sure I saw movement inside, but no one ever opened the door.

Day 15

I called Matt again only today his phone went straight to voicemail, it didn't even ring. I didn't call again.

Day 16

I didn't eat anything all day. I stayed in my bed and pretending to be asleep every time Mum came in to check on me.

Day 19

Mum made me get out of bed today. She ran me a hot bubble bath and said I'd feel better afterwards. I didn't.

Day 21

Dad took me out for coffee today. I ordered a vanilla latte because that's what Matt would have ordered. Megan wasn't there, but our seat was free. Dad and I sat there.

Day 23

Mum took me shopping today. Her and Dad are throwing an end of summer BBQ in a couple of weeks. Apparently they've done this every year, I don't remember that. Mum picked out a dress for me, it's blue and white striped, a bit like the swimming costume I wore on the day Matt and I kissed for the first time. That was a good day. Today was not.

Day 26

Today I spoke to my Gran. She said she missed me, I said I missed her. We spoke for a while but mainly I told her all about Matt. She said there's always hope.

Day 28

I found the song we danced to that night. I listened to it on repeat for hours until I fell asleep.

Day 29

I heard Mum and Dad talk about hope today. They stopped when they heard me coming down the stairs. Everyone always talks about having hope.

Day 31

Mum and Dad decorated the back garden today ready for their BBQ. They made me help them put some lights up, they looked pretty. I asked if they'd invited Matt and his parents and they said yes. Maybe there is hope?

The BBQ

Mia

Unlike most days recently I woke up early today. I hardly slept actually, the thought of me seeing Matt today kept me awake. I had a mixture of feelings about it. I was nervous to see him but I was *desperate* to see him. I thought about what I'd say to him and what he'd say to me, if anything at all. I wondered if he'd stare at me the way he always does, almost like I take his breath away. I hoped he'd hold me, just so I can hold him. I miss his touch, I miss the smell of his aftershave and I miss his voice.

Sometimes at night I would stay awake and just listen to the sound of his heartbeat as I'd lay on his chest. It was always so slow and relaxed. The first few nights at the lake house though there were times that his breathing would change and his heartbeat would quicken. He'd twitch and then hold me tightly afterwards. His eyes always stayed closed though. I'm not sure if he even knew he was doing it, but he did. It's as though he'd dream about me and then realise I was still there.

Does he still reach for me in his sleep?

The sound of our doorbell ringing disturbs me from my thoughts. I've been getting myself ready all morning. I'm wearing the dress Mum picked for me. I've put some makeup on for the first time in a month and decided to make my hair wavy. It falls nicely on my dress and fits the Beach Theme of this BBQ.

"Mia, people are arriving can you come downstairs please?" Mum shouts.

People.

Not Matt.

I look again at myself in the mirror and fiddle with my dress. It's a little figure hugging but not too much and sits just above my knees. I quickly put on my white sandals and spray myself with perfume before joining everyone downstairs.

Mum and Dad are busy being hosts to even notice I've joined the crowd. I scan the garden for him, my eyes search everywhere but he's not here and neither are his parents. I don't actually recognise anyone that's here. My parents said they were inviting work colleagues, family friends and the odd family member who could make it. They've catered for around 50 people and I'd say about 20 people are already here. But they're all blank faces to me. No familiarity at all. Their gazes make me feel like a stranger in my own home.

There's a giant gazebo at the back of the garden where the drink station is set up. I feel like I need to calm my nerves down and I always hear people talk about how they'd have a drink to do that. I don't remember ever having alcohol before. It's not that I'm not allowed it or anything. I've just never felt the need nor has there been an occasion for it. There are buckets of beer bottles in ice, various soft drinks with spirits and then this fountain of pinky orangey coloured liquid. It's pretty to just look at. There's three tiers to the fountain which is plugged into an extension lead that goes into our shed. The liquid trickles out of little funnel shaped hoses into the tier underneath and then at the bottom there's chopped fruit floating around. There's a stack of plastic cups next to the fountain and a sign that says 'Sex on the Beach'.

Inappropriate.

Nevertheless, I grab a cup and hold it underneath one of the funnels from the top tier as it fills my cup up half way. I give it a sniff and it just smells fruity. When I taste it I realise it's just that, fruity. It's really nice actually. I take another sip and then see some vodka on the side. I hope it doesn't ruin the taste of it but I decide to mix the drink with some vodka. I fill the cup up another quarter and then grab a straw from the side, mixing it all together. The vodka definitely adds a kick to it, it doesn't taste as nice but its still ok.

"Mia! I can't believe it's you!"

When I turn around my straw is still in my mouth and I almost swallow it as I gasp. I do my best to take in the bleached blonde curly haired lady in front of me. She's maybe in her 50s but dresses as though she's in her 30s, or younger, and her dress is a lot shorter than mine. It only just covers her backside! She has bright red lipstick on and massive hoop earrings that almost touch her shoulders. She looks a treat!

"Hey?" I frown.

"Oh of course, the memory thing. I'm your Aunt Tess from your Dads side, you can call me Tessie," *Tessie* leans forward and embraces me in a tight, unwanted hug which I don't return. I'm related to this woman? This is Dads sister?

"You look just the same as when I last saw you. Your hair's longer of course and your figure, gosh girl, how have you pulled that off?"

"Um, I,"

"Tess!" Dad snaps and she turns around to face him. I must remember to thank Dad later, I don't even know where he came from.

"Can you help Liz with the Prosecco in the kitchen, now please."

"Prosecco? Only if I can have one of course," Tessie laughs at her own, laugh-less joke and turns back to me. "Come and find me later but don't wait too long, I'm a lightweight!" She laughs again and then pinches my cheek before walking away.

Seriously, I'm related to *that*?

"You ok kiddo?" Dad asks as he comes over.

"That's your sister?" I question. My voice definitely has a tone of disgust to it as I wipe my cheek from where her fingers were.

"Half sister," he clarifies and puts his arm around me as we walk out of the gazebo.

"I don't think I like her very much," I admit.

"Not many people do," he bends down and whispers and we

both laugh.

We then hear the sound of a bottle popping open followed by Tessie laughing loudly drawing everyone's attending to her. She's just so happened to spill the Prosecco down her white dress which has turned see-through. She's *so* classy.

"Don't drink too many of those or you'll end up like her. Your Mum messed up the measurements," Dad signals to my drink.

"Measurements?" I frown.

"Yes, it's a cocktail, Mia. It's got alcohol in it."

Whoops.

"Oh right, of course. I'll be careful don't worry," I smile back at him.

"Tess, stay still," Mums strained voice yells from the kitchen.

"I better go and help your Mum," Dad tells me as Mum starts dabbing a cloth on Tessie who will not stay still. "You good?"

I nod and give him a smile.

I'm not good.

Dad smiles back and quickens his pace over to the chaos Tessie has created.

There's more people here now, but still no sign of Matt. I feel like everyone's eyes are on me as they arrive. Do they know what my parents said about me supposedly dying? Is that why they're staring at me because they think they're seeing a ghost or something? Maybe their stares are out of sympathy because they know what happened? Either way I don't like it, I wish they'd keep their gazes to themselves.

"Is that really her?" Some women not so quietly whispers to her husband as I walk past.

"Yes, Liz said she came home a couple of months ago and she has no idea," he whispers back.

I hate this. I feel as though I'm an animal in a zoo and I'm just here for their entertainment. I take another large gulp of my drink which tastes a bit stronger this time. I wince slightly as I swallow the contents and walk back into the house. Mum's still mopping up the floor from the Prosecco as the doorbell rings.

"Oh Mia, can you get the door please love?" Mum asks desperately.

"Sure," I mumble.

"Are you ok?" She asks after me but I don't respond.

No I'm not ok, this BBQ was a stupid idea because everyone is talking about me or watching me. I only said yes to this stupid thing because I thought Matt would be here. I suck once more on the straw as I open the door and then choke on what's in my mouth. I cough and splutter like an absolute moron whilst blocking the doorway.

"Mr and Mrs Parker," I eventually manage to get out. They smile at me a little awkwardly as my eyes look behind them, looking for him. "He's not here," I breathe sadly.

They give each other a sympathetic glance and then look back at back at me.

"No, no he's not," Mrs Parker's tone is just as sad as mine.

I feel like the wind has been knocked out of me. He must really hate me. He's avoided my calls, he doesn't even open my texts and now he hasn't turned up to this stupid BBQ.

"He doesn't hate you, Mia," Mrs Parker says as she places her hand on my arm.

Did I say that out loud?

"Is he ok?"

"Mia, what are you doing? Move to the side so the guests can come in," Mum rushes over from the kitchen and then sees them. "Oh."

"Hi Liz," Mr Parker smiles at Mum.

"Hi John, Debbie," Mum says cheerfully and gently moves me to the side. "Come in, please. Drinks are out the back and Aaron's just firing up the BBQ."

My legs walk me away from them without me even realising it. I can here them talking behind me but I can't hear what they're saying. All I can hear is my heartbeat pounding against my chest as I do my best to hold back my tears.

"Mia?" Dads voice is full of concern as I storm past him.

"I'm fine Dad."

I'm not fine.

All eyes are on me as I walk back to the gazebo to get another drink. Don't worry people, your dancing monkey is back. I down the rest of my current drink and fill up the cup again with what I now know is a Sex on the Beach cocktail. When I look around again everyone's giving me this disapproving look. Mr and Mrs Parker are talking to my Dad by the BBQ but Mrs Parker's eyes are on me.

"I don't understand how she just can't remember that though?" Some woman says to her friend.

I don't understand either.

My hands grab the vodka bottle that I opened earlier and I walk over to the shed with each hand carrying a drink. Well it's more like a beach house that my parents have decorated which is currently empty. There's a TV in there and lots of big chunky cushions and bean bags dotted around the floor. I drop and land on one of the bean bags before taking a big gulp of the cocktail. Finally I feel like I'm away from prying eyes as I make sure my back is to everyone. I don't want to see them and if all they can see is my back they'll lose interest soon. I hope.

"Fancy some company?" Mrs Parker's sympathetic voice is behind me.

Our eyes meet when I turn around and she gives me a small smile as she stands in the doorway. I only nod, I can't find my voice right now as there's a lump in my throat. I quickly wash it down with a mouthful of vodka. Mrs Parker closes the doors behind us and drops to the cushion next to me. She frowns at the bottle of vodka in my hand and the cocktail on the floor.

"Why is it that without each other you both turn to drink?" There's curiosity in her voice as she asks.

"Has he been drinking again?" I ask quickly, turning to face her.

"I don't know for sure but I don't think so."

"Is he still at the lake house?"

Mrs Parker nods. "Mostly he's there, yes."

"Why didn't he come today."

"He was going to, he drove here and everything. But he felt

like this was probably not the time or place for you to see each other again."

I guess he's right. But I think I'd have coped much better with being everyone's entertainment if he was with me.

"Everyone's staring at me or talking about me out there. I hate it," I mumble and take a sip of vodka again.

She sighs next to me and stretches her legs out. "I know they are."

We're silent for a moment and just stare at the TV that's just got music charts playing. Neither one of us really know what to say but there's something I need to know.

"How is he?"

The selfish side of me doesn't want to hear he's ok without me, but I also want to hear he is actually ok. I don't like the thought that he could be suffering without anyone around him.

"He's," Mrs Parker pauses. "He's hurting too."

"I don't want him to hurt anymore, not because of me or over me," my voice breaks slightly as I talk so I punish it and swallow some more vodka.

"Don't do what he did and use drink to numb the pain, Mia," she takes the bottle from me gently and places it on the floor next to her.

"Did you know he hasn't spoken to me since? He's avoiding my calls and doesn't respond to my texts. It's like he's disappeared," I feel my eyes fill up with water so I blink them away quickly. "How did he cope before. It's been 1 month and I'm at breaking point, how did he cope for so long?"

Mrs Parker looks so sad when she looks at me, her voice breaks as she talks. "He didn't cope though, did he? He ran away from it all and self medicated with alcohol."

"I was so cruel to him," I sob more to myself than her. She doesn't respond because she knows I was. "I hate myself for what I've done to him."

"Punishing yourself won't fix this. He just needs some time that's all."

"But he's had a month and he hasn't even *tried* to contact me this entire time, not once," my voice raises but it's not directed at her, I'm just sad. I'm missing him and to be honest I feel a little tipsy.

"When he's ready he'll contact you love."

"He won't," I sob and then finish the rest of the cocktail that Mrs Parker forgot I had. She sighs as she watches me finish the lot. "He didn't deserve any of this. I don't remember all the years I've lost, but he does and I've just added to that pain. How could I do that to him. *Why* did I do that to him?"

"You've both been through so much," she puts her arm around my shoulders and holds me tightly. "You just have to have a bit of hope sweetheart."

"My Gran said that, to have hope. I hoped he'd be here today and he's not. I have no hope left Mrs Parker I really don't and it's what I deserve. He's only ever done right by me and I just shoved it back in his face. I deserve to feel like this, I deserve all of it for what I've put him through."

"No, you don't."

I hold my breath at the sound of his voice. My sobs stop instantly and my heartbeat starts to quicken.

Please don't be hearing things.

I pull away from Mrs Parker and she gives me a small, reassuring smile. I finally look behind me and see him standing in the doorway. He's wearing black trousers and a smart, plain white shirt. His eyes are piercing through me as his chest rises.

How long was he standing there?

"You're here," I breathe.

I get up as quickly as possible so I can get to him but I tread on one of the bean bags which shifts underneath my feet and off balances me. The alcohol definitely hasn't helped with my balance as I wobble forward. Matt moves quickly and manages to catch me before I tumble over completely. He holds my arms tightly as I rebalance and I lose myself in the feeling of his touch. His warmth, his grip, his eyes... he's really here.

"I'll um, I'll leave you two alone," Mrs Parker says with a happy tone to her voice.

Matt acknowledges her, giving her a small nod as she leaves and then it's just us.

"You're really here," I repeat and he lets go of me. He reaches to his back pocket and pulls out a bottle of water before handing it to me.

"You should drink this," Matt says as he holds it out. I hesitate before taking it from him and just watch as he goes to sit down on a bean bag that was opposite to what I was sitting on. He sighs deeply as he knots his hands together in front of him.

"You haven't answered my calls," I mumble whilst staying in the same place.

"I know."

"Or my texts."

"I know."

The air suddenly feels thick around us. Things are awkward, things a frosty and he's being really off with me. Ok, that's expected but still, it hurts seeing him this way.

"I've missed you," my voice is so quiet I'm not sure if he heard me at first. His focus eventually shifts in my direction and he looks so sad.

"Come and sit down," Matt says but he doesn't say he missed me too.

"You didn't say it back."

"Mia, sit."

My legs are thankful when I give in and crash down on the bean bag opposite him. I take a gulp of the water he gave me and then take two more. I suddenly feel really thirsty.

"How much have you had to drink?" Matt studies my face.

I shrug as I think about it. "I don't know, I had the cocktail but added vodka to it because I didn't know it was a cocktail at first and then when I did, I added vodka again anyway."

"Have you eaten?"

"Not really."

"What does that mean, not really? Have you eaten or not?" Matt snaps slightly as he keeps his eyes on me.

"Not," I tell him as a hiccup falls out.

I cover my mouth quickly but another hiccup escapes against my hand.

"I'm going to get you something to eat," Matt's voice is stern as he goes to push up from the bean bag.

"No, don't. Please just stay with me for a bit and I'll eat after," I reach forward and grab his hand which stops his movement instantly. He turns to face me just as another hiccup escapes.

Crap.

"Come with me," Matt pulls me up from the bean bag so I'm standing in front if him. He grabs the water from my hand and shoves it back in his trouser pocket.

Matt opens the doors and we walk out together. Eyes are on us instantly, obviously. He puts his arm around my shoulder tightly and I can't work out if he's doing it to be protective of me or if he's doing it so I don't fall over. Either way I love his touch. The heat from him is like a radiator against me and fills my whole body with the warms it's been missing.

Dad's well and truly got the BBQ going now, there's a table with trays full of burgers and hotdogs with various other things like kebab skewers and salads on it. Matt keeps one arm around me as he picks up a hotdog.

"Is she drunk?" Mum asks as we walk inside.

"Royally," Matt responds without stopping. "I'm taking her to her room so she doesn't have a garden full of eyes on her!"

Mum doesn't say anything else. Matt's tone was clear that responding to him would not be a good thing. As we turn the corner just before the stairs the bathroom door opens.

Tessie.

"Look at you both, let me just take a picture of you," Tessie shrieks but she has no camera. She just moves her hands into the shape of a camera and makes clicking noises.

"Nice to see you again, Tessie," Matt doesn't mean that, I can tell by his tone. "Excuse us."

Tessie gasps in excitement. "Of course, you two have a lot of catching up to do. Wink, wink, nudge, nudge."

That's another one of her jokes that only she finds funny. She just cackles in front of us which irritates me.

"Your laugh is annoying and your jokes aren't funny," I blurt out.

Matt's face whips in my direction but he's amused by my words. Tessie however stops laughing and frowns at me.

"What did you say?"

"You're actually really inappropriate too and I don't think I like you very much."

Hiccup.

Tessie's eyebrows raise and she has a strange look on her face. She looks around to make sure no ones too close to us and leans down to me.

"I think you've had one too many bangs to the head my dear," Tessie's voice is quiet enough that only we can hear her.

My mouth drops as Matt's grip tightens on my shoulder.

"What did you just say to her?" Matt's angry, he's really angry.

"Oh come on, she's not the same Mia we all knew. But then I'm sure you already know that," she smiles as she talks so that others will think she's saying really nice things to us. But her words are bitter.

"Why does everyone keep saying that about me?" My voice is quiet but not quiet enough.

"Ignore her," Matt tells me firmly but Tessie carries on.

"Both of you, actually, should be ashamed of yourselves. The fact you're getting drunk Mia is so irresponsible. I don't know how you can walk around here like everything's normal when your whole family has been covering up for your mistake all this time."

"What's going on?" Dads voice is firm as he comes up behind us, cutting her off.

Matt's breathing shifts, he's trying so hard to hold it together. He ignores Dad's question but answers him at the same time by simply replying to Tessie.

"I'm only going to say this once. If you so much as look at Mia again I will not be responsible for my actions. You don't have the right to talk to her like that again, ever. I don't care who you think you are but you and your vile words are not welcome here and mean *nothing* to us."

"Well you're nothing to *her* too," Tessie glares back at Matt before Dad steps between us.

"That's not true!" I say desperately.

"Enough, Tessie you need to leave," I don't think I've ever heard Dad so angry before.

Hiccup.

"Why? I'm only saying the truth it's about time they hear it!" Tessie shouts back drawing attention to herself again.

"Out, now!" Dad opens the door and almost pushes Tessie outside before slamming it in her face. He rests his head on the door as his shoulders rise up and down.

Hiccup.

"I'm going to take Mia upstairs but we need to talk later," Matt tells Dad.

Dad turns around and has this strange look on his face. He's angry but there's sort of like an understanding to it. All he does is nod back at Matt and walks back to the party.

Matt starts to walk us upstairs. He's still breathing heavily and his grip is still tight on my shoulder when we get to my room. He walks us over to my bed and puts the hotdog on the side. He finally lets me go as we sit on the edge of my bed together. I miss his touch instantly, it feels colder already.

"Are you ok?" Matt asks.

"You stood up for me," I whisper.

"Your Aunt has always been a bitch."

"She pinched my cheeks earlier and it hurt."

Hiccup.

Matt gives me a small smile and pulls the water bottle out of his pocket again.

"Here," he hands it over to me and I take a sip.

"Your Mum said you wasn't going to come today."

"I wasn't. But then she sent me a text saying you were drinking. Then she said people were talking about you and you were by yourself," he sighs and looks at me. "I didn't like that."

"I didn't like it either," I mumble.

Matt stares at me for a moment and then reaches for the hot-dog. He says nothing and I just watch him, taking in the fact that he's actually here. He holds the hotdog up and I lean forward, taking a bite.

That tastes good.

"I needed some time," Matt breathes as he watches me chew what's in my mouth. "I didn't like who I'd become. I never dealt with anything properly. I turned to alcohol at first and then that night when you told me everything, it felt like I finally snapped."

"Did you see my note, and my diary?" I ask after swallowing what's in my mouth.

He nods slowly. "Yes. I read it when I got home the morning after. It took a while but eventually it helped me sort of understand why you did what you did I guess," Matt holds the hotdog up again and I take another bite. "But only after I spoke to someone about everything," he finishes.

"Who'd you talk to, your Mum?" I ask with my mouth partially full so I cover it with my hand.

"No, not Mum. I spoke to a professional counsellor. I meet with them twice a week," Matt confirms as I swallow again.

"A counsellor?"

"Yeah, I've had I think 6 or 7 sessions now but I feel different already, just more in control of my feelings I guess."

"Is that why you ignored me?"

Matt looks at me sadly and nods. He goes to hold the hotdog up again for me to take another bite but I gently push it away. He doesn't protest and puts it back on the side.

"I didn't trust myself to talk to you. Honestly, I had nothing nice to say," Matt admits and my stomach drops.

"And now?"

"Well I'm here aren't I?" Matt gives me a small smile and butterflies spring to life inside of me.

"I don't want to say the wrong thing," I admit.

"Just tell me the truth, *always* tell me the truth and we'll be ok," Matt says softly.

He reaches forward and gently cups my face, running his thumb across on my cheek. I can't help but close my eyes at his touch.

"I haven't been ok," my voice is a whisper. A sad, desperate whisper.

"I know, I spoke to your Mum daily."

"You did?" My eyes open and stare at him. "She never told me that."

"Because I asked her not to. I can never switch off from you completely, Mia. But if I spoke to you I'd have come straight back and that would have been wrong for me and for you. I needed to focus on getting myself some help," he sounds pained but in control of it.

"I've missed you."

"Come here," Matt pulls me into his arms and holds me so tightly. I wrap my arms around his neck and just breathe him in. His smell, the sound of his heartbeat, the warmth of his skin, everything about him I've missed. He shuffles us backwards and we lay down on my bed. I rest my head on his chest and he slowly starts to play with my hair.

"Isn't it time you had your afternoon nap?" He questions.

The vibrations of his voice ripple through me but I repeat his words in my head. 'Always tell me the truth and we'll be ok'.

"I lied about that before, at the lake house. When I went to have a 'nap' I'd actually read through the scrapbook and try to memorise things in case there was ever an opportunity to talk about a memory with you."

Matt tenses at my words and his breathing changes.

Please don't be angry with me.

"You said to always tell you the truth," I mumble sadly.

He takes a deep breath and carries on playing with my hair again. I grip hold of him a little tighter and he does the same.

He's still here with me.

"Sleeping off your new love for cocktails won't be a bad thing for you though," Matt's voice has a playful tone to it.

"Will you be here when I wake up?" I lift my head from his chest and stare at him.

"I'll be here, Mia, don't worry," Matt says softly.

I don't know if it's the cocktails or just my self control giving in but I reach forward and kiss him. He hesitates at first and then moves his hand behind the back of my neck and pulls me closer to him, deepening our kiss. I gently stroke my tongue against his lips and he opens his mouth instantly.

I've craved everything about this for what feels like forever. How did he manage two years feeling like this would never happen again? I don't think I'll ever understand the extent of what he went through.

The Reveal

Mia

When I open my eyes I'm no longer laying on Matt's chest. My heart drops as I feel around the bed sheets, looking for him. Matt told me he'll be here when I wake up but he's not. When I roll over I have to blink a few times first to make sure I'm not seeing things. I feel relieved to see Matt sitting at my desk, watching me. But that feeling is quickly replaced with dread. He's slumped on the chair and is gripping his hands so tightly that his knuckles have turned white. He's angry, really angry. My mind races with possible scenarios of what's happened and I pray it's nothing I've done. It's dusk outside now so I've been asleep all afternoon, but he was with me when I fell asleep. What an earth could have happened since then?

"What is it?" I ask hesitantly.

"Do you still feel drunk or have you sobered up now?" He questions.

"I'm ok."

I suddenly feel wide awake and definitely don't feel the buzzy feeling from the alcohol anymore. I feel sick, but from nerves and not alcohol.

"They're not telling us something," Matts voice has so much pain to it as he talks it's heartbreaking.

"Who?" I frown.

"Our parents, they're hiding something from us."

"What do you mean?"

Matt sighs deeply and dips his head as he runs his fingers through his hair. He's really struggle to deal with this. What an earth could they possibly be hiding?

"You were right, about me not figuring everything out before. I should have put more effort into questioning it all rather than running away," Matt mumbles and my stomach drops.

"I didn't mean that. I didn't think about it all properly there's no way you could have known," my words rush out as I try to comfort his feelings.

"I'm not angry at you, or what you said because you were right. I'm angry at *them*. I know they're hiding something, Mia, I know they are," I can hear the torture in Matt's voice. He's had years of it and I think it's finally breaking him. Seeing him this way is tearing me apart. He's doubting everything and I can't bear it. Instinct kicks in and I rush over to him. He opens up his arms and pulls me closely to him as I sit on his lap.

"It's ok," I tell him even though I don't think it is. "What makes you think they're hiding something, what do you think's happened?"

Matt cups my face in his hand and has his eyes fixed on mine. He says nothing and I don't push him to. He rests his forehead against mine and breathes deeply against me.

"I just, I just need to hear them say it to both of us," Matt's voice is barely even a whisper.

He breathes deeply again when I run my fingers through the back of his hair. I don't know how to help ease how tense he is. He's acting like he's in actual pain so I do the one thing I'll always want to do and kiss him. He kisses me back instantly, no hesitation, just pure desperation in his touch. It's almost like he's holding on to how things currently are and that terrifies me.

"When the BBQ's over we'll talk to them, ok?" I try to sound confident and reassuring when I talk but my voice shakes slightly.

I want to be strong for him because he's been strong for me so many times but I can't shake that feeling in my stomach that everything's about to change.

"The BBQ is over. It's just our parents downstairs now," Matt tells me.

"What? Mum said it wasn't ending until midnight?" The clock on my wall says it's 8pm.

"After you fell asleep I got up and spoke with your Dad about some stuff. I told him what I thought was going on and he didn't deny it, he ended up asking everyone to leave instead. He said once you wake up we'll all talk, us and our parents."

"After everything that's already happened what could they possibly still be hiding from us?" I ask in shock.

"Is there nothing that you can think of, anything at all even if it's just a fuzzy memory?" Matt's almost pleading with me to remember.

I search his eyes as though they're going to give me the answers but they don't. As I get off of Matts lap and walk over to the windowsill I think, I desperately think. It's just darkness, fuzzy darkness. Almost like when you roll over in your sleep and wake up only for second before going back to sleep again. All you really see is darkness but you're so tired you just close your eyes and drift back to sleep. It feels like that, kind of. My clearest memory is the day I finally woke up in February. I could hear Mum and Dad's voices but their faces were just blinded out by the bright lights above me. There were bleeping sounds and a voice I didn't recognise said 'give her time' but that's it.

Isn't it?

"I, I really don't know. This is making me feel really nervous," I start pacing back and forth in my room feeling more and more anxious as I strain my brain to think but it's just a closed, blank book.

"Calm down," Matt comes over to me and pulls me close against him. His warmth spreads through me like wildfire as he presses his hand gently on the back of my head so I lean against his chest. The sound of his heartbeat starts to calm me down again. Just like it always does. "We'll deal with this together, ok?"

His words are soft and soothing against me. I nod against his chest and breathe him in. When we pull apart he takes my hand in his and leads us downstairs. I can hear all of our parents talking in the living room but their discussion is frantic and unsettled. Hearing their voices that way only makes my heart beat faster and my hands go clammy. When Matt walks us into the living room we see they've put two dining table chairs together, side by side for us which face them all whilst they spread out on the sofas. We get to the chairs and Matt stands in front of me, with his broad shoulders blocking my parents from view.

"Together, ok?" He whispers so only I can hear him. I nod and he gives me a small smile before it wipes off of his face completely. He turns back to my parents and we both reluctantly sit down.

No one talks. My insides are doing summersaults and I have the biggest lump in my throat. Why do I feel like I'm about to lose Matt completely?

"Why don't you start by telling us all what you told me earlier, Matt?" Dad suggests, there's a little sternness to his voice but not in a mean way. Almost as though he knows this is really, really big and that only makes me feel worse.

Matt holds his hand in mine and leans back in his chair, his posture totally dominates the room.

"Here's how this is going to go. You're not going to wait for us to tell you what we know or remember. You're going to tell us, from the beginning, what you've been hiding all this time. No more games and no more secrets. It's *that* simple," Matt's tone screams to me how serious this is but it's also calm at the same time, like he's in totally in control of his feelings even though he's angry. His authority takes me by surprise. His voice isn't raised, his voice is calm but assertive. I don't think I've seen this side to him before. Our parents look uncomfortable but they're not fighting him. There's a couple of nods and 'ok's mumbled between them before they look back at us.

"The beginning would be before the accident and the scrapbook," Mum begins reluctantly.

"The scrapbook?" I frown and Mum nods.

What has a scrapbook got to do with any of this?!

"Well you've seen it's full of happy memories that you both

shared together and then the last page said our next chapter, didn't it?" Mum asks with such caution. All of our parents eyes are on me.

Why are they looking at me like that?

"Yeah, so?" I look at Matt for answers but his eyes are fixed firmly on my Mums as he grips my hand tightly. He knows what's coming and that terrifies me. He's getting more and more tense as he braces himself and I'm oblivious to everything that they all clearly know.

"You planned on giving it to Matt either on the night of the crash or when you got to America. You hadn't decided. But the plan was you were going to ask him to stick a picture on the last page under the words you'd already written, our next chapter," Mum tells me softly.

"Ok?"

Mum pauses and then looks at Matt for a moment. She looks so sad.

"The picture was of an ultrasound," Mum pauses. "Mia, you were pregnant."

Pregnant?!

My lungs struggle to fill for air as I repeat her words. Matt grips my hand as he dips his head next to me. His shoulders rise rapidly but I just feel angry.

Why is she saying this to me?

"I wasn't pregnant!" I spit back.

"You were 9 weeks pregnant at the time of the accident sweetheart," Mrs Parker confirms.

Matt looks up at her words almost as though he believes her. Why is no one believing me? I would *know* if I was pregnant. I'd remember *that!* I remember everything to do with my body after the crash, everything. Why would this be any different?

"I wasn't," I say sternly and then look at Matt and our eyes meet. "I wasn't, was I?"

Please reassure me, please tell me they're wrong.

"You never told me, I didn't know," Matt says softly as he rubs his thumb on my hand. He believes them. He thinks they're tell-

205

ing the truth and that I was pregnant. He knew they were hiding something but surely he didn't think it was this?

"Is this what you thought they were hiding from us?" I ask desperately.

"Yes," Matt whispers sadly. "I just needed to hear it from them."

My head is spinning. Why does everyone always know more about me than I do?

"But you worked it out," I gasp. "When, how?"

Matt's voice is so different with me than it is with my parents, it's full of care, love and sympathy.

"A few things really, my counsellor really helped. But it was things like the scrapbook, the odd comments here and there, and then the scar on your stomach," he explains.

My spare hand instantly holds my stomach as I struggle to process it all. Everyone is staring at me with this look on their face that I can't stand. It's like they pity me and my stupid memory. I'm sick and tired of people looking at me like I'm some type of charity case.

"You told me I had internal bleeding and my spleen was removed!" I shout a little louder at my parents than intended as the anger bubbles away. That's what they told me, I didn't make that up they definitely told me that.

"I know we did, and that did happen. That's what the smaller scar is by your bellybutton," Dad explains desperately.

"And the second scar?" I push. "What's that from?"

I already know what they're going to say. If what they're telling me is true, if I really was pregnant, could the scar be from a caesarean? I'd remember giving birth, wouldn't I? Or would I? I don't think I know anything anymore.

"The second scar is from the caesarean," Mum confirms.

Matt let's go of my hand only so he can wrap his arm around my shoulder, pulling me closer to him. He holds me tightly and places a kiss on my forehead. It's then that I realise I'm crying.

"That's why you were in hospital for so long, Mia. The baby was a miracle, they expected that you both wouldn't make it but by keeping you sedated it meant they were able to keep you both safe. Both alive. We tried to wake you up throughout the pregnancy but when you'd see your bump you panicked and your heart rate went so high it put you both at risk. Your labour was induced earlier than planned because the baby wasn't growing as well as it should have been," Mum rambles on quickly but it's too much, it's all too much.

Stop telling me things about my life!

I don't want to hear anymore.

I can't hear anymore.

"Stop talking!" I cry out and cover my ears. "Stop talking, just stop talking!"

It feels like someone is squeezing every ounce of air out of my lungs and I can't fill them back up with oxygen quick enough. I can feel the colour draining from my face as my head slowly becomes lighter. My shoulders start to feel cold and the cool sensation spreads down my arms. My eyes feel heavy and my body feels like it's floating. I can't hear anything other than my erratic breathing as I try to fill my lungs, but it slowly becomes more and more quiet as everything fades away.

"Put her legs up on the chair, John pass me a cushion for her head," Mrs Parker's panicked voice is barely audible.

"Mia, it's ok I'm here," Matt squeezes my hand. At least I think it's him. When I open my eyes it is him, but I'm on the floor now. I'm flat on my back and my legs are up on a chair in front of me. There are five pairs of panicked eyes watching me and my tired eyes are watching them. When I try to sit up I feel incredibly woozy, the room spins and I feel so cold. Matt's arm flies around my back before I know what's happening and he steadies me in place. His warmth slowly starts to spreads through me.

"You fainted sweetheart, take your time," Mum says with worry in her voice.

"I'm fine," I manage to say as I remove my legs from the chair and grip onto Matt. I search his eyes and they tell me everything. He believed it before my parents confirmed it to us. Something inside of him knew it happened. I was pregnant and,

"I had a baby," I breathe.

Saying the words out loud feels strange, really strange. How could I have a baby and not remember it? How is that possible?

"You're ok, let's just stay on the floor for a bit," Matt says reassuringly and leans us back against the chairs but he keeps his grip tightly on me. It's almost like he's holding me up still. Everyone else slowly goes back to their original seats on the furniture and remove their eyes from me. Then this horrible feeling hits the pit of my stomach. Matt asked me to be honest with him, he said always tell him the truth.

Does he think I've kept this from him?

Does he think I'm still punishing him?

"I didn't know Matt, I haven't lied to you I promise," my words are rushed as I turn to him. My hand grips his shirt tightly almost as though I'm stopping him from leaving me.

Please don't leave me.

"I know, I know. Shh relax ok, I told you we're in this together," Matt says as calmly as possible even though his voice breaks too.

"How can I not remember this?" I ask in disbelief.

"It's ok," Matt continues to comfort me but he doesn't know what else to say. He doesn't understand it either, I can tell. Matt just holds me as everyone stays silent, giving us time to process it all.

I had a baby.

But, but where is the baby?

I've never seen him or her?

Or have I?

"Did the baby survive? You said the baby came early," my words come out so quick I'm surprised they even understand what I'm staying. However, Mum smiles at my words and nods her head. Actually, for the first time both of our parents all smile at the thought of the baby.

"Yes love, she's absolutely perfect," Mum sounds so proud as she talks.

A daughter.

I have a daughter, *we* have a daughter.

"She?" Matt asks as his voice breaks.

Our parents nod back at him, still smiling.

"What's her name?" I ask.

Mrs Parker talks this time. "She gave us all hope during such a difficult time and continues to give us hope daily that everything will be ok in the end. So we all decided on calling her Hope, Hope Parker."

"Hope," I repeat.

Is that why everyone keep mentioning hope me?

"You've met her?" Matt asks his Mum.

"Hope stays with each of us one weekend every month. With you being in America and you being in Scotland it was just a simple routine for us all," Mrs Parker explains.

"But where is she now?" I ask desperately suddenly feeling this sense of needing to protect someone I've not even met.

"She lives with my Mum, Matt's Nan, Dorothy. She's been with her since she was discharged from hospital," Mrs Parker tells me.

"She lives with Nan?" Matt asks again.

"Yes love. When you're both ready we'll transfer full custody back to you," Mrs Parker says with a reassuring smile.

When we're both ready. How will I know if I'm ready?

"When was she born, what's her birthday?" Matt asks snapping me out of my thoughts.

"She was born on 4th January. Mia you were only just 34 weeks pregnant at the time. Hope was so tiny, she was 4lb and 3oz. She had to stay in the hospital for a while until she got a little bigger but don't worry, one of us was with her everyday," Mum pauses and then smiles again. "Would you like to see a picture of her?"

I look at Matt who's eyes are glassy.

"Yes," he confirms and blinks a few times.

Dad opens a drawer on the table next to him and pulls out a picture that's framed. He hands it over and we both grab it together. The picture shows our parents smiling at the camera behind a little girl, well Hope, who's sitting in a highchair. She has a pink birthday cake and a giant candle that says 1 on it. It was her first birthday. Hope is laughing and has her hand at the base of her cake. On top of her cake is a picture of Matt and I. Hope is really laughing in the photo and I can't help but smile at her. She has my green eyes and Matt's dark hair with a small pink bow clipped in. She's got a pink dress on that says Mummy and Daddy love me. She looks so happy.

"She has your eyes," Matt chokes.

"She has your nose," I smile and wipe my face.

"What's she like?" Matt asks no one in particular. His voice feels broken as we stay in a heap on the floor. One of his arms is still wrapped tightly around me whilst we both grip onto the photo frame. We keep our eyes locked firmly on our daughter.

Even though we don't look up, I can hear the joy and can picture the smile from Mr Parker as he talks. "She is the spitting image of you both. She started walking shortly after she turned 1 and now she just runs everywhere, Matt, which is exactly what you used to do. It's almost like I'm raising you again. She has this almighty giggle when you tickle her too. She looks just like you, Mia, when she laughs."

His words fill me with some sense of warmth that I didn't know I needed.

"We're on her cake," I point out quietly.

"Hope knows who you both are," Mrs Parker sounds sad but reassuring. "We talk to her about you all the time. She's surrounded by pictures of you and sometimes when she can't sleep we'll put on some old home videos of you both. She relaxes immediately. It's the most bizarre, beautiful thing. She points to you both on the screen and says, Mama or Dada.

Matt and I both look up at the same time.

Hope knows who we are?

"She knows who we are?" Matt gasps and his Dad nods.

"Can she say anything else?" I ask.

"She likes the word no, she uses that with me a lot when I want her to do something," Mr Parker laughs and I can't help but laugh with him. "It's just a few bits here and there that you can sort of work out what she means. A bit like 'ack', she means snack."

Silence fills the room as my head spins with all this information. I keep looking at her in the picture, she really does look so happy.

"Why did you keep her from us?" Matt asks.

Gosh his voice sounds so betrayed.

They all sort of shift in their seats and look at each other.

"We were always going to tell you about her," Mrs Parker says softly.

"When? When she's going off to college?" Matt spits back angrily.

"No of course not!"

"Well then when? I left the country and everything I needed and everyone who needed me was right here the whole time! How could you let me do that?" Matt's losing his cool so I hold his arm gently.

"The doctor was very clear with us all that Mia and the baby were not expected to survive," Mrs Parker continues trying to stay calm and keep her voice low. "We didn't know Mia was pregnant, we found out when we got to the hospital. It was one of the first things Liz told us. It just made everything so much worst. Eventually we all agreed that it was better for you, Matt, if you didn't know about the pregnancy and if you already thought Mia was gone. You had been in a coma for 11 days yourself and it wasn't an induced coma, you just didn't wake up. We had to protect you, we couldn't have you wake up and find out that Mia was alive and that she was pregnant but both weren't expected to make it. That would have destroyed you and you know that deep down. At the time that's what we thought we were faced with. Of course if we were told that there was a chance for Mia or the baby then we'd never have lied."

"But you did lie," is all Matt responds.

Mum takes over now as she talks to me. "Mia we didn't tell you because it was all about your recovery. Once Hope was here safely and you woke up, you didn't remember her. You were so confused, about everything, and that wasn't helping you move forward. So the last thing we wanted was to tell you about Hope when you were already really struggling."

"We all agreed that once Matt was back from America we would sit him down and tell him the truth about you being alive. Your Mum and I were then going to fly to Scotland and slowly tell you about Matt. The idea was that you both would get to know each other again and then when the time was right we'd tell you about Hope. We never planned on keeping her from you, or keeping you apart from each other. The lies just sort of spiralled out of control and we didn't know how to fix it." Dad explains.

"You should never have lied. It's not hard," Matt scoffs and no one responds.

I rest my head on Matt's shoulder and sigh deeply against him. I'm so tired of everything. I don't feel sad, I don't feel angry I just feel, numb.

"You ok?" Matt leans his head to the side so he can see me.

"It's just, it's just a lot to take in," I mumble sadly.

"I know," he breathes and places a kiss on my forehead before resting his head against mine.

"Why don't you both go back to the lake house and take a bit of time to yourselves to process this. When you're both ready we can arrange for you to meet Hope and we'll go from there. We can go at whatever pace you need," Mrs Parker says softly as she watches us.

Matt nods buts doesn't say anything.

I don't feel like I can say anything.

We just sit there in a heap on the floor for a little longer and stare at the picture of our daughter.

Hope.

The Doubt

Mia

The drive back to the lake house was quiet. I don't think either of us said anything to each other the whole drive. Well, Matt would ask me every now and then if I was ok but that was it. When he could, he would place his hand on my thigh as he drove. I could feel his gaze on me when we'd sit in traffic or stop at traffic lights. But my head was too jumbled with everything to really pay attention.

How could I not remember having a daughter?

When we got to the lake house, again, neither of us really said anything. It was late by the time we got there and I just felt like my mind needed to shut off for the night. Matt brought in our bags and I just headed straight upstairs but froze when I got to my bedroom. The memory of us is in there. Matt's broken face when I told him I'd been lying to him was all I saw when I looked into that room. It was almost as though Matt could tell what was going through my mind. He came up behind me, placed his hands on my shoulders and walked me to his room instead. I felt relieved as we walked inside and I saw his bed. I felt like I was finally home. We both got changed for bed in silence and he immediately pulled me to him so my head was on his chest. His grip was so tight around me. I gripped him back just as tightly before finally letting my mind sleep.

The sound of Matt's heartbeat slowly wakes me up the next morning. It's so peaceful, so calm and so comforting. We're in exactly the same position that we were when we fell asleep last night. I move my head ever so slightly and Matt gives me a little squeeze to let me know he's already awake.

"Morning," his voice is tired and raspy.

"How long have you been awake for?" I question still laying on his chest.

"A while," Matt slowly rubs my arm with his hand. "You looked so peaceful I didn't want to move."

I smile at his words and squeeze him tightly before sitting up. His eyes are on me as I rub my face and take a breath. All I can think of is Hope. She's going round and round in my head followed by a tremendous feeling of guilt.

"Are you ok?" Matt asks as he sits up next to me.

His voice snaps me from my thoughts of Hope and I look back at him. I do my best to smile and nod but it's a weak attempt.

"Yeah, I'm just tired," a sigh escapes my lips as I push the sheets to the side so I can get out of bed. "I'm going to make a drink, do you want one?"

Matt watches me from the bed as I walk to the door. I stop in the doorway and turn back to him, waiting for his response.

"Sure," he mumbles sadly and looks away.

It's my fault he hasn't met his daughter. He must hold that against me, even if it's only a little bit.

I would.

The floorboards creak underneath me as I walk down the stairs, through the living room and into the kitchen. I can hear him walking around upstairs as I put the kettle on and then go over to stare out the kitchen window. My thoughts slowly start to take over.

I wonder what Hope is doing right now? Does she think I didn't want her? Does she *really* know who I am or were they just saying that? Does she actually call me Mama or was that a lie too? Is she happy? Is she sad?

Oh god, please don't be sad.

What's Matt's Nan like? Is she nice to Hope? Does Hope like her? Would Hope prefer to stay with her rather than us? Are we even ready to have Hope stay with us?

"Mia," Matt's soft voice has entered the room, snapping me

from my thoughts. But all it takes is one look at him and my thoughts take over again.

Is he angry at me? Does he blame me? If I'd have told him I was pregnant before the accident everything could have been avoided. He'd have woken up and known about her, so they wouldn't have lied to him about me would they? Or would they? Does he think of that too? Does he blame me for not telling him? Were we trying for a baby? Was Hope unplanned? Would Matt have been angry? Is that why I didn't tell him?

"Mia, stop it," Matt comes over to where I'm standing and stops in front of me. "You're shutting me out, don't do that. Whatever you're thinking, just stop and talk to me."

Matts voice is sad, there's no sense of anger or frustration in it at all. He just sounds hurt. Well, he is hurt isn't he, because of me. All of the pain he's suffered and continues to suffer is because of me.

It all starts and ends with me.

"Mia?" Matt's eyes search for mine but I can't look at him. How can he even look at me after everything? I just feel so numb. My mind is racing but I still feel so numb to it all.

Matt waits so patiently for me to respond to him but I don't, I *can't*. My voice has totally disappeared. I don't even know what I'd say if I felt like I could speak. What even is there to say other than...

"I'm sorry."

You'd have thought I'd just punched Matt in his stomach. My words seem to have caused him physical pain again. His hand reaches for mine and immediately it's like he sets me on fire again, just by his touch. He pulls me gently encouraging me to follow him, which I do, as he walks us into the garden. At the back of the garden there's a decking which is almost like a hut as there's a wooden roof to it. Inside the hut there's a giant square sofa with massive chunky cushions all around. The fresh morning air hits my skin as the sunlight sneaks through the trees. This place really is beautiful.

Would Hope like it here?

Matt sits down near the corner and pulls me down to him. The seats are wide enough for us to lay on it side by side so we do just that. Matt holds me closely against him as we stare back at the house inhaling the fresh air.

"What did I say to you yesterday?" His voice is almost a whisper as he talks.

Yesterday.

Lots of things were said yesterday.

"I told you we're in this together, didn't I?" He confirms after I don't reply. "I meant that Mia, so don't shut me out ok. Talk to me. What's going through your head?"

My eyes close at his words.

What isn't going through my head?

"A lot of things," I manage to say.

Matt's arm rests gently around me and he rubs his thumb against my skin softly.

"Do you want to know what I'm thinking?" Matt says and I nod, bracing myself for him to blame me, which he should do. "I wonder if Hope is truly happy or if she thinks we didn't want her. I'm doubting whether I can be what she needs me to be and honestly, I'm worried about how much blame you're putting on yourself."

"What if she thinks we abandoned her?" I ask sadly when I look at him. "I'd never have done that if I'd have known about her."

"I know, neither of us would have done that," Matt reassures me as he continues to stroke my arm.

"Was she planned? Did we want a baby or was she unplanned and that's why I didn't tell you? Would you have been angry?" I twist my body completely so I can study every bit of him. I want to see if any part of his body language gives me a different answer to what he tells me. Will his shoulders tense? Will the rhythm in his breathing change? Will he keep eye contact or will he look away? However, his body gives *nothing* away.

"We weren't trying for a baby, Mia, so I would have been surprised when you told me. But I'd *never* have been angry about starting a family with you. Even if it was a little sooner than I'd have thought. I always knew you and I would have a family one day, I didn't doubt that for a second."

I can't hide the smile that escapes my lips as he talks. How did I get so lucky to meet him, twice.

"But if she wasn't planned, then, do you remember how I got pregnant in the first place?" I ask him hesitantly as he truly is the only one who can give me these answers.

Matt breathes deeply but he doesn't break his eye contact with me, not once.

"I've thought about this so much, we were always so careful, Mia, we really were."

"But?"

Matt grins a little and I can't help but smile with him.

"The only time I can think of was actually here."

I look around the cushions that we're sitting on and then look back to him.

"We conceived Hope on this?" I question pointing to our seats.

"No, not right *here*. I mean whilst we were at the lake house. Well, specifically, in the lake," Matt laughs slightly as my mouth drops.

"The lake, as in *we* were in the lake?"

"Uh-huh," Matt laughs at my reaction and rubs his temples. He hates talking about this sort of stuff. He was like this when he told me about our first time but he always elaborates eventually. "It was my birthday, I think. My birthday is in May so the dates add up and match what happened that night."

"Did we not use protection or something?"

Matt shakes his head and looks a little uncomfortable but in a funny sort of way. Talking about how Hope was conceived has definitely helped lift the mood a bit.

"We'd been drinking, not massively but enough to feel a little tipsy. We were watching a film called What If, it has the same actor in it who plays Harry Potter so you wanted to watch it. There's a scene in there where he goes skinny dipping with a girl he likes and we both starting talking about it. Before I really knew what was happening we were running into the lake without our clothes on."

"What if someone saw us!?" I shriek out whilst laughing a bit. There was clearly a wild side to me that I'm yet to experience.

"By who? Mia, there's no one close to here within a 3 mile radius," Matt laughs and carries on. "Neither of us really anticipated how cold the water would be so you wrapped yourself around me. We were just bobbing around in the water, naked, and I guess we had a healthy sex life," Matt laughs again, shrugging his shoulders.

"So we knew what we were doing?"

Matt nods and sits up slightly. "We knew we didn't have a condom, yes. I guess we just got caught up in the moment of it all. But the next day once we sobered up we drove into town and you took the morning after pill."

"I did?"

"Uh-huh, which clearly worked as well as a chocolate teapot."

The way Matt is able to make me laugh during all of this is something I think I'll be forever grateful for. *Nothing* about this situation is funny and he knows that too. But the laughter helps take away the pain of it all.

"We have a daughter," I breathe.

Will it ever feel real saying that out loud?

"We do," Matt leans forward, pulling me closer to him again which I didn't know I needed. He gently places his forehead against mine and breathes deeply. "And she's absolutely perfect."

Matt cups my face in his hands. I love how it fits so perfectly in it. I reach up and place my hand on top of his making sure he keeps it there as I relax against him. The fire between us ignites the second his lips touch mine. He breathes deeply against my mouth as he swipes his tongue against my lips. My hands thread to the back of his hair as I give him total access. I love the feeling when he gets goosebumps against my skin. I wonder if he even realises it happens. The moment is suddenly broken by the sound of his phone ringing in his pocket. He pulls it out and I see the name 'Jenny' on the screen trying to FaceTime him.

Who's Jenny?

"Shit," Matt breathes heavily as he shifts away from me slightly.

Why do I suddenly feel really jealous of whoever Jenny is and the fact that she didn't just ruin our moment but Matt *let* her ruin it. He could have cancelled the call and he hasn't.

"Jenny's my counsellor, I have an appointment with her at 11am," Matt seems to hear my thoughts and always makes me feel better or reassure me if he can. Which he does.

Counsellor, Jenny is his counsellor.

"Over FaceTime?"

"Virtual appointments are kind of easier. It makes me feel a bit more in control when I open up if I'm around familiar things," he shifts a little uncomfortably as he sits up straight.

"Oh, ok, no problem. I'll go back inside and cook us something for when you're done," I tell him as I go to stand up but he grabs my hand.

"Actually, can you stay with me? I think this might be good for both of us," Matts voice sounds vulnerable as he ignores the ringing phone and looks directly at me.

"Sure," I reply feeling hesitant.

Matt smiles and lifts his arm up for me to sit against so it wraps around my shoulders. I quickly sit against him as he slides his finger across the screen, connecting the call. Jenny is a redhead with dark black glasses and I can see she has a blazer on. She looks maybe our parents age and actually looks very friendly. Matt has the camera on him for the moment so she can't see me there.

"Hi Matt, I thought you weren't going to answer for a second," Jenny smiles.

"Yeah sorry, I um, I actually have someone here with me if that's ok?" Matt moves the camera back revealing both of us on the screen. "This is Mia."

His voice sounds so proud as he talks I can't help but smile at him before I look back at Jenny who is also smiling.

"The famous Mia, it's so good to finally meet you!" Jenny sounds so friendly. I just smile at her response. I don't really know what to say back to her.

"So I can see you've made some progress since our last session, Matt, and that you've worked things out, that's really good," Jenny writes something down and then looks back at us.

"Yes, but it's been a really eventful 24 hours. It turns out I was right," he tells her.

"You were right?" Jenny gasps and Matt nods before looking at me.

"We have a daughter, she's called Hope."

Gosh, he sounds so proud.

"Wow, I mean congratulations to you both of course but wow! That must have been quite a revelation for you," Jenny asks with a bit more sympathy to her voice.

"Yeah I guess. But our last few sessions together helped me brace myself for it. I ended up going to the BBQ Mia's family put on and her Aunt Tessie was there. She said some things that just helped confirm it enough for me to confront Mia's Dad. He didn't deny it. Then it all sort of came out from there."

"Mia, did you have any idea about your daughter?" Jenny asks.

"Um," I pause and feel really vulnerable at her question. Matt grips my shoulder tightly encouraging me to talk. "No, I didn't know."

Jenny nods sadly and writes down on her notepad again.

What are you writing?

"How does that make you feel, that you didn't know?" Jenny pushes gently.

"Horrible," I admit.

"Why horrible?" Jenny looks at me and then to Matt.

"Because I should have been able to know. Matt figured it out. He'll be a great Dad I know he will. But Hope was inside of me and I don't even remember that or figure it out. What sort of Mum does that make me?" It feels weird saying this out loud, everything is still so jumbled up inside my head.

"Mia no, don't ever think like that," Matt says softly as he kisses the side of my head.

"You figured it out though, Matt. Your instinct kicked in and you knew,"

"That's not true," Matt interrupts me. "I was clueless until I started talking to Jenny. I told her about our first time since, well, our first time after the accident, and I spoke to her about how sad it made me when you panicked about your scars. I'd also told Jenny that you were sedated for months and Jenny said she knew someone who'd experienced something similar but it was because she was pregnant. Everything sort of fitted. Then Mum and Dad always questioned whether you remembered anything from the hospital. Of course some of the things Tessie said just stuck too. I wasn't going to say anything for a while. I was going to just sit back and observe but Tessie got me so angry I just went with it and asked your Dad. Now we're here."

I don't know what to say, so I say nothing.

"Mia, your memory loss doesn't define your ability to be a parent," Jenny says with such sadness in her voice.

"But I don't know how to be a Mum," I choke.

"None of us do, your maternal instincts will kick in," Jenny smiles as she talks as though she has complete faith in me. How could she, I don't even know who I am.

"My maternal instincts didn't kick in to even remember I had a baby," I point out.

"That's because of your memory loss and nothing more. It's natural to have doubt. You'll both feel that, but you'll also get each other through the times you have the doubt. That's what love is, being there for each other even on the darkest days."

"And the guilt, what do I do about that?"

"Guilt? Mia, you have nothing to be guilty for," Matt says firmly next to me.

"My memory loss kept you from your daughter all this time. All of your pain is linked to me."

"My pain is because I didn't *have* you," Matt strokes the side of my face gently as he stares directly into my eyes.

"Mia the guilt you feel will go in time. Do you want to know why?" Jenny asks and I nod. "Because love is the strongest feeling we all have the pleasure of experiencing. Your guilt is triggered by love and will be replaced again by love. Yourself, Matt and Hope now have your whole lives ahead of you to replace all of these horrible feelings with happy ones. Eventually, all of that pain that you both feel will ease, simply because you love each other. It truly is that simple, it just takes time."

Is it, is it really that simple?

The Preparation

Mia

The next couple of days sort of merged into one. We'd have moments of silence, moments of laughter, moments of pure denial and moments of complete anxiety. All of these feelings are so conflicting that we're both just so mentally exhausted. I've tried to let Matt in more, Jenny told me to do that. She also told Matt to have some faith. His reality for so long has been that everything goes wrong or everyone lies. Which is true, even I did that to him.

"It's almost time, are you ready?" Matt shouts up the stairs for me.

"One sec," I shout back.

We're about to do a group video call with our parents, we haven't talked since they told us about Hope and we think maybe it's time we do. We've been so hesitant with making any sort of decision around Hope purely because we're terrified of failing.

Matt's fiddling with the laptop on the coffee table by the time I've come downstairs. He's trying to get it into a good position with the camera so we'll both be seen whilst sitting comfortably on the sofa.

"Why do I feel so nervous?" I question as I walk in and take a seat next to them.

"I'm asking myself the same question," he smiles back at me reassuringly. "I think it's because all of this matters, you know?"

I only get the chance to nod before the laptop starts making a noise.

"Here we go, are you ready?" Matt asks.

"Yeah," I mumble and sit back against the sofa.

Matt answers the call and sits back next to me, taking my hand in his. The call takes a couple of seconds to connect and then our parents pop up on the screen. Mum and Dad are sitting at their dining table and Matt's parents are sitting on their sofa. They both smile when they see us, almost like it's a relief. I don't think Matt and I return the same smile. I know I certainly don't.

"How are you both?" Mrs Parker asks sounding hesitant.

"Ok, I guess," Matt responds. "We had a session with Jenny and I think that helped."

"Who's Jenny?" Mum questions.

"Matt's counsellor," when I say it out loud it makes that guilt inside of me spring to life again.

"*Our* counsellor," Matt corrects me. "She's helping us deal with everything that's happened."

"You're seeing the counsellor too?" Dad asks.

"Yeah," I can't help but shift uncomfortably as the attention turns to me.

"Why the change of heart love? You refused help before. No matter what we tried you just didn't engage with it even though we knew it was something you really needed," Mum sounds sad but curious as she speaks. Matt turns to me as he also seems intrigued but to me it's really quite simple.

"Yeah, well, I guess I didn't understand back then that there was a past I'd want to remember so it seemed pointless talking about it," everyone looks sad as I talk but this time I'm talking only to Matt. "Things have changed now, I have two reasons as to why I need to try."

The sadness from Matt's face changes to an expression I don't think I've seen from him before. His smile just melts my heart and he leans forward, kissing my cheek softly. Tingles rush through me as the smile is still on his face. We lean back against the sofa but this time Matt puts his arm around me.

"How have you been with the drinking, Matt?" Mr Parker asks him.

Why does it feel like we're being interviewed?

"Good," Matt responds instantly. "The last time I had anything was the day I came back from America. I came close that day when we were all at yours but the reason I drank so much was because I missed her."

Matt sounds so confident and in control when he talks. I'm so proud of him. I didn't really see the drinking side of him but from what I've been told it really wasn't pleasant.

"You've not even been tempted?" Mr Parker asks again.

Matt pauses and squeezes my shoulder gently. "The night Mia and I had that argument I was tempted then. But I left the house instead and realised I needed help. I don't want to be that person anymore, Dad."

"You're not, you never were that person to me," I whisper against him so only he can hear me. I can see his face in the camera smile which makes me smile too.

"Have you thought much about Hope?" Dad asks and Matt and I nod instantly.

"I don't think we've *stopped* thinking about her," I reply.

"How is she?" Matt sits forward a bit as he asks.

"She's good," Mrs Parker smiles. "She's coming here for the day on Saturday actually. We're not meant to have her this weekend but Nan's running a stall at a fair for her local church so she asked if we could have her for the day."

"Hope's going to be at yours?" There's something different to Matt's voice, there's excitement but he's sort of apprehensive too.

"Would you like to come over as well?" Mr Parker asks encouraging.

My skin goes cold at his words and I suddenly feel really anxious. Of course I want to see Hope, truth be told I'm dying to meet her but I'm so terrified. What if she hates me? I feel like they're expecting us to just know what to do and I haven't got a clue. I don't know the first thing about parenting or being a Mum. If I get this wrong it's Hope that suffers and I feel like she's suffered enough already. We all have.

"It's not that we don't want to," Matt answers sounding like he's being tortured again. "We just, what if,"

"We don't want to get it wrong," I mumble sadly.

"Oh sweethearts," Mum says. "You could never get it wrong even if you tried."

"You don't know that Mum. She's just this tiny little human who's settled in her life and then we just turn up and flip it upside down. We don't want to do that to her," I protest knowing exactly what it feels like to have everything you know change in a heartbeat.

"You wouldn't be doing anything other than what she needs, which is to have the both of you with her," Mrs Parker points out with her usual calm, soothing voice.

"The thing is though Mum I already know what's going to happen. As soon as I see her I'm not going to want to be away from her a second more. Mia and I have nothing ready for her. We don't have our own place, we know nothing about raising a child and the thought of doing wrong by Hope is eating us both up."

"Oh honey," Mrs Parker looks like she wants to reach through the screen and hug Matt. "Look, your Dad and I have already made some decisions to help you both."

"What do you mean?" Matt frowns.

"The lake house, it's yours, on one condition that we get to have little holidays with you all there."

"What?"

"You're giving us the lake house."

"Yes, and as for getting things for Hope. When she comes to live with you, your Nan won't need the stuff she has anymore. So you can just have that? Or you can buy your own with the compensation money you've both got from the accident. It's not like you don't have enough of it. As for the parenting, you learn it as you go. Hope is still teaching us things, isn't that right Liz?" Mrs Parker asks.

"Absolutely! The last time she was here she managed to find a tub of sudo cream and smother herself in it," Mum tells us.

"And the time before that it was talcum powder everywhere, and I really do mean everywhere," Dad laughs and Matt and I join in.

There's sort of some weird satisfaction knowing that she's given them a hard time, but not too hard of course.

"There's really nothing to be afraid of. We all make mistakes and we're all constantly learning but we're doing our best. That's all parenting really is," Mrs Parker has such a reassuring tone to her voice she could make anyone agree to something.

"Ok," I mumble and look at Matt. "We can do this, for Hope."

Matt gives me a small, nervous smile and nods in agreement.

"For Hope," he confirms.

"Dad's picking her up at around 9am so she'll be here by maybe 9:30am. You can come round whatever time you want though she'll be here all day," Mrs Parker says cheerfully. "Liz and Aaron, the same goes for you both of course."

"We're really going to meet her," Matt says in disbelief almost to himself but he's taken the words right out of my mouth.

I'm going to meet my daughter.

After the phone call ended Matt and I started preparing for the day when Hope comes to live with us. We decided on giving her the spare bedroom next to Matt's room, well, our room now I guess. I picked out baby pink paint and then added silver glitter to the paint just to make it a bit special for her. Painting her room didn't take too long to do between us and it made us feel so excited.

The next day we went shopping to get furniture and necessities for Hope. We purchased all white furniture for her room from IKEA and various other bits and bobs from Boots. The wardrobe went up fine but the cot is currently half complete on the floor.

"What is this bit even for?" Matt mumbles with a screw in his mouth. He's looking at the instructions and comparing them to the piece of wood in his hands.

"I think that bit connects to that bit?" I frown and look at the pile of wood in front of us.

"No, the instructions look like that bit connects to that," Matt sighs in frustration and looks at me. "Did we pick the most complicated cot that's ever been made?"

I can't hold back my laugh as I take in the image in front of me.

"Oh here we go," Matt says triumphantly as he manages to fit two pieces together that connects to the base.

I leave him to it and start rummaging through all of the bags we purchased full of things for Hope. I feel like we have enough nappies to keep us going for a year. We have dummies, baby bottles, toiletries, clothes and...

"Um, Matt? What's this?" I frown holding up the box.

Matt looks up for a moment and then goes back to using a screw driver. "It was in the baby aisle."

"In the newborn section?" I smirk and he stops again. "It's a breast pump, Matt."

"A breast pump?"

"Uh-huh."

"Right," he laughs and shakes his head. "I take it you don't need that then?"

"Not so much," I giggle and put it back in the bag.

Getting Hope's room ready has made everything feel very real but in the best way. It's amazing really how filling a room with furniture can give you a bit of confidence and make you feel prepared.

"Can you picture her in here soon?" I question as I rummage through another bag of new clothes and pull out a cute dress with bunny rabbits on it. "Or wearing this?"

Matt looks up and smiles even though he has yet another screw in his mouth.

"I'm starting to, yeah. Can you come and hold this bit in place for me?" He asks whilst trying to balance two bits of wood together. "I'm also trying to picture that this cot will be worth the headache it's giving me."

Matt gives me a playful wink as I sit next to him and hold what he needs me too. His sense of humour just makes me fall in love with him even more every single day.

"When do you reckon she'll come and stay here with us?"

Matt pauses and looks at me just for a moment before he goes back to screwing two more pieces of wood to the base of the cot.

"I meant what I said the other day. As soon as I meet her I'm going to want to bring her home. But that's probably not right for her. I think we just need to see how she reacts to us and take it from there."

"I haven't even met her yet and I already know I'm going to hate saying goodbye to her tomorrow," I admit as Matt looks for another piece to match the instructions. "It's that bit you want," I point to a piece on the floor next to him.

"I knew that," he laughs and grabs it. "Are you nervous about tomorrow?"

I nod and hand him a screw. "Yeah, but getting her room ready has made me really excited."

"Same, it's strange isn't it? Where's the screwdriver gone?"

"You're sitting on it," I can't hide my laugh. He is so useless at this but in the best way.

"Let's hope my parenting skills are better than my DIY skills eh?" His tone is playful as he tilts his head. "This doesn't look right."

"You're looking at it from the wrong angle, it looks fine to me."

Matt leans nearer to me to have a look and shrugs his shoulders before carrying on. I hold the bits he needs me too, when he needs me too and continue to pass him a screw when he's ready rather than him holding them in his mouth.

I feel myself drift away and I start thinking of how much my life has changed over the last few months. I've gone from feeling like I was just existing to feeling like I've got a purpose. I have everything I've ever needed and I didn't even *know* it was what I needed.

"Mia?" Matt's voice snaps me back from my thoughts as he looks at me with a slightly raised eyebrow. "Can you pass me that bit, please?" He says hesitantly as he keeps his eyes on me.

"Sorry," I smile and hand over the piece of wood to him.

He's trying to figure me out, he does this all the time. I think he's worried somethings wrong sometimes and then tries to figure out if I'm hiding something from him. He eventually pulls his eyes off of me and screws the bit of wood in place.

"What are you thinking about over there?" He questions, giving into his curiosity.

"When she's older, I want her to find someone like you," I tell him.

Matt's head snaps up immediately. His eyes burn through mine and then he shakes his head. "Well that's not happening. She's not allowed to date. Ever," he says firmly but with a small sense of playfulness.

"What if my Dad said that about me?" I raise my eyebrow at him, teasing him slightly. "Would you have listened?"

"No," Matt answers instantly as a slight laugh escapes his lips. "No one can keep me from you. But I'll keep every scallywag away from Hope."

"Did you just say scallywag?" I laugh as I hand him the final piece.

He laughs back and screws it into place before sitting back and looking at it. "Why doesn't it look right?"

We both get up from the floor and look at the crib, our daughters crib. Matt has his hands on his chin as he studies it. He's actually not bad at doing DIY. He's just worried it's wrong or won't be good enough for Hope. But it's perfect. *He's* perfect.

I grab the mattress from the floor and place it inside the cot which makes Matt nod.

"That looks more like it," he grins and walks over to me. He drapes his arm around my shoulders and admires his handy work. "That wasn't so bad."

"You're joking, right?" I nudge him playfully and he laughs.

"What's next on the list?"

"Umm, well all the furniture is done. I've got a few clothes to put away and then I'd say her room is ready."

"Shall I put these up on the wall?" Matt asks as he holds up giant letters H and P which are Hope's initials.

"Oh my god," I gasps. "HP."

"Yeah?" Matt frowns.

"Harry Potter," I laugh. "Our daughter has the same initials as Harry Potter."

Matt looks at the letters and then laughs too.

"I'm sure our parents did that on purpose."

The Reuniting

Mia

"How are you feeling?" Matt asks as he turns off the engine to his car.

"Terrified, but I'm so excited."

"Me too."

Matt and I left the lake house so early but we hit a lot of traffic on the way. We planned on getting to his parents before Hope arrived, I'm not really sure why. I think in our heads it would help calm us down. Although I don't think anything will calm us down now.

We're about to meet our daughter.

"She's literally behind that door," Matt breathes next to me as he looks at his parents home.

My mind is racing right now with so much doubt about how this will go. My hands are incredibly clammy from nerves and every time I breathe in my body feels as though it shudders.

"What if she doesn't like us?"

"What if she does?" Matt says confidently next to me. "Remember what Jenny said to us. Every time a bit of doubt creeps in, replace it with something positive. What if she does like us, Mia. Which she will. We made her, she is *literally* us."

Matts right, Jenny did say that and I've been trying my best to do it. It's helped, more than I thought it would actually. It sounds so simple doesn't it? Just thinking of something positive every time something the complete opposite happens or creeps into your mind. But it has helped.

"Come on, we can do this," Matt gives my hand a squeeze

before opening his car door and getting out. He's already at my door by the time I've unbuckled my seatbelt. I can't work out if he's trying to be extra confident to help me relax or if he's just genuinely confident. Either way I'm thankful.

"You good?" Matt asks as we walk up the path to his parents home.

"I'm ok, you?"

Matt nods and knocks on the door. Immediately the giggling shrieking sound of Hope can be heard through the door. I think every bit of oxygen leaves my body when I hear her. Our heads whip round to each other and I think our expressions are the same. Hearing her just made this all very, very real. Matt threads his fingers through mine and his heat spreads through me, settling my nerves. He then smiles at me like he's a child on Christmas morning. Pure excitement is on his face and it slowly transfers through his touch into me.

Mrs Parker looks flustered when she finally opens the door for us. She has an apron on and has little sparkly stickers down her arm.

"Come in, come in," she says cheerfully. "How are you both?"

"We're good, you?" Matt raises his eyebrows as he looks at his Mum.

Mrs Parker laughs a little and nods. "Hope would only eat her breakfast if she could stick these all over me," she points to the stickers on her arm.

"That's my fault, I shouldn't have given them to her when we got here," Mum walks out of the living room to meet us. "How are you both feeling?"

"Nervous, but excited," I tell them.

"Understandable sweetheart," Mum says with a sympathetic smile.

"Come through, get yourselves comfortable," Mrs Parker says to as both. "I think she just ran out into the garden."

Matt and I say nothing, we just follow them both into the living room. Dad is sitting at the dining table with a newspaper which is opened but he's no longer interested in it.

"Morning, it's good to see you," Dad says cheerfully.

"You too," I smile back.

Matt walks us over to the sofa and we sit down, getting comfortable. All eyes are on us but the excitement on everyone's face is something I don't think I've ever seen before. I'm so used to seeing sadness or sympathy from all of them but this time it's different. It feels like the start of a new chapter for all of us.

"Where's Dad?" Matt asks.

"With Hope in the garden. She through a ball at him just as you knocked and ran away laughing as he chased after her," Mrs Parker explains.

"I think we heard that," Matt smiles. He seems to quite like the idea of Hope doing that to his Dad.

"Can I get you both a drink?" Mrs Parker asks but neither of us respond.

As soon as she finishes her question all we hear is the sound of little footprints running through the kitchen getting louder and louder as they approach.

"Hope, slow down," Mr Parker yells after her.

The sound of her giggle makes my heart melt as the anticipation inside of me builds. Our eyes are fixed on the doorway as we wait for her to run through into the living room. It feels like we're waiting for hours but it's actually only a few seconds before she enters.

She's real.

Matt and I both squeeze each other's hand at exactly the same time without taking our eyes off of Hope. She hasn't seen us yet. She just struts in like she owns the place but in the cutest way. She looks behind her to see how close Mr Parker is and then looks back in front of her with a smile that reveals two front teeth. She's wearing a baby pink dress with white tights and shiny pink buckle shoes. The very top of her dark hair is tied into two pigtails but her hair is so thin and short it looks like little paintbrushes on the end. She picks up a silver glittery ball from the floor and turns to Mum, her eyes then travel to us on the sofa.

Hope freezes, her smile fades and she slowly lets go of the ball. She looks nervous and unsettled which makes me feel nervous and unsettled. In the corner of my eye I can see Matt swallow, he doesn't look as confident anymore.

"Hope, look who's come to see you!" Mrs Parker says cheerfully as she walks over to where Hope is frozen in place.

Hope eventually takes her gaze away from us and looks at Mrs Parker.

"Would you like to say hello?" Mrs Parker asks her.

Hope immediately shakes her head and runs to hide behind Mr Parker's legs. She wraps her tiny arms around them and peeps out to the side.

She's scared of us.

Why does no one else seem worried by her reaction?

"Hope does this with everyone she meets, don't worry," Mum says causally.

"Here," Dad reaches forward for the ball Hope dropped and chucks it to us. Matt only just manages to let go of my hand in time to catch it. "She loves that thing. When she's ready she'll come and get it from you."

Matt holds the silver glittery ball in his hands and looks at me. Hope watches behind Mr Parker's legs, her eyes are fixed on the ball.

"She's watching you," I tell Matt and he looks back at Hope.

Matt bounces the ball once on the floor and catches it again. Hope steps out to the side from hiding behind Mr Parker's legs so she can watch what Matt's doing. He looks back at me and this time he smiles a little.

"Do it again," I encourage and he does.

This time Matt bounces it twice and Hope takes a step closer to us. She still looks nervous but her shoulders have relaxed slightly. She's not just watching the ball anymore, she's looking at both of us too. When I look at her I see my double and then I look at Matt and realise she's his double. It's the strangest, most beautiful thing.

She's perfect.

"Would you like a go?" Matt asks Hope.

She nods slowly and takes another step closer to us. Everyone in the room is silent as they watch them both. Matt gently bounces the ball to Hope. It bounces around her feet as she bends down and tries to grab it. When she stands back up with the ball in her hand she wobbles slightly and then throws it back at Matt, revealing her two front teeth again as she smiles. Matt reaches forward to pick up the ball and then he passes it to me.

"Your go."

I take it from him as he turns back to watch her. I bounce it a couple of times, just like what Matt did and Hope takes two more steps towards us.

"Ready?" I ask her and she nods excitedly.

I bounce the ball at her gently and she wobbles again as she bends down to pick it up. A little giggle escapes her lips as she holds the ball. She doesn't throw it back to me though, instead she takes a couple of steps closer to us both.

"Ball!" Hope shouts a little louder than expected. She doesn't quite pronounce the B, it almost sounds like she said 'all'. Her voice is high, a bit like her giggle. Her eyes search our faces, it's like she recognises us but can't understand where from. Her eyes go from Matt's face to my face over and over.

Mum gets her phone out and then comes closer to Hope. She kneels on the floor next to Hope and shows her a picture.

"Hope, who's that?" Mum points to the photo and Hope follows her finger. She looks at the photo for only a second before she shouts.

"Mama!"

Hope almost drops the ball as she gets excited.

"That's right, well done," Mum praises her and then points to the photo again. "And who's that?"

"Dada!" Hope shouts even louder this time and throws the ball at Matt in excitement, hitting him in the face. Everyone laughs at her which earns us all a giggle from Hope. Matt looks at me and has such an overwhelming expression on his face. I don't think either of us fully believed our parents when they said Hope points us out in pictures.

"So who are they?" Mum points to us on the sofa this time as she puts her phone away.

Hope takes a small step closer towards us, she's in touching distance now. I feel like I'm holding my breath as her face searches mine, trying to work it out. Then her eyes turn to Matt and she frowns before looking back at me. Her tiny finger points at us both as she wobbles again.

"Mama, Dada?" Hope says but she doesn't sound as confident this time.

Matt and I nod quickly to reassure her. "Mummy and Daddy." He confirms as he points to us when he talks.

"Ball!" Hope screams at Matt and we both laugh at her.

Matt gives her the ball again and she trots off to the middle of the room. She bounces it a couple of times and then accidentally kicks it with her foot. It hands at Matt's feet so he kicks it back to her.

"Dada," leaves her lips as she carries on playing followed by. "Mama."

Over and over again she repeats those words to herself as she plays leaving my heart feeling so full.

The Goodbye

Mia

The day literally flew by. Hope wanted Matt and I to play in the garden with her so of course we did. We spent probably an hour with her just kicking or throwing the ball back and forth. She laughed for what felt like the entire time.

Before lunch she had a nap. I thought Mr and Mrs Parker had a cot for her but instead they just put removal bars on Matt's bed and she slept in there. Matt read her a story whilst I gently played with her hair. She fell asleep almost instantly. We then just stayed in his room and watched her sleep. Neither of us dared to talk in case we woke her up, but we couldn't leave her. Watching her sleep felt so relaxing to us. I think we're both trying to process that she's actually real. Watching her helped us understand that Hope is *very* much real.

We worried about how she'd be after her nap and whether we'd have to start again with the ball to earn her trust. But when she woke up we were still sitting there, in exactly the same place that she last saw us before she fell asleep. Hope gave us a tired smile when she saw us and reached out her arms.

"I think she wants a cuddle," Matt whispered to me even though Hope was awake.

I didn't know what to do. I've never held a child before but I trusted my instincts that everyone kept telling me about and lifted her out of Matt's bed. Hope showed me what she needed. She wrapped her small arms around my neck and rested her head on my shoulder as she yawned against me. When I turned back to Matt his eyes were glassy as he watched us.

"Are you ok?" I whispered.

Matt nodded and got up from the floor. He wrapped his arm around me, resting his arm on Hope and simply said, "My girls."

Once we went downstairs Mrs Parker made everyone a roast dinner. Hope sat on a highchair in between Matt and I and had a very small portion. She fed herself with cutlery at first and then started playing with her food with her hands occasionally eating bits. Mum said that's what Hope does when she starts to get full.

The conversation was relaxed, it almost felt like what a normal conversation around the dinner table should be like with your family. All I've known when we're together is arguments or sadness. But this actually felt nice. Matt told everyone about how we'd transformed the spare room into Hope's room. We laughed about how hard the cot was to put up and I boasted about the pink glittery walls. Matt questioned about Hope's initials being the same as Harry Potter and everyone just laughed. At times it almost felt like Hope was listening to us, which I'm sure she wasn't but it felt like she was.

After dinner Hope and Matt went back to the garden to play with her ball again whilst I helped Mrs Parker and Mum wash up.

"You don't have to do that dear," Mrs Parker told me.

"I don't mind honestly, it's nice giving them both some time together," I explained as we watched Hope and Matt in the garden. She'd run around giggling as Matt chased her. When he caught her she shrieked so loud I think it even made Matt jump. They looked so happy and just in their own little world together. When Matt put her on the floor he tickled her sides and her legs gave way underneath her. She started rolling around laughing louder than ever and my heart just melted.

"Are you ok love?" Mum asked and put her arm around me.

I blinked away my happy tears and nodded back at her.

Once we'd finished the dishes our parents insisted Matt, Hope and I had a picture together so I joined them both in the garden. Hope ran up to me as I approached so I bent down to pick her up. She put one arm on my shoulder and twisted her body back to look at Matt.

"Stand by the roses in the corner," Mrs Parker instructed as each of our parents got their phones ready.

We moved over to the roses as instructed and I held Hope to my side where Matt was so she was in the middle. Matt wrapped his arm around my shoulder and placed his other hand on Hope's shoulder.

"Hope, look over here," Mum shouted waving her arms but Hope's eyes were fixed on Matt.

"She's obsessed with you," I told him.

"I'm obsessed with her," Matt admitted and he gave her a little tickle on her side.

Hope shrieked and giggled instantly as we watched her. She truly is such a happy baby, well, toddler I suppose.

For the next hour or so Hope, Matt and I stayed in the garden together. We'd have moments where we'd play and moments where Hope just wanted cuddles. She looked like she was getting tired now, her blinks were getting longer and she wasn't as energetic as before. Matt and I knew it was getting closer and closer to having to say goodbye to her. Neither of us wanted this day to end.

Matt and I are currently sitting next to each other and Hope has somehow managed to lay across us. Her legs are on Matt and head is on my lap whilst I gently fiddle with her hair. One of her hands is still touching her silver glittery ball.

"I don't know why I was even nervous," I tell Matt quietly.

"I know, me either. She's made this very easy," Matt smiles as he looks down at Hope.

"She looks like she shouldn't be comfortable right now, but she is?" I laugh looking down at her.

"It's the hair fiddling that's done it," he laughs back.

"Guys, Hope and I should start making a move," Mr Parker comes outside to tell us. He knows he's now the bad guy but we understand his hands are tied.

Hope's head snaps up from my legs as she looks at him.

"No!" She shouts.

I remember Mr Parker said she liked saying the word no to him.

"I stay," she grips my legs with her tiny arms.

Matt sighs next to me, we knew this would be hard but this really is so hard.

"Nanny Dot is waiting for you," Mr Parker tries to sound cheerful as he approaches. Matt's Nan's name is Dorothy, but I guess Nanny Dot is easier for Hope to says.

"No!" Hope shouts louder this time and sits up but manages to balance herself on both of our thighs.

"You'll see us again," Matt says reassuringly.

"No! I stay!" Hope's voice is tired and filled with anger.

"Maybe next time we see you, you can come to our home?" I suggest.

"You could stay over?" Matt pushes gently.

"No Dot," Hope sniffs and her bottom lip starts to wobble.

"It's ok," I try to comfort her and pull her closer to me. She twists her body to face mine and clings onto me as though her life depends on it.

"I stay," she sobs tiredly into me.

Matt looks at her with sadness and then looks at his Dad as we both get up from the grass.

"Is she always like this when it's time to go?" Matt asks him.

"She's not usually this bad," Mr Parker confirms as he reaches us.

Hope hears his voice is closer and grips onto me even tighter.

"I stay!" She cries desperately against me.

"Shh, it's ok," is all I can say to her.

I want you to stay too.

I carry her through the garden and back into the house where her cries seem to multiply. Matt rubs his hand on my back as we walk through the living room. The lump in my throat returns as she cries. I never want to hear her crying and if she does cry, I don't want anyone to comfort her other than Matt and I.

"Have you got her bag?" Mum asks Mr Parker.

"Yes it's in the car already," he tells her as she opens the door.

"I stay," Hope repeats once more through her sobs.

"Bye bye darling," Mrs Parker kisses the top of her head as I continue to hold her. Hope doesn't even acknowledge her, she just holds me tightly.

"Bye munchkin," Dad tickles her back gently but she doesn't react at all.

Mum says nothing, she looks really emotional so she just kisses the top of Hope's head like Mrs Parker did. The fresh air hits us as we walk outside again and she sobs once again.

"I stay."

Mr Parker walks ahead of us and unlocks the car. He climbs in and starts the engine whilst Matt, Hope and I wait by her door. Matt swallows the lump in his throat as I lean back to kiss Hope's cheek.

"Do you want to give Daddy a cuddle?" I ask her.

Hope nods slowly and reluctantly loosens her grip on me. Matt's hands grab hold of her gently as he pulls her off of me and holds her tightly against his chest. He kisses the top of her head as he holds her with one hand and then reaches for the door handle with his spare hand. The sound of the door opening makes her grip Matt tighter but he carries on. He leans down and positions her into her car seat. She lets her arms drop from his neck and sobs as he starts to buckle her in.

"I stay."

"Next time you'll stay with us, I promise," Matt tells her as he makes sure she's buckled in safely. He places another kiss on her cheek as she watches him closely. "Mummy and Daddy love you."

"Wuv you," Hope mumbles back as she struggles to pronounce her words.

I can tell it takes everything for Matt to pull away and close the door.

"Drive safe."

"Will do, Son."

Matt steps back from the car and keeps his eyes locked on Hope as he pulls me close into his chest. Her faint cries drift

away and the car goes out of sight as I remember.
"She left her ball in the garden," I choke.

The Unexpected

Mia

When Matt and I got home we felt so deflated. All we wanted was to have Hope with us and it seemed like that was what she wanted too. Instead we're both at home without her and our last memory is of her crying in the car. Dad text us when he dropped her off to let us know Hope fell asleep within minutes of driving away. That sort of made us feel a little comforted. But what about when she wakes up, how would she feel then?

"What do you think she's doing?" I ask Matt.

He's laying on the sofa with his head on my lap whilst throwing her silver glittery ball up in the air and catching it again. We decided to take it home with us so we could be the ones to reunite it with her.

"I'm hoping she's asleep," Matt sighs. "And not missing us as much as we're missing her."

That's true. He continues to throw the ball up and down whilst I thread my fingers through his hair.

"She adored you."

Matt smiles as he thinks of her and throws the ball up again.

"This ball literally saved our arses."

I laugh at his comment and genuinely couldn't agree more.

"I can't believe she really knew who we were."

"I know, when she said Dada it really hit me. And I'm not talking about the ball in my face. I mean it hit me that I'm her Dad."

Matt's phone starts ringing on the table which stops our conversation. He catches the ball again and sits up to see who it is.

"It's Mum, she wants to facetime?" Matt frowns and looks at

me. "It's late?"

"Do you think something's wrong?" I ask as I shift in my seat. Dread starts to bubble away in my stomach. Why would she be calling us at 10pm for a chat when we've been with her all day.

Matt doesn't respond to me as he answers the call. He sits back so we're both on the camera and his Mum eventually comes into view once the line connects.

"Mum? Is everything ok?" Matt asks quickly and frowns as he looks at the screen. "Where are you?"

Behind her I just see white. All the walls are white and the ceiling panels look familiar, I've seen those before. They're squared with faint grey dots on them and I can see the corner of the chair Mrs Parker is sitting on. It's a pale beige colour and her back is against a red sponge cushion. I know this place.

"She's at the hospital," I breathe and Matt's head snaps in my direction.

"I can't hear you both hang on, the signal is bad," Mrs Parker tells us as she gets up. She walks out of the room she's in and down a corridor where you can see the odd Nurse or Doctor walk past her.

"Oh my god she is," Matt gasps as he realises where his Mum is. He tenses immediately and I grip his thigh gently.

Hope.

"Is that any better?" Mrs Parker asks as she gets outside.

"We could hear you fine, can you hear us?" Matt says desperately.

"Oh yes I can now. Good. I'm sorry for calling you both so late."

"Mum what's happened, why are you at a hospital?" He interrupts her.

"I don't want you to worry, everything is ok. Nanny Dot, I mean Nanny Dorothy has had a heart attack but she's ok."

"She had a heart attack?" Matt gasps.

"Yes, earlier this evening."

"What about Hope where is she?" I rush out.

"She's fine sweetheart, she's with Matt's Dad," Mrs Parker

smiles and I relax slightly.

"Will Nan be ok?" Matt questions hesitantly.

Mrs Parker changes the hand she's holding her phone with and nods. "It was a mild one so she's ok. They think they can help her with just medication, no operations or anything. They're going to keep her in for observations whilst they trial the different medications," Mrs Parker explains. "I'm going to stay with her and as I said Dad has Hope but we were wondering if maybe you'd want her for the night? Dad said she asked for you both when he picked her up."

"She asked for us?" Matt questions and Mum nods proudly.

We look at each other in pure amazement and smile. Matt grabs my thigh and squeezes it gently.

"We'd love to have her here," I tell his Mum.

Mrs Parker smiles and nods. "Good because Dad's already on his way. I meant to call you sooner to check with you first but the doctor came in. They both left a while ago now so they'll be with you soon."

"They will?" Matt asks as he looks at me with a smile. "She's coming home."

"She really is," I smile back at him and lean against his shoulder.

"We might need to come up with a plan though. I don't think Nan will be ok to look after Hope anymore."

"That's fine Mum. Hope is going to stay with us," Matt tells her firmly.

Mrs Parker looks so relieved. "She's only ever needed you two, I hope you know that."

We're distracted by some headlights that shine through the curtains and light up the living room.

"I think they're here," Matt tells his Mum as he stands up.

"Ok love, I hope it goes well. If you have any questions just call or text us."

"Thanks Mum, send our love to Nan for us," Matt tells her and Mrs Parker nods before disconnecting the call.

"She's really here," I breathe and then look at Matt. "Are you ok?"

Matt tells me he's ok by leaning down and placing his lips on mine. He pulls me close to him only for a moment before letting me go again and walking to the door. I grab her ball from the sofa, just in case we need it again. Matt opens the door as his Dad comes up the porch steps. Hope is wrapped tightly against him with her head on his shoulder.

"She's just woken up," Mr Parker says quietly as he hands Hope carefully to Matt.

Hope gives us a few tired blinks and then looks at the ball in my hand.

"Ball," Hope's tired voice says.

I smile and hand it to her.

"I stay?" She asks as she looks at us both.

Matt wraps one arm around me pulling me closer to him as he holds Hope.

"You stay," he whispers.

Epilogue

Hope

5 years later

It's been a year since Mummy and Daddy got married. I got to wear a blue dress that day and was allowed to play with rose petals. Everyone cried a lot at the wedding but they insisted they were happy tears. I don't know what happy tears are. I only cry when I fall over and Mummy or Daddy have to kiss my bump better. That doesn't happen often though, mostly we just have fun.

Today my Nanny, Grandad, Gran and Grandpa are coming over for the afternoon. I love it when we're all together, everyone is so happy.

Daddy spent the morning hanging up homemade bunting around the garden which is pictures of us three. I like the picture of when I was almost 2 years old. We're in my Nanny and Grandad's garden by some roses. Mummy is holding me as her and Daddy watch me laugh. It's cute. There's pictures of me in the lake with Daddy in an inflatable boat. I remember that day, it was so fun. Mummy and Daddy look so happy in all of the pictures with me except for one. I'm on Daddy's shoulders and Mummy is standing next to us. We were at M&M World in London. I was holding a massive plastic M that was filled with lots of M&Ms. I remember that day, that moment. There was a sticker on the giant M that I was fiddling with and I managed to pull it off. But it opened up the M and all of the sweets fell out just as the picture was taken. Mummy and Daddy have their mouths open in shock but I'm laughing. That was a fun day and I didn't get in trouble. Mummy said something to Daddy about it being in my blood to destroy an M&M store. I still don't know what she meant by that.

"Hope come here, quickly," Mummy calls from the kitchen.

"Coming," I shout back and throw one more handful of confetti on the table that's in the garden.

Mummy looks strange when I walk into the room. She's sort of happy but confused at the same same time. Daddy's next to her and has the same expression on his face as he holds her stomach.

"What is it?" I ask as I approach.

"The baby has hiccups, quick come and feel," Mum says excitedly.

Mummy has been pregnant for what feels like forever now. You can really see her bump through her dress, it pokes out and gets in the way. Sometimes we play games together and see what we can balance on it.

"Hiccups?" I gasp as I run over to them.

Mummy nods and grabs my hand when I get to her. She places it on her bump where her hand was. She then rests her hand on top of mine and presses down slightly whilst looking at me.

"I can't feel anything?"

"Just wait," Daddy says as his hand is fixed firmly on her stomach still.

My eyes watch her bump as we all wait patiently. Suddenly I feel something. There's a tiny little vibration that I can feel on my fingertips followed by another, then a pause, then another.

"I can feel it!" I shriek in excitement.

"It feels so strange," Mummy giggles to herself.

Daddy gives her a kiss and then rubs his hand on my head, messing up my hair which makes me laugh.

"Dad!" I moan playfully and nudge him.

"Everyone will be here in a minute, do you want to help me carry this cake outside to the table?" Daddy asks.

"When can we cut it, it looks so yummy!" I tell him as we

both grab the base. Mum picks up the last of the balloons and follows us outside.

"After we've done the gender reveal we can then cut the cake," Daddy explains.

"Can we do the reveal as soon as they get here please?" I beg.

"Yes, the baby wants some cake too so we'll do it as soon as they arrive," Mum tells me as she watches us.

Dad and I position the cake around the pink and blue confetti that I've scattered onto the table. Mum puts the pink and blue balloons behind it next to a giant black balloon.

"Do you really not know what you're having?" I frown at them both.

"No," Daddy laughs. "We've told you this."

"We'll be finding out the same time as you," Mummy explains and then smiles as she rubs her bump. "I think it's another girl."

"I want it to be a girl," I tell them.

"Why don't you want a boy?" Daddy frowns.

"Because boys are gross."

It's true, they really are. Well the ones at my school are anyway.

"Yes, yes they are. Make sure you remember that when you're 16 years old," Daddy tells me.

"Why 16?"

"No reason, your Dad is just being silly," Mummy wraps her arm around me and nudges him playfully. "Pack it in Matt."

"I told you, she's not allowed to date and I meant it," he laughs and shoves a handful of M&Ms in his mouth that are in a bowl on the table.

"What's does date mean?"

"Nothing that you need to worry about," Daddy runs forward and starts tickling me.

I can't hold back the laughter that escapes my lips as I try to get free from him. But his arms are so strong he manages to hold me in place whilst tickling me. I laugh continuously as I lower to the floor and curl up into a ball. Daddy comes down to the floor with me though as Mummy laughs.

"Stop it," I continue to laugh the entire time.

"Don't get your clothes dirty," Mummy tells us both. "Matt, be careful of her dress."

"Relax Mia, her dress is fine," Daddy laughs and sits back on his knees finally removing his hands from me.

"Knock knock."

Grandad.

I wriggle away from Daddy completely and run over to Nanny and Grandad as they walk through into the garden.

"We could hear your laughter all the way from the car," Nanny tells me as I give her a cuddle.

"Daddy was tickling me again," I explain and then give Grandad a hug

"Of course he was," Grandad laughs and then shakes hands with Daddy. "Hi Son."

"Alright Dad, Mum, any sign of Mia's parents out there?" Daddy asks them.

"Yeah they were right behind us," Nanny explains.

"Oh good, I want some cake," Mummy claps her hands happily as she greets Nanny and Grandad.

"How are you feeling love?"

"Hot, hormonal and uncomfortable," Mummy laughs as she rubs her bump.

"Baby had hiccups! I felt it and it was so cool!" I tell them both as Gran and Grandpa come into the garden.

"You did? Baby must like it's big sister," Nanny tells me and I nod.

Just please be a girl.

"Where's my little munchkin?" Grandpa picks me up and gives me the tightest squeeze.

"Are you ready to find out if you're going to have a baby sister or baby brother?" Gran asks.

"Yes!" I shriek as Grandpa puts me down again. "Mummy, Daddy, can we do it now please?"

"Ok, ok." Daddy replies.

I run over to them both and grab each of their hands. "What

balloon is it?"

"The black one but don't do anything yet," Daddy explains firmly.

I run over to the table and grab the string to the giant black balloon, which is almost bigger than me.

"Stand over by the flower bed," Nanny tells us.

Mummy and Daddy walk over to the flowers hand in hand as I skip over with the balloon.

"Do you want to hold the balloon or do you want to pop it?" Mummy asks as we face everyone. They've all got their phones out videoing us and look so excited.

"I want to pop it!" I scream and everyone laughs.

"Ok, give me the balloon then," Daddy says as he takes it from me.

They both lower down to my level and Daddy holds the balloon just above us all.

"Here's a pin but be very careful with it," Mummy says as she hands it to me.

"Countdown?" Grandad shouts followed by.

10...

9...

8...

Please be a girl.

7...

6...

5...

I don't want a brother.

4...

3...

2...

Please.

1...

I look above and see the giant balloon in Daddy's hand. I lift my arm up and hit the balloon with the pin, bursting it instantly. The loud pop makes me jump so I close my eyes but I hear lots of cheers from everyone around me. My eyes open and

I see pink confetti dropping around us and tiny pink balloons floating away that were inside the giant black balloon.

It's a girl.

"It's a baby sister!" I scream in excitement.

Daddy sweeps me off my feet before I know what's happening and pulls me into cuddle him and Mummy. But Mummy's crying.

"Why are you crying? Did you want it to be a boy?" I ask worriedly.

"No, no, these are happy tears," Mummy tells me and kisses my cheek. "I promise."

Happy tears again.

"Another daughter," Daddy gushes and kisses Mummy before kissing my cheek. He's holding onto us both so tightly.

"I know," Mummy smiles.

"I'm so excited!" I grab some confetti that was sitting on top of Daddy's head and start playing with it.

"Oh no," Daddy says to Mummy.

"What?" She asks him.

"Now I have to stop two daughters from dating."

The End

Acknowledgements

This has been such an incredible journey for me which started back in 2015. Yes, 6 years ago! Something that started out as a bit of fun with my friend, Taylor, slowly turned into a passion for writing. I will be forever thankful to her for encouraging me to write. I guess she was the first person who saw I had potential and she pushed me to continue with it.

Then of course my Husband Kurtis, who has absolutely no interest in books and will probably never even read mine. But he has always supported me. He would encourage me to continue with it, no matter how long it took. He understood it was important to me and therefore, it was important to him too.

My parents of course, they have always supported whatever I've done whether it be cheerleading, playing darts or writing. They're in my corner, always, and I'm thankful for them both.

During one of my many self doubting phases I sent a handful of friends a couple of chapters to read for some feedback. My favourite response would be from Nicole. Her excitement and demand for answers or more chapters really pushed me to carry on. She helped me believe that it was good enough.

Last but not least I want to thank George, who without his help this book would not be available for you to read today. I didn't understand how to self-publish my book so he found out how and helped me do it. I'm forever thankful for his help and humour.

Printed in Great Britain
by Amazon

78523783R00146